The Anonymous Man

by Vincent L. Scarsella

The Anonymous Man

by Vincent L. Scarsella

DIGITAL FICTION

P U B L I S H I N G   C O R P

Edition 2.01 Copyright © 2016 Digital Fiction Publishing Corp.
Story Copyright © 2016 Vincent Scarsella

ISBN-13 (paperback): 978-1-927598-29-0
ISBN-13 (e-book): 978-1-927598-31-3

Part One First Betrayal

The Anonymous Man

Chapter One

It's my funeral! Jerry Shaw thought as he watched in his car from a safe distance. It was not his actual funeral, of course. He was obviously not dead.

First to arrive that crisp, sunny October morning was Holly Shaw, Jerry's wife, playing the part of the grieving widow to perfection. She was helped from the car by her younger brother, Raymond. She leaned against him and moved forward with a slow, mournful gait, even faking a misstep along the way. As she reached the wide oak entrance of Marzulak's Funeral Home, one of the funeral director's sons pulled the door open, allowing her a slow, dramatic entrance with a grief-stricken sigh.

The other somber mourners arrived steadily after that. They included four of Jerry's fellow sales reps from Micro-Connections, the computer software distributor for whom he had worked the last six and a half years in what had disappointingly evolved into a dead end job after so much early promise. Next, college chums from New York City and Long Island, including Dan Cormack, his best friend from those days, Andy Schneider, now a doctor, and little Stu Holman, drove up in a rented Ford Mustang and walked gingerly into the funeral parlor after a long night of partying and remembering funny things about Jerry. Like the time he spent the afternoon "pennied" in his dorm room and had to pee in an empty Coke can. Even Joe Reed, Jerry's best friend from high school, whom Jerry hadn't seen since the summer after graduation, showed up.

The usual array of old aunts and uncles and three or four distant cousins arrived, including, on his mother's side, Aunts Judy and Bernice with Uncle Lenny in tow; and, of course, his moronic, bachelor cousin, Lenny Junior who, as far as Jerry knew, still lived at home with Uncle Lenny and Aunt Judy. Jerry remembered Aunt Bernice's sauerkraut pierogis and mushroom soup and regretted that he'd never be able to taste another mouthful.

At a quarter to nine, Jerry's older sister, Joan, dropped their father, Big Pete, off and pulled his ten-year-old Buick Century into the space in back of Holly's car directly behind Marzulak's long black hearse. Another of Marzulak's sons came rushing down to help Jerry's father up the steps to the front door. Jerry noted that Big Pete looked ashen, feeble, and grim–faced, every bit his seventy-four years.

No wonder, Jerry thought. Now, both his sons were gone.

His oldest, Peter Shaw, always Petey, the golden boy of the family, had died fourteen years ago. Petey had everything, as Jerry was repeatedly reminded—athleticism, good looks, a winsome personality. He'd been a high school football star, a solid, fast safety and tight end, six foot one or something. He had signed a letter of intent to attend Michigan State on the day he was killed after the last game of the football season his senior year. Joe Denz, one of his teammates, had guzzled too many beers at a post-game party and lost control of his father's pick-up on the rain and ice-slicked asphalt of old State Route 391 and smashed into a tree. Petey was thrown from the truck and killed instantly. Naturally, the drunken Joe Denz survived the wreck.

His parents' grief over Petey's death never seemed to stop after that night. And it seemed to Jerry, and his sister, Joan, that after Petey's death, Big Pete and their mother simply gave up on life. Jerry and Joan had their good points, but their parents never seemed to notice. They could never quite match the awesome promise of the golden boy. The letter of intent granting him a full scholarship to Michigan State was framed and hung forever on a wall in his parents' bedroom, an unhappy reminder of what might have been.

Of course, Jerry's mother and father acted with appropriate pride upon his graduation from college. They seemed equally proud when Joan received her nursing degree. But somehow, these accomplishments were far too ordinary when compared to what Petey had seemed destined to accomplish—a stellar college, then a pro football career—and the celebrity that his certain fame would have brought to the household and the family name.

Mrs. Shaw had died in her sleep one night two years ago, still grieving, and Big Pete had carried on thereafter in his same silent and empty way. And so, as Jerry watched the old man arrive for his funeral that morning, he could not help but feel a pang of remorse. No man should have to face burying two sons in a single lifetime.

Jerry's co-conspirator, Jeff Flaherty, finally pulled into the lot in his silver Lexus. It was a minute after nine and Jeff was again fashionably late. He got out of the Lexus and strode toward the funeral parlor with the confidence and aplomb of the up-and-coming lawyer that everyone touted him to be.

The ceremony inside the funeral home was brief. At ten past nine, Holly ambled unsteadily back out into the cool October morning, now completely supported by her brother's wife. Jerry had to laugh. She was some actress. Well, wasn't that what she had aspired to be some lost time ago? Now the only thing that seemed to motivate her was money. Jerry found it ironic that she had to call upon her old acting skills to pull this off.

His father was next to the exit, arm-in-arm with Joan, his face a solemn mask. Immediately behind them walked Father Mike, a young associate pastor from Our Lady of Victory Church, the parish where Holly and Jerry had been married but never had attended after that.

Finally, the rest of the family and friends spilled out into the bright, chilly morning. They wore grim expressions, having paid their last respects to the closed coffin inside of which, they had been led to believe, was the burnt cinder of flesh that had once belonged to Jerry Shaw.

Next, the funeral home associates assembled the pall-bearers—including Jeff; Paul Castelli, one of the sales reps at Micro Connections with whom Jerry had grown somewhat close; Joe Reed, Jerry's old high school chum;

Dan Cormack, his best friend from college; his cousin, Lenny Jr.; and, finally, Holly's brother, Raymond. Upon their somber assembly, the pall bearers were directed by the associates to march alongside the casket as it was wheeled, then glided, into the back of the hearse. Once it was safely deposited, each of the pall bearers scampered to their own cars for the short half mile ride down South Park Avenue to Our Lady of Victory Basilica for the funeral mass.

Jerry waited until the last car in the funeral procession had driven out of the parking lot before starting after it. A minute or so later, he pulled into a space in the deserted rear of the basilica parking lot just as the last of the mourners had meandered into the basilica as the solemn bong of church bells beckoned them inside. From a paper bag on the passenger seat, Jerry pulled a long-haired auburn wig, a fake goatee, and a pair of thick, black-rimmed glasses. He carefully put them on in the way he had practiced back at his motel room the previous night. He gave himself a long last look in the rear-view mirror before deciding, with some amusement, that he was disguised just enough to get away with attending his own funeral mass.

Jerry left his car and hurried past several rows of cars, each of which were marked by a blue Marzulak's funeral home flag. He took the narrow walkway leading to the front of the basilica and, upon entering the foyer, he stopped a minute to catch his breath. He smoothed down his wig, adjusted his glasses, felt the goatee one last time and went on ahead into church.

Chapter Two

Jerry dipped his right index finger into the large marble bowl of holy water offered up to worshipers by one of two bucolic, life-sized marble angels standing at the end of the main aisle of the church. The long center aisle ended at a fabulously ornate main altar with its nine-foot tall, sixteen-hundred-pound marble statue of Our Lady of Victory herself. She had been sculpted in Italy and blessed by Pope Pius XI eighty-five years ago. Four thick swirling columns of rare red marble flanked the altar, reminiscent of St. Peter's Basilica in Rome.

After making a quick sign of the cross, Jerry took the aisle seat of the last empty, dark African mahogany pew. Father Mike had already started the funeral mass as Jerry sat down and lowered the kneeler. As Father Mike bellowed the opening prayer, Jerry looked up above the altar and was suddenly humbled to the core. The Holy Spirit and several saints hovered along a bright blue dome as if peering down from Heaven itself. By faking his death, Jerry thought at that moment, he and his co-conspirators, Holly and Jeff

Flaherty, seemed to have mocked God Himself. The worrisome hex was broken when one of two pre-teen altar boys shook the ritual bells for the first reading.

From among the sparse mourners, occupying only the first half-dozen or so rows of pews, Jerry's cousin, Lenny, took a deep breath and hesitantly stood. Pursuant to Jerry's request, he had been nominated to recite the first reading. A crumpled piece of paper shook in Lenny's hands as he lumbered forward and stepped onto the altar.

The day before his death was staged Jerry had sat down in the living room with Jeff and Holly in yet another post-dinner review of their scheme. After Jeff had led them, for the hundredth time, step by step over how they were going to stage the death the following morning, Jerry took another long gulp of his cheap bottle of Cabernet Sauvignon, stood up, and announced to Holly and Jeff that he wanted to plan his funeral.

"Plan your what?" Holly had frowned dubiously as she sipped her own low-priced white zinfandel, but Jeff immediately agreed with Jerry, saying, yes, Jerry boy, that makes perfect sense. He even gave Jerry faint praise for thinking of it and suggested that doing so would be at very least a symbolic break for Jerry, a way to purge his old life. He then asked Jerry what he had in mind. In the next half hour or so, Jerry laid it out, jotting down plans on a yellow legal pad while Holly rolled her eyes and mumbled to herself. Jerry noted what funeral home to use (Marzulak's, of course); found the old bible his Aunt Bernice had given them as a wedding present and flipped pages to locate the readings that he wanted to be given at the funeral mass and added who should give them; finally, Jerry announced firmly and directly that Jeff should give the eulogy.

"Me?" Jeff grinned. "Why me?"

Jerry shrugged. "Why not you?"

"Sure, why not you?" Holly chimed in. "You're his best friend." She gave a short laugh, took a sip of wine and added, "Well, his only friend."

That wasn't quite true. Jerry did have friends down at Micro- Connections. Only, he hardly associated with them outside work so she was quite right.

Jeff accepted the honor with an exaggerated bow while twirling his right arm up and around in an extravagant gesture for Jerry's benefit. During this display, Jeff gave Holly a sidelong glance and, although Jerry could not fathom what this glance might signify, if anything, he decided to let it go and not make anything of it.

That was all ages ago, it seemed, in another galaxy far, far away. Jerry now focused on the ridiculous sight of his daft cousin at the pulpit on the altar about to give the first reading at his—*his funeral mass.* Lenny held his breath momentarily before tapping the microphone, looking something like a comic playing a dumb-struck, dim-witted character about to launch into his act. He stared out at the mourners and it soon became apparent that a bad case of stage fright had incapacitated the poor man and that he was incapable of speech.

After a time, Lenny lifted and pulled a hand through his thinning blonde hair. One of the altar boys leaned forward and pulled at the hem of Lenny's sport coat and there was an inappropriate titter from the mourners. Then, because Lenny continued to appear transfixed, Father Mike stepped forward and was about to intercede when, from the audience Uncle Lenny barked something up to his son. Not encouragement exactly, just something to get him going. Lenny Junior squinted down at Lenny Senior, seemed to get it together with a nod, and feebly began to speak.

"A...a...a reading from Wisdom 3:19," he said, his voice quivering, difficult to understand. Then, after a pause, Lenny closed his eyes, took another breath, opened them, finally launched into it.

"The souls of the righteous are in the hands of God," he read and stopped a moment to look up and out at the mourners. He muttered the rest of it stiffly, painfully, without emotion, but it was understandable and without any further significant hitches. When finished, a small smile formed on Lenny's thin lips and he nodded with ultimate relief. He stepped back from the pulpit, looked up at the monstrous statue of Our Lady of Victory and the small, suffering Jesus statue behind her. He made the sign of the cross before at last exiting the altar.

The next reading, from Corinthians, was given by Joe Reed, Jerry's best friend from high school. Jerry hadn't seen Joe or had anything to do with him since the summer after graduation and he regretted that. Therefore, it seemed appropriate that he select Joe for this special honor. Jerry noted that Joe appeared to have become a solid citizen as he walked briskly to the pulpit, turned to the mourners and started the reading in a clear, confident voice. When he was finished, Joe left just as confidently as he had come.

Next was Holly's younger brother, Raymond. Halfway through reading, he broke down and sniffled for a time though the text of the reading was not all that stirring or memorable. Jerry was surprised, and a little embarrassed, that the kid had apparently been so fond of him.

The remainder of the mass consisted of the usual prayers and rituals of any other mass. Father Mike's sermon was a tad long, sprinkled with clichés including the one about the need to simply accept God's will because He must surely have some good reason and plan for snatching life from someone as young as Jerry. A smile formed on Jerry's lips as he agreed that certainly there had been a plan but not necessarily God's.

There came the point in the mass, like every Roman Catholic mass, when the worshipers were asked to extend a sign of peace and goodwill toward their fellow churchgoers. Thankfully the row Jerry was in, and several rows forward were empty. Still, an old woman, a daily worshiper who often attended funeral masses of people she didn't know, hobbled from her seat down the few rows to where Jerry was standing and extended her hand. She looked at Jerry as he shook her hand. For a panicked moment, he wondered if the old lady knew what he was doing there.

In a voice just above a whisper, she said, "May peace be with you."

"And also with you," Jerry said with a nod. She returned the nod and hobbled back to her pew.

During the offering of communion, when most of the mourners got up and made their way to receive the Eucharist from Father Mike, Jerry felt the need to look up.

At that moment his gaze locked upon Mary Grace McDonnell, Holly's beefy cousin a few years her senior, staring down from the marble rail of the balcony. She was the family soprano who was always called upon to sing at funerals and weddings, celebrated for her stirring, hearty voice though she had never made it past local productions. Jerry gasped as their eyes met and quickly looked down, sick to his stomach.

Perhaps because her glance had been so fleeting or her mind too clouded, worrying over singing the final song in his memory, or because his disguise was that good, Mary Grace did not appear to recognize him. Jerry sighed as she turned to watch as the last of his mourners glumly received God in the form of a wafer and returned to their seats for the ritual Eucharist prayer.

After Father Mike deposited the remaining wafers in the tabernacle and proceeded to the front of the altar, he scanned the mourners in the pews to his left and then reached out his hand to call forth Jeff Flaherty. Jeff strode up to the altar, ready to give the eulogy. After looking over the mourners for a time, he glanced toward the back of the church until his gaze settled on the solitary, overweight figure sitting in the last row.

Jerry tensed, knowing he'd been spotted. He knew Jeff was going to be furious that he had risked everything for the privilege of watching his own funeral mass. In the next moment, he heard Jeff clear his throat.

"Most of you don't know me," Jeff began, his voice affecting a slight, delightful drawl as it settled over the mourners. "My name's Jeff Flaherty and I work with Holly

Shaw, in the same law firm she does. I'm a lawyer, but don't hold that against me. And by the way, I'm not charging for this eulogy." There was a smattering of laughter among the mourners, along with one or two uncomfortable chuckles. "I don't need to be paid, or to be a lawyer for that matter, to say nice things about Jerry Shaw. I didn't know him for very long, not as long as some of you, but what I do know is that he was a great guy. And for this to happen to him, and to Holly, is deeply troubling and like the Father said, makes you question your faith and all that goes into it.

"But I don't want to dwell on that. I want to dwell on the kind of guy Jerry was, and ask that you all remember what was good and decent about him, the fond memories you have. I found him to be smart and funny in that quiet, self-deprecating way. As I am sure all of you are aware, he was way too worried about the way he looked, his long battle with the weight demon. And what is really sad about all this was that Jerry had just started a new diet, thinking that this time it was really going to work. Anyway, he, he—" Jeff broke up a beat and took a breath to compose himself. Jerry marveled that his acting skills rivaled Holly's, watched him weep on command. Maybe that was something all lawyers learn in law school.

"Anyway," Jeff went on, "there are so many complexities about a person. Some we know about, others we don't. Some we see, some we don't. I bet most of you don't know this about Jerry—that he was one damned good illustrator and in his spare time drew comic books that were quite good. He especially liked to draw storyboards regarding the adventures of this one particular guy, a unique superhero he called the Anonymous Man."

Jerry frowned, more than a little perturbed that Jeff had brought up this rather secret aspect about himself. It was conceived while he was still in college not long after 9/11 and he had kept it hidden from most everyone over the years except Holly, and later, Jeff.

"Yes, the Anonymous Man. A guy whose family and friends think he's been killed at his job in the World Trade Center on 9/11. In truth, he had gotten to work late that morning and so survived but decided to use the disaster as a cover to escape his humdrum life, beset with financial and marital problems, and start a new life as an anonymous man. And the really neat part about the story, showing how keen of a mind Jerry had, was that this anonymous man uses his anonymity as a kind of cloak to help people escape from their own bad or miserable lives. Anyway, that was the special something about Jerry that I'll always savor, his unique talent, and I really think that had he lived, Jerry would have worked at that comic book and gotten it published. Who knows, there may have been a movie made out of his Anonymous Man.

"But unfortunately for us, in his real life adventure, Jerry died. He did not become anonymous. And a great guy was taken from all of us."

At that moment, Holly let out a wail and Raymond wrapped his arms around her. Jeff let her display of grief linger for a time, and while doing so, stared out at Jerry's solitary figure in the back pew. Jerry looked down again, certain now that Jeff knew it was him in the church.

Finally, Jeff looked heavenward and said, "From all of

us, goodbye my friend. And goodbye to the Anonymous Man."

That was it. The mass concluded with the ritual spreading of incense by the altar boys. The pall-bearers were called forth and started to wheel the casket down the aisle while Mary Grace McDonnell started bellowing "Ave Maria." Some of the mourners, including Holly, of course, wept as they shuffled after the casket.

Jerry had slipped out ahead of them. He hurried to his car and crouched below the steering wheel as the funeral procession re-formed and started on its way out of the parking lot to Holy Cross Cemetery. When the last car took a left turn onto South Park Avenue Jerry started his car and pulled out after them. All the while, Jerry held onto the woeful thought that this really had been his funeral and that now his life was over.

But he was not dead.

In fact, he had truly become the Anonymous Man.

Chapter Three

Someone rapping at the passenger side window woke Jerry from a near wet dream involving Marcy Teresi, the slim, sultry, dark-haired, ample breasted receptionist who cheerily greeted visitors from behind a half-circle information kiosk in the lobby of the squat, modern Micro-Connections building. Marcy was partial to short dresses, clinging low-cut sweaters, and, on especially good days, fishnet nylons.

Jerry gasped as he stumbled out of the haze of the dream. He feared he had screwed up the perfect crime. But he saw it was only Jeff Flaherty at the window, wearing a cynical sneer that distorted his good looks. He mouthed, *Open it!*

Jerry yawned and fumbled for the switch that unlocked the doors of the silver Chevy Malibu. It had been purchased three months ago in the name of the New Mexican limited liability company in which he, Jeff, and Holly had each become silent partners. The faint red numbers on the Malibu's dashboard read 11:17 am. He hadn't slept for long.

The Malibu was parked along a narrow road crisscrossing the sprawling Holy Cross cemetery that stretched literally from one side of the city to the other. Jerry had parked in clear view of the mausoleum where the service for the cremated ashes of his fictitious corpse had just concluded. He had closed his eyes for only a moment while waiting for the mourners to proceed from the cemetery to the funeral breakfast at a nearby Italian restaurant when he had fallen asleep.

Jeff slid onto the passenger side and slammed the door. "What the fuck are you still doing here, Jerry boy?"

"Watching my funeral," Jerry said. "I couldn't resist."

Jeff sighed and a slight curl of a smile finally formed on his lips. "I hear ya."

Jeff lit a cigarette, took a deep drag, and blew out a thin line of gray smoke. After almost three years of their inexplicable acquaintance, it was the first time Jerry had seen Jeff smoke. Lately, Jeff seemed full of surprises.

"I couldn't believe you came to the church this morning," Jeff went on, "sitting alone back there as if you didn't exist. What the fuck is going on in that mind of yours? I couldn't believe your stupidity. And your balls. What if someone saw your fat ass?"

Jerry shrugged.

Jeff took another drag, leaned back. "You could have ruined everything. In fact, it's a miracle somebody didn't see you."

Jerry thought of Mary Grace McDonnell looking down but somehow not seeing him and passed it off with another shrug.

"I know," he said. "I know. It was stupid. But again, I couldn't resist."

"Stupid is right," Jeff said. "Stupid is becoming your middle name."

Another thing Jerry had noticed lately was that Jeff was becoming more and more insulting toward him, and not only about his weight. Only a few days ago, Jeff had labeled Jerry, "a stupid fucking useless lazy fat bastard oaf." What made it even worse was that Jeff seemed to spew these insults whenever Holly was around.

But Jeff was right about one thing. It had been criminally stupid for Jerry to be lurking around the funeral parlor the last couple of nights, and to have attended his funeral mass, not to mention the graveside service. Jerry had simply been overcome by the curiosity of watching one's "loved ones" and "friends" paying their last respects. But what he had observed had been frankly disappointing.

Last night, for instance, at his wake, except for Holly's fake numb look which had been part of her role all evening, and the sad, lost frown of Jerry's father, there hadn't been much display of sorrow among the mourners. Jerry attributed that to the closed casket. It was as if the deceased wasn't even there. Without a body to look at and grieve over, Jerry reasoned, there was no ultimate reminder of the tragedy of a young life cut short. The mourners had no object giving rise to an expression of grief.

Still, corpse or no corpse, Jerry had been to enough wakes to know that people weren't in the habit of spending much time grieving. They were gatherings of living human beings, desperate not to be reminded of death's inevitability. Thus, wakes had become merely a reason to socialize, to catch up on news, or have a good laugh at old times. At various points during the evening, the rise of laughter from the mourners even became somewhat embarrassing. This inevitable occurrence took place during Jerry's fictitious wake. Once the mourners recognize that the wake has been transformed from a solemn ritual into a kind of impious revelry, the noise level subsided and everyone settled into a kind of acknowledged glumness, reminded temporarily at least of the purpose for the occasion. This lasted only a few minutes until the talk and laughter rose up again. Through all that, the coffin and the corpse of the dearly departed are mere props.

"You should be in Binghamton by now," Jeff said. "Setting up your new life."

"I was just leaving," Jerry said. "Guess I fell asleep."

"Damn straight you did," Jeff said. "And damned straight you are leaving. Where have you been staying, anyway?"

Jerry described the cheap motel out on Route 20 near Ralph Wilson Stadium. It was forty-five dollars a night with smoke-stained cinder block walls run by some sullen, swarthy Arab.

"You keep a low profile at least?"

"Yeah, sure," Jerry said. "You know how many people they see at those places, day and night."

Jeff grimaced, unconvinced. "How's Holly?" Jerry asked.

Holly seemed a million miles away from him right

then, completely out of his life. Jerry was surprised how much he missed her. Over the last couple of years, things hadn't been quite right between them. What was wrong had been difficult for Jerry to pin down, and Holly was not inclined to want to talk about it whenever he broached the subject by asking her exactly that—what was wrong between them? Maybe, Jerry thought, it was the fact that he couldn't get her pregnant. Or maybe it was because the reason for her initial attraction to him, his affecting, boyish chubbiness, had worn off like a bad habit.

Jerry's tendency toward obesity all the way back into childhood had made him shy, lacking in confidence. And, until Holly had come into his life, he had operated on the usually correct assumption that fat guys didn't get pretty girls. How he had ever won Holly's heart was still largely a mystery to him, and a matter of much speculation and wonder for most of his as well as her friends and relatives.

Jeff shrugged. "Holly? She's alright, I guess. Nervous. But she was damned impressive as the grieving widow, don't you think?" He laughed. "Tomorrow she puts in the claim on your life insurance policy. Four million bucks."

"Four million?" Jerry asked, frowning. "I thought it was two."

The plan had been to make the claim on the one-million-dollar life insurance policy with Global Life & Casualty Jerry had taken more than a year and a half ago, shortly after they had first hatched the scheme. With the accidental double indemnity rider, it would pay out a flat two million, certainly enough for all of them to live comfortably for a lifetime even split three ways; provided, of course, they used discretion in how their respective shares were spent and otherwise invested the nest egg wisely.

Jerry had rejected right off the two-million-dollar figure suggested by Holly as simply too much. They shouldn't get greedy, he had argued, keep the claim reasonable so it wouldn't arouse any more suspicion than necessary, so the insurance fraud investigators wouldn't feel absolutely compelled to become hound dogs—they might wonder about a married guy without any kids leaving his widow so much money. In the end, they had all seemed to accept the wisdom of this. But apparently, Holly, at least, had a change of heart somewhere along the way. Jerry was peeved she hadn't told him.

"Yeah," Jeff said. "Holly told me last night. I mean, during the wake, she told me that she had upped your million policy to a two mil a few months back. Guess she forgot to tell us about that. Somehow she got your signature on the form without you even knowing what the fuck you were signing. She flatly denied that she had forged it."

Jeff laughed and Jerry immediately took it as a mocking sneer. It gave Jerry the distinct idea that maybe Jeff knew more about what Holly had done than he was telling him.

"We got one conniving bitch of a partner on our hands," Jeff added. "Lucky for me, it's you that has to spend the rest of your life with her."

"That play on her part could fuck us over real good," Jerry said, seething over Holly's lack of judgment, and Jeff's nonchalance over it. "Worse than me being here."

Jerry tried to think back to what document Holly could have snuck under his nose that had turned out to be the policy addendum. Perhaps, contrary to her denial, she had brazenly forged his signature, hoping that it would never become an issue.

"Anyway," continued Jeff, "what's done is done. They still don't have the slightest proof your death was anything but a tragic accident, no matter how much money she claims. And the body is nothing but a pile of ash at the bottom of an urn. No way to extract DNA out of what they think is left of you." He smiled. "So, as long as we keep the real you hidden—anonymous, right, the way you put it—we're in the clear."

Jeff was probably right. As long as they kept quiet, and he kept hidden, anonymous, they were in the clear.

Chapter Four

Jeff had proposed the plan almost two years ago on a cold, blustery night a couple weeks before Christmas during what had become his regular Tuesday night dinners at Jerry and Holly's house.

It was about an hour or so after they had finished off another of Holly's crock-pot concoctions and retired to the living room to drink yet more wine and gossip about work or mutual friends while a nonsensical sitcom mumbled in the background.

"How much life insurance you got, Jerry boy?" Jeff had asked as he took another long sip of his wine. He was sitting on the floor looking up at them on the couch.

"Not much," Jerry said. "Through work, a little, maybe twenty grand, plus a term policy, maybe another fifty. Not really sure.

"Why?"

They had just finished griping about how sick they were of all the bullshit, tired of the everyday toil of life, of the cold, gloomy weather and a winter that went on far too long; and then, of the injustice of money, why some people had it, and others, like them, didn't, and probably never would. How they were destined to remain hopelessly locked in the struggle with an unknown force that controlled everything, with the prospect of fame and fortune certain to remain beyond their reach.

At one point, while staring morosely into the dying embers of that night's fire, Jeff had lumped himself in with the losers, "pure and simple, just plain losers." Yes, Jeff had concluded remorsefully, their fate was set. They were destined to forever feed at the bottom of the pecking order. Unless, he added while still gazing into the fire, unless they acted affirmatively and decisively and, yes, criminally, to change their destinies.

Holly had laughed and, after silently burping up some of the wine, lifted her glass to toast the comment. But there was no stopping him.

"For example," Jeff continued as he turned to Holly, "you had wanted to become an actress, a movie star. Some Hollywood starlet. Live in a fucking mansion or something, like the guys on that HBO series, 'Entourage.' Instead, you answer calls all day long from disgruntled clients and lawyers and law clerks, file boring papers for boring, arrogant lawyers for their boring, stupid cases. The rest of the day you sit on your ass behind your computer screen listening to those same arrogant, stupid lawyers spinning out letters or motions, typing sentences and paragraphs that have no meaning to you. You come home exhausted and disgusted with your life and take it out on Jerry boy over here."

Jeff sighed and looked over at Jerry. "I bet you and her hardly even screw anymore."

That was an understatement, Jerry thought, as he glanced over at Holly while she sat there, stone-faced, looking at Jeff.

"I bet the two of you are so comfortably numb in your lives you don't even realize how miserable you are," Jeff went on, on a roll. "And you, Jerry boy, you had wanted to be an astronaut or something."

"Astronomer," Jerry corrected, smiling. "Yeah, when I started college. But I had no aptitude for calculus, so I switched to accounting, then business management. What I really should have done, what I eventually want to do, is become an illustrator, a cartoonist. You know, drawing comic books. For my superhero."

Holly looked at Jerry and smirked.

"Yeah," she said, "the infamous Anonymous Man."

Jeff nodded, remembering back to the evening a few months back when an enthusiastic Jerry had first revealed the existence of the Anonymous Man. He had been high from too much wine and, after rambling on about his comic book hero, Jerry proceeded to dig out from an old, musty cardboard box down in the basement his old journals filled with comic book storyboards that he had drawn throughout his college years and a couple more years after that. He had spread them out on display for Jeff and Holly on the living room floor.

Most prominent among the faded drawings were the storyboards from the first issue of *The Anonymous Man*, and some other strange superheroes, each with a superpower the novelty of which was that it wasn't truly a superpower, like super strength or flying, but instead was something ordinary involving some human frailty or defect used to confront and defeat crime and overcome general human unhappiness. After staring at them for a time, Jeff had remarked that Jerry's drawings were actually pretty damned good. And he had meant it. Jeff had seemed especially impressed as he repeatedly leafed through Issue #1 of *The Anonymous Man.*

The Anonymous Man, a nebulous, dark figure clinging to the shadows of some city storefront, had come into being the moment his former self was presumed dead when the World Trade Center went down on 9/11. Nobody realized that he had miraculously escaped death because he had been late in arriving at his cubicle for the financial firm on the seventy-third floor of the north tower, and so had escaped its collapse into a monstrous heap of ash and twisted steel beams. Photographs of him were posted by his wife on the wall with hundreds of others but soon she and his other loved ones gave up all hope that he would be found. Finally, he was presumed dead and because his life had not been so wonderful anyway, he became anonymous, a living dead man. He was happy to be off the grid, to have escaped the matrix of his sour life.

That evening, Jerry went on to narrate what his comic book drawings depicted: how the Anonymous Man had rescued a damsel in distress who was being chased by a vicious wife-beater; he hid her under his cloak of anonymity and she helped him as his front to interact with the world.

"This is good, man," Jeff had said. "Real good. You

should have continued it, gotten it published."

Jerry had shrugged and told Jeff he had drawn a few more storyboards for *The Anonymous Man* but could never find the time to finish another complete issue of the adventures of his superhero.

"Waste of fucking time," was Holly's belated, mumbled comment. Then she had laughed.

In retrospect, Jerry wondered if it was that reading of Issue #1 of *The Anonymous Man* that had sparked in Jeff's mind the scheme he was now proposing.

"What if," Jeff said, continuing on the living room floor, "we bought a bunch more life insurance on old Jerry here, a million bucks, say. Then, after a few months, maybe longer, fake his death." He looked at Jerry. "You know, make it look like an accident, then collect the insurance money. You know, you could become like your Anonymous Man. For real. We all could escape this comfortable numbness."

Just then, an ember exploded and popped from the wood smoldering in the fireplace onto the cheap oriental rug, which was laid out across the oak floor before it. Jeff ignored the heat as he pinched the ember off the floor and flicked it back into the fireplace.

"So," he asked, his face aglow from the heat emitting from the fire, "what do you think?"

Jerry frowned for a time, took a sip of wine. His first inclination was to laugh, but he soon realized that Jeff was serious. Holly just sat there next to Jerry on the couch, her legs under her slender frame, poker-faced, seeming to be sizing things up.

"How could we make it look like an accident?" Jerry asked. "What would happen to me to make it look like an accident?" He felt the wine course through him. "And then, what about my body?"

"We'd set it up so you burn," Jeff said. "You know, in some kind of accidental fire. A garage fire or something. Burned beyond all recognition. No DNA left."

"But, whose body would it be?" Jerry asked.

"One of those bodies from the medical school," Jeff said, indicating that he had thought through certain messy details, and even done some research. "You know, one of those cadavers donated by someone for use in anatomy class for dissection by medical students. They have dozens of them at the university medical school, right here in town. We could get one of them, bribe a worker who takes care of them or something. As far as the autopsy, the medical examiner would have no cause to doubt that burning or smoke inhalation was the cause of death."

There it was, the seed of a seemingly crazy, if not entirely stupid, criminal conspiracy. Insurance fraud of the highest order. And the million-dollar policy subsequently became two, purportedly by Holly's selfish scheming, meaning a take of four million dollars because of the double indemnity rider. Meaning, of course, that the three of them could and would be set for life if they did the improbable and actually went through with it. And even more improbably, pulled it off.

"It's called pseudocide," Jeff said. "It's been done before. Lots of times. There's even a TV series on it, I think. Most people do it without a lot of planning. We have to be careful, we have to be good. We have to be patient. Go slow. Real slow. Wait a year or more to pull it off." Jeff laughed. "You know, someone even wrote a book on it. But don't worry, I didn't buy a copy. That would leave a trail. You have to be careful about those things these days."

The fireplace had long grown cold, reduced from a once crackling blaze to a few hunks of black dying embers. Outside, it had stopped snowing and a cold full moon produced a stark blue glaze along the blanket of white covering the front lawn of Jerry and Holly's modest, split-level Colonial as if were made-to-order to give atmosphere to Jeff's bizarre proposal.

With Jeff apparently finished, Jerry looked over at Holly. Her legs were still pulled tightly under herself, and her eyes glazed over as she stared forward with a simple, fathomless Giaconda smile. It was at that moment when Jerry first suspected that Holly had already known about the plot. That Jeff had already secretly discussed it with her at some point previous to this, and that this meeting had been not been spur-of-the-moment but a set-up to convince him to do it.

They continued discussing what was then only the fantasy of a criminal plot, massaging it, adding and subtracting details. At around midnight Jeff proclaimed with bold conviction that this was something that they could and would actually do.

"You will need a front, of course," Jeff had stated somewhere along the way. "Like in your comic book. To be your interface with the world so that you can survive. Someone to secure your shelter and your food, the basic necessities. Just like your Anonymous Man."

Jerry mulled that over for a time. "Why not just get me a new identity? There are ways of doing that, right?"

"Too fucking risky," Jeff slurred, by then having consumed six or seven glasses of red wine. "Too much paper."

Jerry nodded. Yes, as Jeff stated, the perfect way to commit the crime, and to avoid risking detection in the future, was for him to become his comic book hero.

Jerry looked over at Holly. She was still playing dumb.

"So," Jerry said, still looking at her, now himself slurring his words, "I presume you will be my front?"

Holly turned to him. "Of course. Who else would do it? Not the girl from your comic book drawings. What was her name?"

"Karen," Jerry said. "Her name is Karen Smith."

He held up his wine glass and toasted the plan as eagerly and enthusiastically as Jeff and Holly did. Following the toast, he joined in the embrace in a symbolic ménage a trios consummating the conspiracy, proclaiming that it was real, that they were going to do what needed to be done to fake his death and fraudulently collect the two million dollars.

Part two of the plan concerned Jerry's exile to Binghamton, New York, three hours away, until the claim on the insurance policy was filed and paid. Then Holly could join him to become what Jeff had called his "front."

Jeff had sensed Jerry's unease with this part of the plan. For the first few weeks, certainly no longer than two or three months, Jerry would have to go it alone in

Binghamton. He certainly could never return to Buffalo. Once they had the money, they could go wherever they pleased, provided he remained anonymous.

"Just take my advice," Jeff continued. "Lose some weight. Get a different haircut. Grow a beard. Become a new man, totally different, in looks anyway. And it couldn't really hurt, could it, for you to lose a few pounds?"

Jeff smiled, and there it was for the first time, Jeff's first cruel reference to Jerry's abundant waistline.

"Then," he went on, "once Holly joins you, you can both start a new life with money in your pocket this time around."

Start a new life. Yeah, that's what Jerry and Holly needed, big time. Maybe Holly would even get pregnant, and all the dreams they used to talk about in those wonderful first couple of years of their marriage might actually come true. Back when Holly still thought she would become an actress, and had studied scripts late into the night.

For his part, Jeff had talked about moving out west, buying a ranch, settling down. Hunting, fishing, golfing, relaxing 24/7.

"Fuck the world," he said. His idea of romance, of finding the woman of his dreams, he added with a wink toward both Jerry and Holly, was to "pork" half-way decent looking escorts three or four times a month, a different one each time. Or finding a country girl, some rugged Sarah Palin type who believed in the right to bear arms. Not like the women in these parts, intellectual bitches who became lawyers and had daddy issues.

"All you have to do is keep a low profile, my friend," Jeff said and patted Jerry on the shoulder. "Then we'll be millionaires. Set for life."

"No problem," Jerry said. "What other choice will I have?"

They gave themselves two years to pull it off. Two long years, a timetable Jeff insisted upon and Holly debated. Jeff needed time to find the right medical school employee to bribe for a body. And all the other details needed to be hashed out before they even remotely tried to pull it off.

Almost a year to the day when it was first proposed, just a week or two before Christmas, Jeff came beaming over to their house and exclaimed that he had found "the body guy." That was when they finally picked a relatively certain date for Jerry to become the Anonymous Man.

Chapter Five

"Look," Jeff said, "no more time to chit-chat. I have to get to your funeral brunch and you have to get your fat ass moving before something bad really does happen."

As he opened the passenger side door, Jeff reached back and patted Jerry on the shoulder.

"Everything's going to work out just fine, Jerry boy," he said, smiling. "We pulled it off, man. They really think you're dead. Once Holly gets the money, she'll come down to Binghamton and you guys will live happily ever after while I slink off alone to Wyoming or Montana or wherever-the-fuck I find that ranch I've been blabbering about."

He patted Jerry one last time.

"You have become your creation, pal," Jeff said as he left the car. "The Anonymous Man."

Jerry nodded, suddenly unsure of anything right now. He started the car and drove away.

He should have gone directly to the Thruway entrance ramp for the two-and-a-half-hour trip east to Syracuse, then another hour south on I-81 to Binghamton. Instead, Jerry took the route for one last look at 320 Northview Lane, the first and only house he and Holly had ever owned.

The modest three-bedroom split-level Colonial was in a relatively new subdivision representing the kind of lifestyle pursued so thoughtlessly by young, aspiring middle class, credit-card-crazy-keeping-up-with-the-Joneses   couples. They had bought the house six years ago. Jerry had just been hired by Micro-Connections, then an upstart company with few assets but fueled by the dreams of its two owners. Kent Grant, one of the sharp, fast-talking gurus who had started the company, had employed Jerry fresh out of the State University of New York at Binghamton, or SUNY Binghamton. Jerry had been awarded a degree in business, with a relatively impressive GPA. At the time he was sufficiently motivated to convince Grant, himself a SUNY alum, that he could not only adequately serve the existing customer base, fledgling as it was at the time, but also, and better yet, substantially increase it. For that, Grant had agreed to pay Jerry what seemed a generous $50k a year to start, with the promise of making a lot more in salary and bonuses with the increasing client base.

But after six years, Jerry had settled into to a kind of melancholy competence, a comfortable numbness, and general obscurity in the company chain-of-command, satisfying existing customers and developing just enough new ones to keep his managers unaware of his lackluster and uninspired performance. He got lost in the mix as the company burgeoned and Kent Grant and Arthur Bay, the other owner, another Binghamton grad, became too far removed from the day-to-day trenches to notice what guys like Jerry were doing. Jerry had settled somewhere between the cracks, so as the company increased in size and profits, Jerry became professionally anonymous. And at times, true to form, he found himself wasting an hour or two during the drudgery of the nine to five drafting storyboards on his computer screen concerning the latest exploits of the Anonymous Man.

Holly was working part-time as a retail clerk in a jewelry store at a nearby mall back then. She was also getting some shoots for clothing catalogs arranged by a somewhat suspect modeling and talent agency that had sucked a bushel of money out of them with the promise of serious TV commercials or stage roles that never seemed to materialize. There was a side offer to do a soft porn series which Holly had flatly rejected. It once led to a really big argument between Jerry and Holly when, during one of their rare love-making sessions late one night, Jerry was stupid enough to admit that the thought of her making soft lesbian porn genuinely excited him.

Only a year or so after that, having completely settled into the house on Northview Lane, and, having still not yet gotten pregnant, Holly took a full-time job as a secretary in a medium sized law firm, Carlton and Rowe, that specialized in handling personal injury cases for accident victims. It was at this point that Holly truly and sadly seemed to give up on her modeling and acting career. She had stopped talking about it with Jerry and stopped seeking auditions or reading lines from some script late into the night. It was as if someone had operated on her brain one night and excised all interest in the thespian art.

On the day of his funeral, Jerry turned onto Northview Lane just before noon and slowed as he approached number 320. The street was deserted, with everyone in the neighborhood working and their kids at school or in daycare, so Jerry did not believe there was much risk of being spotted. He pulled the car to the curb almost directly in front of the house. The attached garage up a short driveway was a burned out shell. What used to be the garage door had already been boarded up with several sheets of plywood and there was a bright red sign on it from the salvage company, Brewer & Sons, Inc.

To the disappointment and chagrin of Jerry, Holly, and Jeff, the firewall between the garage and the house had worked gloriously to specifications and saved the house from complete destruction. So far, this had been the only glitch in their scheme, which had included not only faking Jerry's death, but destroying the house as well. The fire had been called in to 911 by the cell phone of Dan Kleingensmith, a neighbor from down the other end of Northview who had been out walking his ornery fox terrier and observed smoke billowing out from under the garage door and flames shooting out of a side window. Kleingensmith was the same neighbor who after making the call burst into the house and, after hearing someone taking a shower in the upstairs bathroom would forever believe that he had rescued Holly from the blaze.

Their failure to burn down the house had caused a momentary panic among the three of them, a lack of confidence that their perfectly planned and executed crime had not been so perfectly executed after all. The thought finally occurred to each of them at that moment that there were a million things that could and would go wrong. It had been their intention all along not only to collect on Jerry's life insurance policy, but also on the homeowners' casualty policy as well. Holly said the house was insured for twice its value. Together with their personal belongings, the homeowners' claim would put another four hundred fifty grand or so in their pockets. But with the house proper withstanding the blaze, the destruction of the garage and some smoke and water damage would merit only fifty or so.

Not to mention that confining the damage to the garage might make it easier for the arson investigators to pin down the cause of the blaze as intentional rather than accidental. Jeff had read that the more damage inflicted on a structure during the course of a fire, the less likely the arson guys would be able to prove arson.

Jerry stayed parked along the street not far down from 320 Northview for at time with the car idling, remembering all that and other things while staring at the house he had lived in every single day for the last six years. Finally, he surprised himself by choking up. The sight of the house and its burnt-out garage confirmed once and for all that he was never going to live there again, that his former life was over. That indeed his life as Jerry Shaw was over. Or, if he ever lived as Jerry Shaw again, he would do so in jail.

Glancing up into the rear-view mirror, Jerry saw a car cruising toward him from the far other end of the street. He put the Malibu in drive, and slowly pulled off from the curb. After passing six or seven houses in the subdivision, he pulled back to the curb and let the car pass. He took one last look over his shoulder. What had used to be his house looked empty and quite alone right then, forlorn and forgotten, an innocent victim of their crime.

That was when Jerry really started crying.

Chapter Six

As Jerry merged onto the New York State Thruway for the three and a half hour ride to Binghamton, he thought back to how he and Holly had met. It had been the first weekend of his junior year at the State University of New York at Binghamton. He had gone with his two housemates, his best friend, Dan Cormack, and Steve Fisher, to *Bo Jangles*, a newly opened singles' bar in Johnson City, a poor, working class town squeezed between its equally poor, working class neighbors, Binghamton and Endicott, hugging the meandering Susquehanna River, together making up the so-called Tri-Cities.

Having lost his buddies among the wall of bodies in the crowded bar after visiting the cramped men's room, Jerry situated himself into a dark corner. *Bo Jangles* thumped and roared with inaudible music and conversation. To be heard by the person next to you, you had to shout.

Jerry observed the crowd of people around him with disinterest. He wanted to find Dan and Steve if for no other reason than to tell them he was leaving, going home to watch Saturday Night Live or some old, silly Japanese spy movie on TV when really he would probably end up jerking off to porn on the Internet.

Jerry's decision to abandon the bar was related, of course, to his complete lack of confidence or hope that he'd find a girl to make it with that night. He was self-conscious of his bulging stomach, his lack of even a hint of pectorals, and the assurance that, because of these attributes, no respectable girl between eighteen and twenty-one could find him even the slightest bit attractive.

"I wouldn't fuck me if I was a girl," he had recently told Dan.

But as he stretched up on his toes to try and glimpse the whereabouts of Dan and Steve, Holly happened by, nudged him accidentally. In the process of saving himself from falling sideways into the bar, he corrected in the other direction and fell flatly into her.

"Oh, Jesus," he said as he nearly smothered his face in her neck and bosom.

She laughed. "Did you just give me a hickey?" she asked.

While he backed off and straightened himself, apologizing profusely at what an awful klutz he was, she smiled and said that he had "great blue eyes."

"I love eyes," she said. "Especially blue eyes." Then, she added the clichéd, "Did you know, the eyes are the windows into the soul?"

It was the first time Jerry had ever heard such a thing. In fact, he thought it was clever and nice and could think of nothing to say or do so he simply shrugged and said, "I guess."

"No, really," she insisted, thinking perhaps the shrug and his comment was an indication that he doubted her sincerity. "You have really nice eyes."

"Really?" He thought a moment, then added, "What, you mean, like a teddy bear or puppy dog?"

"Yep, that's exactly what you remind me of," she said, and smiled, "a big, sweet, huggable puppy dog."

Jerry smiled too, and they somehow transformed that lame initial discourse, which Jerry would never forget, into an engaging and ultimately sweetly intimate conversation that somehow, over the roar of *Bo Jangles*, lasted almost an hour. Finally, with his voice growing raw, Jerry felt entirely secure in suggesting that they take a walk outside. That walk led to a stop at Jerry's car, fifteen minutes of necking and panting and massaging, and, finally, to Jerry's utter astonishment, a trip to the bedroom of the apartment she shared with three other classmates for sex.

"Maybe she simply has a thing for fat guys," Dan Cormack had suggested the following morning when, in answer to Dan's question as to where the hell he had gone off to last night, Jerry had, with some hesitation, narrated his surprising evening of sex with this rather pretty, in fact quite gorgeous co-ed, Holly Connors, and her inexplicable attraction to him.

"Or maybe it's a beauty and the beast kind of thing," Dan added as a sort of armchair psychological evaluation.

Whatever her reason for being attracted to him, Jerry and Holly were inseparable after that first night. She had literally and inexplicably fallen in love with him, and, quite understandably on his part, considering her looks and winning personality, he for her. After only six weeks of courtship, Jerry asked Holly to marry him, and to his utter astonishment, without the slightest hesitation, she said yes. Of course, they would have to wait until after graduation, another year and a half or so. But during the time remaining, they spent almost every waking and sleeping moment together, when not attending classes, as if they had already been married in some secret ceremony.

No one in Holly's family, and certainly none of her friends, could understand her attraction to the "blob," as he became un-affectionately known to some of them. Sure, Jerry was a nice guy, someone who would take care of Holly and treat her with unwavering respect and fidelity for the rest of her life. Handsome guys invariably cheated. So what was wrong with loving an insecure fat guy? Plus, there was something about Jerry's looks, something beneath or behind or hidden by his rotund midsection and chubby jowls suggesting that he was really a good-looking guy waiting only for Holly's kiss to bring the best out of him. The princess kissing the frog and awakening a prince kind of fairy tale.

Jerry started working out regularly, nearly every day after he first started dating Holly, and he lost a good amount of weight, to the point where he reduced himself from the category of obese to merely stout. Still, when compared to the striking, sexy, svelte young woman Holly was flowering into, with the looks and shape of a budding actress and model she still dreamed of becoming back then, the pair of them, walking across campus hand-in-hand, dancing together at some dorm or house party, or, simply standing next to each other talking or whispering into each other's ears was certainly an incongruous study in contrasts meriting disbelieving stares from classmates.

But none of that seemed to bother Holly. She brushed off the cruel comments. She had fallen in love with Jerry, was under a spell of sorts, and though some of her girl friends giggled behind her back, knowing surely, in her case anyway, that love was truly blind, none of that mattered. Jerry was her soul mate, and his body size truly did not matter to her. At least, not at the time.

Much later, when the dust had settled over their relationship, and Jerry had some time to think about it, he began to suspect that there was something darker at work regarding Holly's attraction to him that had nothing whatsoever to do with the Beauty-and-the-Beast syndrome. Not that reaching the final analysis was all that complicated. The truth was: Holly was a controlling bitch. She got a perverse thrill out of dominating men. But strong, virile men weren't easily dominated. What she needed was an imperfect, self- conscious man lacking in confidence. And Jerry was the perfect fit.

Their first couple years of marriage went just fine. Jerry was busy at work, putting in long hours, learning more than he ever thought was possible about selling computer software and making call after call to present and prospective customers, dedicated to keeping old accounts and adding new ones.

After long days, Jerry came home from work and after

a quick supper, usually pizza or some other fast food that certainly didn't help his weight problem, he crashed on the couch with Holly snuggling in his arms as a low flame from the fireplace lit the room with a warm glow. Sometimes, especially on cold winter nights, they skipped dinner and simply sat there before the fire after spreading out some cheese and crackers, perhaps some ham and salami on a platter, opened a bottle of wine and had an indoor picnic. They talked and laughed and kissed long into the night, forgetting to turn on the television, and sometimes, when Holly felt in the mood, they would make love right there in front of the heat and dying embers of the fireplace.

During those evenings early in their marriage, they talked of having children, finally settling on a maximum of two, debating names for the boys (David, Paul or on a whim, Lane or Nevada) or the girls (Cynthia, Dana, or simply, Mary), and fantasizing whom their sons or daughters would look like and grow up to be (professional athlete, actor, congressman) and even marry. They dreamed of moving out to some rural berg, where it seemed better to raise a family, and once the kids had grown and deserted them, of spending the long Buffalo winters in a retirement community down south, in Arizona or Florida.

But Holly couldn't get pregnant. After a while, they began to wonder if there was some physical problem. Their sex life was decent. Holly never seemed repulsed by Jerry's weight, even during certain phases when he let himself balloon due to stress or boredom and started overeating up to the almost gross obesity level. He'd invariably wake up to the fact that he had miserably let himself go and pursue some kind of intense, desperation diet and start working out again until he lost as much as fifty pounds.

Holly eventually grew tired of doctors telling her that there was nothing wrong with either of them, that there was no medical reason for their inability to procreate. She had eggs, an anatomically correct and functional uterus, and Jerry's sperm count was just fine. He could lose some weight, obviously, but that had nothing to do with the results of their coital episodes.

Holly sometimes hinted that Jerry was to blame. He wasn't virile enough, and though the doctor said there was nothing physical preventing him from getting her pregnant, she once suggested that like him, maybe his sperm collectively lacked the confidence to do the deed.

Then one day they simply stopped talking about having kids, raising a family, moving out to the country, and ending their golden, retirement years as Florida snowbirds. Kid names became a discarded, sad memory. There simply came a point in time when Holly seemed oddly content with the idea that they were going to be one of those childless couples whose reason for marriage was selfish companionship or simply habit, rather than doing their marital duty of adding numbers to the species.

One day became the next and they started acting more like roommates than husband and wife. Their relationship eventually lost any semblance of intimacy. There were no more living room picnics by the fireplace. Even the memory of those happy events seemed unreal, like a faded photograph of a long-lost love. Lately, they had settled into a benign numbness. They sipped their respective wines keeping their interests and worries to themselves, Jerry in front of the TV watching sports or the Food Network, or in front of the computer surfing social network or porn sites; Holly in bed reading her romance novels or sometimes, if the mood possessed her, a script or a play.

The odd part was that Jerry hadn't become overly concerned with the lack of intimacy, believing it merely a natural part of the marital aging process. The honeymoon was literally over, but everyone knew it could not last forever. Many of his co-workers at Micro-Connections talked about a similar lack of passion in their marriages. Sure there were some couples that ended up separated or divorced, but that was usually due to infidelity or alcoholism, and Jerry couldn't conceive of that happening with him and Holly, even though he had become horribly jealous of Holly's close proximity, day after day, to the snobby and often handsome young associate lawyers at the firm.

Jerry worried, of course, that the magic spell that had made Holly blind to their physical differences had worn off. He no longer saw the sparkle in her eyes when she looked at him. Could it be that she had finally come to the realization that he was a fat, ugly man with whom she had no business being forever tied? If so, it would be only a matter of time until she walked out. Without any kids, or a financial stake in the relationship, why not?

When out of fearful desperation one night, in their sixth year of marriage, Jerry brought this fear to Holly's attention, she looked at him coldly at first, then with amusement. "You will always be my chubby darling," she had said, and squeezed his flabby belly handles. He was in one of those periods where his weight had ballooned to close to two hundred seventy pounds.

Jerry decided that in order to preserve his sanity, his only recourse was to take Holly at her word and ignore this concern. Life went on, and his worry over Holly dumping him, though ever-present, became more or less a minor annoyance in his life, like a dull and persistent toothache.

One day Jerry realized that seven years had somehow come and gone all too fast. Somehow he and Holly were still together, despite the boredom and lack of passion in their marriage and respective lives. After all those years, Holly and Jerry were now simply living together, like wary friends. Like most married couples become after a while, Jerry supposed.

And then Jeff Flaherty came into their lives.

Chapter Seven

A couple of days after Jerry Shaw's funeral, Jack Fox sat in Dick Reynolds's dingy, cramped office. Reynolds was the white-haired, grizzled Chief of Global Life and Casualty Insurance Company's Special Frauds Unit. Only three weeks ago, Fox had been hired by Reynolds after a long and distinguished career in the Philadelphia Police Department. Like Reynolds, Fox was considered by his fellow Global Life colleagues as a throwback, a cliché of sorts, of the crusty cops of old detective pulp fiction magazines.

Fox had been waiting for some minutes that morning while Reynolds, scowling in his typically methodical and careful manner, finished perusing the contents of a file folder opened before him on his ridiculously undersized and cluttered desk. Two piles of similar investigative folders, each a foot high, had been precariously set on opposite sides of the desk close to Reynolds's bony elbows. Should Reynolds move a couple of inches to the right or left, or perhaps sneeze, Fox thought, the piles would be knocked right off the edge of the desk to the dusty floor.

"Whatcha got, Chief?" Fox finally asked as he squirmed in the uncomfortable chair before Reynolds's desk, wondering if the Chief had forgotten that he was sitting there.

Fox was short, solid as a boulder. In his early sixties, his hair, which he meticulously kept as short as a Marine Corps drill sergeant, had become a mixture of brown and gray and white. All his life he had dutifully battled his weight, first in order to get into the Marines, then after he had gained fifty pounds a couple years after his honorable discharge, to get a spot in the police academy. But over the past year or so, Fox had really let himself go, for whatever reason, and now observed, with a measure of exasperation and alarm, that his once granite, athletic frame was dissolving into a kind of ripened corpulence. When gazing in the mirror the other morning, he was reminded of goddamn Buddha and grumbled to himself as he vigorously brushed his teeth that it was goddamn time to get back to the goddamn gym.

In most other respects, however, Fox had aged gracefully, and, as his wife of thirty-six years could attest, his always handsome features had remained youthful, and there remained in his deep blue eyes a sparkle that told everyone he remained alert and vigilant as the diligent, hard-working, honest kid who had completed Marine Corps boot camp now over forty years ago.

Chief Reynolds finally looked up at Fox. "Four-million-dollar claim," he said, seething. "Something ain't right."

It always bothered the Chief when a large claim like

that came in, thought Fox, as if he would be paying it out of his own pocket.

Fox whistled, truly impressed by the size.

"Any markers?" he asked. "Markers" was the word the Global Life special frauds guys used for indications of fraud in a claim.

Reynolds shrugged. He had been Chief of Global Life's fraud unit from its establishment in the early nineties when insurance companies finally started getting serious about cracking down on the millions lost to fraudulent claims. The Chief had retired from the FBI to take the job and regularly reached out to retired, ex-cop buddies like Jack Fox. Reynolds had learned that Fox wasn't doing much, just some part-time PI work that meant long hours, boring cases, and lousy working conditions, and called him in.

"Markers? Yeah, maybe." Reynolds gave a slight shrug and looked back down at the file. It contained the policy, premium payment history, the UC 505 claim form, a two-page report from the sheriff department's arson task force investigator, and the adjusters' intake/analysis sheet. "The amount of the claim, for one thing. And purchase history."

"When was it bought?" Fox asked.

"Little less than two years ago," said the Chief, "the first million anyway. Six months later, the insured increased it to two. A term policy for a decent enough monthly premium. The insured was married, but no kids. No real reason for such a large policy. Why it wasn't earmarked, I have no idea. Somebody missed it, I guess."

Fox shrugged. The size of the policy, its increase, and

the lack of a need for it were interesting and curious facts, but hardly proved fraud. And what the Chief was talking about went beyond fraud. He was talking murder.

"How'd the insured die?"

"Burned," Reynolds said. "Garage fire. The insured had bought an older model, a Pontiac Sunfire. Apparently, it had a leaky gas tank. He was working under the car trying to fix it. At least, that's what the widow said.

"Anyway, the water heater was out in the garage instead of downstairs in the basement. Not sure why. Gasoline dripped from the leaky gas tank and formed a puddle under the old car right next to where the insured had crawled to get a look at the defective tank. The arson investigator's guess is that a spark arced from the water heater somewhere right into the gas and blew him up. Probably never felt a thing. At least, that's the hope of it. His body was burnt to a proverbial crisp. Some luck for the poor sap, eh? A spark from the friggin' water heater picks that moment to arc."

"Geez, yeah," Fox agreed and shivered from the awful thought of dying like that, burnt alive. "A spark from the water heater could just happen like that?"

"Apparently," Reynolds said. "According to the arson report, it's been noted before as the causative agent."

Reynolds closed the claim folder and, after a wide nine-thirty a.m. yawn, placed it on top of the pile of folders to his right. In the process, they almost came crashing to the floor, but at the last moment, the Chief grabbed and straightened them perfectly back in place.

"So the arson unit up there concluded it was an

accident,"

Fox said. "Isn't that it? Game over for Global Life? Lack of proof, despite the obvious financial motive?"

"I guess," Chief Reynolds said, noncommittal. "The policy was accidental double indemnity?" Reynolds made a face and nodded.

"So the beneficiary, the widow, gets four mil?"

"Yep." Reynolds scowled. "Four mil."

"And all we got is a dead insured," Fox said. "That's it, right? I mean were they having marital, financial problems? Anything?"

"No," he said, more like a bark, as he looked at Fox, "Not to our knowledge anyway. Nothing. Dead insured and that's it."

The Chief looked away, brooding.

Something beyond just the size of the policy was bothering him, his famous intuition perhaps. Fox had heard about it from some other cops and had seen it in action once during his time on the force, and had accepted it was equal to his own.

"But I opened a file anyway," Chief Reynolds said and turned back to Fox. "The numbers alone justify it." After a sigh, he added, "I just don't like it. Too clean, too spic and span. Just like that, four million dollars goes to the poor childless widow. Like winning the lottery, she's set for life at the expense of her poor, dumb-ass husband. Anyway," the Chief said, "I assigned you to the file. You okay with that?"

"Sure." Like the Chief, Fox too felt there was something not quite right about the claim. And if the Chief wanted to dig, he was the Chief. Might cost a couple days poking around, maybe a few hours of surveillance, but what the hell. It would cost a small fraction of the four million dollars the company was about to pay out. And if the Chief was right, and somehow Fox found something incriminating that scuttled the claim, the fraud unit would gain a huge vote of confidence from the company bigwigs not to mention the shareholders. But, if after a few days, a week or so, he found nothing out of the ordinary, not to suggest murder, they'd close the file and authorize the adjuster to pay the claim. Four million bucks. Easy come, easy go.

"So where's the action?"

"Buffalo," said the Chief.

"Buffalo?" Fox rolled his eyes. "Thanks, Chief." Not a popular place, cold, even this time of year. They get big snowstorms sometimes in late October.

"You'd better get going," Reynolds said.

Chapter Eight

Jerry and Holly met Jeff Flaherty almost three years ago when he sat, uninvited, at their table at the annual Christmas party of the law firm, Carlton and Rowe, where Holly had been working as a secretary going on three years. He had been hired as an associate attorney the previous September and Holly had brought him up a few times at home to Jerry. She had described Jeff as some brash new kid who had become the firm heart-throb, making all her secretary colleagues all aflutter with lustful thoughts.

"What about you?" Jerry had asked. "Are you all aflutter?"

Holly had simply smiled and told him with a peck to his cheek, "Course not, I'm a married woman."

Moments before Jeff sat down at their table, the firm's bossy office manager, Grace Stackpoole, had barked from the stage at the front of the grand ballroom in the Hyatt Hotel, where the firm held its party every year, that everyone needed to take a seat "immediately," and repeated, "immediately," so that the hotel caterer could start serving dinner—the usual tiny cube of filet mignon, garlic mashed potatoes, and a handful of green beans.

Jeff was fashionably late arriving at the party, and, of course, late obeying the sit-down order. He wandered over to the lone empty chair at Jerry's immediate right, hovered for a long moment before it, holding a full glass of some reddish-brown mixed bourbon drink just as the army of caterer ladies started delivering salad bowls. After a favorable glance toward Holly at Jerry's left, his stare lingering a moment too long at her generous show of cleavage in the black evening dress, Jeff asked no one in particular at the table, "Mind if I sit?" Without allowing for a response, he abruptly did just that.

Jeff struck up an immediate conversation with Jerry, not the usual small talk about the lousy weather or the prospects of the local sports teams, but complaining what a bore life was for a single guy in a dying city like Buffalo. Jeff was moderately intoxicated, enough that he was slurring his words ever so slightly and leering at some of the ladies' bosoms regardless of whether or not they were attached to some other male companion who might not appreciate such impolite gawking.

"You're not an associate at the firm, are you?" he said to Jerry as he took another sip of whatever drink was in his glass. Before Jerry could answer, Jeff looked across the table past him and raised his glass to Holly. "But you do look familiar."

Holly introduced herself and added that she was Jim Moore's Legal Assistant, the important-sounding title the firm used for secretaries like Holly to make them work harder for little pay. Jerry, she added unenthusiastically, was her husband. And no, she added further, he was not an associate at the firm.

Jeff nodded absently at Jerry, then returned his gaze to Holly, focusing on her chest. She looked quite lovely that evening in her low cut, sleek black dress, with the hemline just above her knees. As for Jerry, he looked like a plump stuffed sausage in an old suit that was worn out and clearly too small for him. While putting it on, he had complained to Holly about failing to buy a new one before the annual event after she had paid so much for her dress, and about letting himself get so goddamned fat.

"And you are?" Holly asked Jeff, though she already knew perfectly well who he was: the newest firm hunk fresh out of the DA's office.

"Jeff Flaherty," he said, and smiled at Holly, "I work for Condon." Ed "Too Tall" Condon (and he was literally that), headed the Litigation Department and was the most highly regarded litigator in the city.

During his brief tenure at Carlton & Rowe, Jeff Flaherty had become the topic of much discussion among the female employees, especially the support staff. The consensus was that he looked like the late Heath Ledger, especially as the sensitive, gay cowboy in *Brokeback Mountain*. Jeff had been tagged as the lovable rogue kind of guy. He was confident, determined, and prone to flirt with anyone wearing a skirt without regard to age or marital status. All women were fair game. Gossip had spread that he was banging Carla Anderson, Condon's slim, beautiful and quite married, black paralegal. It was also rumored that he was also screwing Grace Stackpoole, at least twice his age, whom everyone joked must surely be a dominatrix behind bedroom doors.

"You just started, didn't you?" Holly said as if she hadn't noticed. "Haven't really seen you."

"Three months, next week," he said and laughed. "But who's counting. Our place is such a factory, it's easy to remain anonymous."

Holly nodded in agreement. There were eleven partners and twenty-one associates.

"Plus," Jeff went on, "they don't exactly give young associates much time to fraternize. All I do is research, research, and more research, and after that, case memos up the ying-yang. You know what they say, all research and no trials makes Carlton & Rowe associates dull boys—and girls, I should add, to be politically correct."

Holly smiled at that.

"They'll throw you into court soon enough," she said.

Undoubtedly, Holly was already the envy of her fellow legal assistants to have been lucky enough to share the table with the young and dashing Jeff Flaherty. And Monday morning, in the law firm kitchen, Holly would be peppered with questions from the likes of Gail Morgan and Sue Kowalski (as if she ever had a chance at him) such as: What did he say? What does he smell like up close?

They finally started in on their salads, drenched with some kind of sour vinaigrette dressing. As Jeff ate, and pretty much during the rest of the meal, he directed his conversation Jerry's way, wanting to know exactly what he did for Micro-Connections, whether he liked his job, or did he have designs on doing something else.

Jerry didn't have a ready answer. He stumbled around a minute, knowing full well that he had long since tired of Micro-Connections and was content to stay anonymous, hidden between the management cracks. He told Jeff that his position was secure and interesting enough, and though the opportunity for advancement at Micro was slight, some said non-existent, he had decided to play it safe for the time being until he and Holly gave up entirely on having kids. That comment, overheard somehow by Holly from her side of the table as she conversed with one of the RNs from the Personal Injury Department, caused her to glance disagreeably at Jerry.

Jeff didn't seem to notice. "So you guys don't have any kids?" he asked. "How long you been married?" He chomped on a wide leaf of lettuce with dressing dripping off like syrup into the bowl right under his chin.

"Seven years," said Jerry. "We've been working on it seven years."

Jeff lifted his head from his salad bowl, frowned, and leaned back in his chair. He picked up the glass of bourbon and drank. "Seven years?" He drifted toward Jerry and whispered into his ear. "Shooting blanks?" Jeff then backed away and tossed the rest of the glass of bourbon into his mouth.

"What?" Jerry thought the comment, joke or not, was inappropriate, considering that he had known Jeff Flaherty for now going on ten minutes. Jeff's mouth formed into a kind of smirk that seemed to be something of an assessment of Jerry's masculinity. Drunken asshole, Jerry thought.

"Oh, sorry," Jeff said after another few moments. "Just wondering if you knew what the problem is? Why you can't have kids. Is it medical or something?"

But before he could respond, Holly answered for him from out of nowhere across the table. "Yes, we think he's shooting blanks," she said.

While the other guests around the table tried not to gawk at Holly over the odd and unexpected comment, she gave Jerry a sympathetic look.

"No, not really," she said, then turned to Jeff. "It's all my fault. I'm just not woman enough to give him a son."

Wherever this conversation was going was thankfully, as far as Jerry was concerned, interrupted by one of the caterer's waitresses removing the salad bowls and replacing them with the main course.

As if all was forgotten and they were old buddies who had just exchanged some friendly banter, Jeff laughed, reached over and patted Jerry on the back, told him that he considered him a lucky man to have settled down. In that department, Jeff went on, he had been unlucky in his ability to find the woman of his dreams.

Jeff sliced off the corner of his filet mignon and shoved it into his mouth. In the process of chewing, he leaned over toward Jerry and, after saying, "Ya know, Jer," confided that he regretted ever having become a lawyer. That his true love was hiking, fishing, hunting, the great outdoors (his favorite all-time movie was *Jeremiah Johnson*) and that if he had it to do all over again, he would have gone to forestry school and then moved out west to police one of the national parks. But what was done was done, and if nothing else, the plan was to use his talent for the law to earn him a ton of money in the shortest amount of time possible, retire rich and move out to a hunk of land adjacent one of those national parks and be where he wanted to spend the rest of his days.

As they talked, Jeff glanced across every now and then at Holly. No doubt, thought Jerry, Jeff was wondering, like so many others before him, what it was that Holly saw in this flabby, unimpressive software sales rep guy, her husband, sitting next to him; wondering what it would be like to take her to bed and show her how a real man with tight abs who wasn't shooting blanks made love. But Jerry forced himself to stop thinking that, knowing that it was more a function of his own insecurity than what Jeff and other guys might be thinking.

By the time the plates were cleared from the table, a DJ had set up his sound system and started playing some mild dance tunes. Jerry and Jeff got up to stretch, and surprisingly, Jeff remained in their company as if they were old chums. Holly finally got to her feet and, with a flushed look from too many glasses of white wine, started sashaying at the side of their table to the soft music. After a few moments, with an evil grin, she sauntered around to the side of the table where Jeff and Jerry stood.

"Jerry doesn't like to dance," she told Jeff, nudging up to him, and laughed. "And when he does, he looks like a wounded water buffalo."

"You dance?" she asked Jeff. Jeff nodded. Of course he did.

A moment later, they left Jerry standing there and

went off, hand in hand, onto a cramped dance floor in front of a small stage and started wiggling with a few other couples to the sound of some ancient disco tune. Jeff had moves alright, he was athletic and bold and smooth. Square-jawed dark and handsome, former star of his high school football and track teams. In short, he was everything Jerry wasn't, a live version of what his brother Petey might have morphed into.

After a couple more dances with Jeff, a slow song started playing and Holly came over and pulled Jerry onto the dance floor, her way of making up to him for dancing with Jeff.

"This you can do," she whispered as they edged toward the dance floor where several couples had collected. They swayed with them, going round in endless circles, with Holly standing erect and stiff, hoping that Jerry wouldn't step on her toes as sometimes he was prone to do.

Jeff had moved over to the other side of the room and had engaged a ravishing blonde in a strapless mauve dress in gentle conversation. Next to them stood Condon's legal assistant, Carla Anderson, with her big black husband, Earl. She scowled as she observed Jeff cavort.

After the slow dance, Holly led Jerry back to the table and told him she had a splitting headache and wanted to go home and get to bed. Jerry supposed now that she didn't have Jeff to dance with anymore, the firm's annual Christmas party had become just about as dull as they usually were. She didn't have to ask Jerry twice. He had always despised the mandatory public gatherings of her firm, the Christmas party especially.

As they were walking toward the exit in the rear of the hall, Jeff was suddenly upon them.

"Hey, you folks leaving?" He was wide-eyed, huffing.

They nodded, and looked at each other. Holly said Jerry was tired.

"Mind if I walk out with you," he said, and he strolled with them into the lobby.

"Look," Jeff said as they stood for a moment awkwardly eyeing the revolving door leading out of the place. "Want to stop at that bar across the street for a nightcap?" he asked and looked at Jerry. "Resume our discussion of what troubles the world these days?"

Jerry gave Holly a sideways look and she shrugged as if to say, why not? Her headache was mysteriously cured. Although none of them realized it then, it was the acceptance of Jeff's invitation that sealed their fate.

They went across the street to a noisy bar and had several drinks. In the process, they struck up a friendship of sorts. Jerry even joined in after Holly invited Jeff over for dinner sometime after the holidays. What surprised Jerry most that first night was that in the bar, Jeff didn't even hint at making a pass at Holly. He acted like a simple, nice guy, someone who from a distance over you might have reservations, but once you got to know him, convinced you that he was really the decent sort. They sipped their drinks and talked over the din and rush of the place until one or all of them suddenly noticed that it was almost 2 a.m., and started yawning because the booze they had consumed that night wasn't affecting them anymore. That was when it was mutually decided to call it a night and part ways.

But Jeff had not forgotten their dinner invitation.

Late one afternoon toward the end of January, he peered around Holly's cubicle and reminded her. On the spur of the moment, she offered next Tuesday night and he cheerfully accepted.

Jeff didn't bring a date, as Holly had suggested, and instead came alone. At the table, as they ate, Jeff and Jerry resorted to guy talk, discussing the local sports teams, and for a time, hunting and fishing (about which Jerry feigned interest).

With dinner out of the way, a simple yet delicious roast Holly had shoved into the oven the moment she had walked in the door from work, they retired to the living room at close to eight o'clock with glasses of wine. Jerry stroked some embers to life in the fireplace and they resumed the same thread of conversation they had started at the firm Christmas party now already more than a month ago. Jeff mentioned again how much he detested the work at the firm, and being a lawyer in general. When Jerry asked him why he had taken all the trouble and expense of going to law school, Jeff had answered, "It was either that or becoming an accountant or school teacher, or even worse, working in my father's carpet business." He rolled his eyes. "Jesus Christ, that would have caused me to go frigging nuts."

Holly laughed and took a sip of wine. "You can say the 'fuck' word in this house," she said with a wink, tipping her glass to him. "We're old friends."

"Alright, then," Jeff said and smiled. "Working in my

dad's business would have made me go fucking nuts."

They all laughed at that. But soon enough, what Jerry came to believe was that it was not so much that Jeff detested being a lawyer, accountant or teacher, or a seller and installer of carpets, but working at something in general. He enjoyed leisure time, and the great outdoors, being free of obligation.

They gravitated to national politics, movies and TV shows. What they soon realized was that they had a decent amount in common. And Holly and Jerry soon decided that Jeff was a decent guy, a nice guy.

Finally, at about nine thirty, Jeff thanked them for a pleasant evening, sincerely hoped they would do it again soon, and left for parts unknown. Once he was out the door, Holly suggested with almost envious certainty that he was going from their humble abode to one of his favorite singles' haunts downtown, on Chippewa Street, in search of another of his many conquests of the ladies.

Jerry shrugged and thought there was nothing wrong with that, as long as they were single, even though he knew from Holly that whether or not the particular lady was attached was not a prerequisite and indeed, he seemed to have a penchant for married ladies. After all, rumor was that not only was he still banging Condon's legal assistant, as well as Gloria Stackpoole, but he had taken up with the married legal assistant of yet another partner, Wade Boswell.

"He was nicer than I thought he was going to be," Jerry admitted. "I didn't know what to think at the Christmas party. He seemed so full of himself at times, a nice guy at others."

"Yeah," Holly agreed. "Funny how your perception of a person is different before you really get to know them. I always had thought of him as a conceited fool."

Jerry laughed. "Well, in many ways, he is a conceited fool," he told her.

But Jerry had truly enjoyed Jeff's company. It was a similar feeling a kid gets when he is allowed to hang out with the most popular and brash kid in school or the neighborhood. Though he would not have admitted to himself back then, it may have been Jerry's hope that Jeff's charisma might rub off if they hung out together.

And perhaps from the very beginning, Jerry later thought, that is exactly what Jeff hoped would happen. Befriending Jerry would get him close to both him and Holly, enabling him to move toward the implementation of his plan to obtain a life of luxury by faking Jerry's death. But could Jeff really have been that sinister? Could their friendship have been orchestrated for no other reason but to find the perfect patsy? And worse, was Holly in on it from way back then?

But Jerry wasn't thinking that after their first dinner date only a month after they had met. The experience of being with Jeff had been so intoxicating for both Holly and Jerry, that, with his express approval, Holly invited Jeff over the following Tuesday, and the Tuesday after that, until it became a set ritual.

And after eating whatever Holly threw together, sometimes gourmet, but more often, something simple, like a tuna casserole, they never seemed to tire of adjourning to the living room for some wine and conversation, or on rare occasions, to watch something on TV, settling into the same spots they came to habitually occupy—Holly sprawled out on the far corner of the couch across from Jeff, with Jerry curled up on the loveseat adjacent the couch. Only sickness, two or three times in all those weeks of Tuesdays, prevented this ritual gathering. In fact, there came a time on some of these nights, when, for whatever reason, usually because they had all drunk too much wine, Jeff slept over.

After six months of this, Jerry considered Jeff a close friend. Not a best friend, however. Jerry could never quite get close enough to Jeff where he thought he could confide his inner self to him. Jerry had no other close friends. He wasn't particularly close to anyone at work, although he did go out for drinks with several of his fellow sales representatives from time to time, especially to celebrate someone bagging a new customer, and he was a member of the office fantasy football league. So Jeff's friendship was welcome, even though it ranged to the distant kind.

It seemed to Jerry that Jeff and Holly had become close as well. They would sometimes speak privately, whispering about troubles he was having with his latest girlfriend or deciphering office politics. At least, that's what they told Jerry whenever he attempted to venture into their conversation space and asked them what they were talking about. But Jerry never felt threatened by Jeff. After all, he had so many girlfriends, he didn't need another. And he seemed to prize their Tuesday dinners enough to avoid ruining them by making Holly unfaithful, however much she (and Jeff) may have fantasized about that happening, a possibility Jerry quickly chased from his mind whenever it popped in.

The Tuesday dinners were expanded to other days when they became a curious threesome at various entertainment and sporting events. They bought a 20-game package for the Buffalo Sabres though none of them knew anything about hockey, and rarely missed a Broadway musical at Shea's Theatre of Performing Arts. That summer, Jeff dragged Jerry out to his small cabin in the middle of nowhere to lay around a couple weekends, drinking beer and fishing in the creek a mile or so into the woods behind the place. That was when Jerry decided there was a quirky, lonely side to Jeff, an emotional vacuum the result, at least from an armchair psychologist perspective, of an unloving and demanding mother. But once again, Jeff refused to confide anything beyond the superficial, the names and places from his childhood, but nothing else, and so their relationship remained friendly though not particularly deep.

It was nearly a year later, after one of those Tuesday night dinners as they lazed around the living room in front of a blistering fire a couple weeks before Christmas, having drunk way too much wine, Jeff finally brought up his crazy plan to fake Jerry's death.

Chapter Nine

The first thing any decent private investigator masters, after many long and arduous hours of on-the-job training, is how to conduct an effective and discreet stakeout.

Jack Fox had learned over the years that a professional, high-quality surveillance depends first and foremost upon one's vehicle. Windowless vans were best, preferably with a fake logo of some home service contractor, followed by vans with darkly tinted windows, then SUVs or cars similarly equipped. Of course, if a regular car was all you had, then you needed to augment your efforts to make it, and yourself, inconspicuous. The bottom line was that your car should, ultimately, blend in with the surroundings. No matter what kind of vehicle was used, it was crucial that it be parked in a location that would not arouse curiosity or suspicion in the mind of some nosy neighbor, or of course, the target.

The next thing, of course, was to learn how to kill the inevitable long stretches of time, hours or days perhaps, when absolutely nothing happens.

Last, but certainly not least, it was important to take note of suitable, nearby places with a clean public toilet in the vicinity of the stakeout where you could run and pee or crap; or, if leaving the stake-out was not possible, a suitable container that would at least hold the piss and not stink up the car was essential.

Believe it or not, such items are available for purchase. The couple of surveillance vans belonging to Global's Fraud Unit back in Philly were equipped with mini porta-potties but Chief Reynolds had told Fox that they were unavailable for this job. So he would do, as he had done countless times before, with an ordinary rental sedan and have to rely on the nearest public restroom.

Jack Fox had probably conducted a thousand stake-outs in his thirty-two-year career as a detective, then a private investigator, and now insurance fraud agent, and thus, he had become adept at the art of surveillance. He knew exactly where to park his vehicle in order to best observe the target, and, once there, to remain unnoticed for hours or days or weeks. He always grabbed several newspapers, some magazines (specializing in hunting and fishing), and a couple bestsellers to kill the time, provided there'd be enough light to read anything at all; and, in the last few years, Fox had even taken along a Walkman and listened to music (country in his case) on CDs or, more recently, his iPod. A small cooler filled with sodas and ice had also become a part of his supplies.

After flying into the relatively small, subdued and dreary Buffalo airport late Sunday night, Fox rented a basic model, inconspicuous navy blue compact sedan. The clerk apologized that despite his request, the model available did not have tinted windows. Fox thought a moment, then said it was no problem.

He checked into a decent enough hotel near the airport and got his usual bad night's sleep on a queen-sized bed with a hard mattress and pillows the size of dishrags. His wake-up call came at 6 a.m. sharp. Bleary-eyed, he brewed a pot of weak, lukewarm coffee in the mini-coffee maker in the bathroom and drank it while sitting on the edge of the bed thinking how lousy it was to grow old. In five years, six months, he'd be seventy. His father had died at seventy-one. And where had all the time gone?

Fox took another sip of coffee, sighed and clicked on the TV to get some light in the room. He turned down the volume so low he couldn't hear the banter among a pair of chirpy hosts of a local morning wake-up show. Finally, after a deep yawn, Fox trudged into the bathroom and took a quick hot shower, shaved, and brushed his teeth. Still groggy, he slipped into new, gray dress pants (disgusted that the waist had bulged out to size 40—in his heyday, he had been a 34), and tossed a sweater over his head. With the outside world still in the grip of cold darkness, and only a few unlucky souls moving about, Fox visited the bathroom one last time and relieved himself just to make sure the urge would not hit him the first minute of the stake-out. Then he threw on a jacket and stumbled out of the hotel.

In an insufficiently lit parking lot, Fox walked around in circles a minute, trying to remember where he had parked the rental car, found it, then finally began his journey out to

Northview Lane in Hamburg, New York, wherever the hell that was, to stakeout the very house where the insured, Jerry Shaw, had burned to death. Along the way, contrary to his best intentions, he stopped at a McDonald's and ordered the Sausage and Egg McMuffin breakfast value meal with a cup of strong black coffee.

With all that grease sludging around in his gut and bowels, Fox found his way to the target residence. Initially, he spent some time driving up and down the plain, mostly treeless wide streets of the newer subdivision, which, in addition to Northview, included other unimaginative names such as Southview, Westview and Eastview lanes. Fox spotted a decent place to park to watch the comings and goings of the insured's house—an access road to a deserted parcel of land about a tenth of a mile across from the main subdivision. The parcel had been plowed into a rough-strewn mud and rock heap but that was it. The access road was a narrow dirt path that led nowhere. The builder had likely run out of money, or run off with it, and no one had yet thought there might be a profit in picking up the slack.

Fox did a U-turn and parked along the curb on the access road to nowhere. He nodded to himself, pleased that he had a straight, clear view of the insured's former house where he could watch his widow come and go either with the naked eye, or as was more likely, with a pair of top quality Spytek 4-in-1digital camera surveillance binoculars. Fox also had with him a decent enough digital video recorder but, being an old-timer, he preferred the glossy permanence of a photograph of a target caught in the act. His most lucky and famous was snapped twenty-five years ago while working as a part-time private investigator for a Philadelphia firm to supplement his measly Police Department salary. He had been following a particularly nasty guy, Dan Goss, for a couple weeks before finally catching him late one night in his Jaguar getting a blowjob from his latest paramour in some lonesome public park. As Fox snapped a series of incriminating photographs for use by his soon-to-be-ex-wife, Goss pointed a silver revolver at him. The lawyer who had hired Fox to follow Goss had framed the photograph and given it to Fox and Fox stuck it on his wall.

By the time Fox parked, it was already eight-thirty. Only three days after the funeral, Fox doubted Mrs. Shaw had gone back to work for the law firm where, he already knew from the police arson report, she had been employed as a paralegal for the past five years.

Fox picked up his binoculars and brought the Shaw house into crisp focus. It was a decent-sized, nicely manicured raised ranch with white vinyl siding with a large deck attached to the back overlooking a fairly bland yard. All told, Fox guessed the house probably measured something like twenty-two hundred square feet of living space, with a fair-sized kitchen and living room, a den, and three upstairs bedrooms. In short, it was a decent spread. But it was unlikely the insured's bride of seven plus years would stay there once the nearly four million plus dollars of life insurance proceeds was paid. In that new life, this house would seem more like a servant's quarters.

Fox snapped several shots and looked back at the camera screen to make sure it was working. An old dog, high-tech gimmickry had never been his forte. Satisfied that it was working just fine, Fox resumed what he did best, watching. The sun was, by now, hovering above the rooftops and some of the residents of this sleepy subdivision were just starting out to their tiresome jobs.

The garage of the insured's house was still boarded up with a sheet of plywood. Fox would have loved at some point to sneak inside and have a look around. Sometimes the local arson team was a bunch of incompetent chumps who hurried through the job so they could go to the nearest donut shop and kill a few more hours of another boring shift talking about the local football team's chances that coming Sunday.

But Fox had to admit that this case seemed a cinch anyway. It was more likely than not that the arson guys weren't chumps, but decent enough cops who had gotten it right by calling the scene a tragic accident. According to their report, what had happened was that some hapless yokel, Global's deceased insured, had the bad luck of finding himself lying next to a small pool of gasoline that had leaked from an eight-year-old Pontiac Sunfire he had purchased just a week earlier for a couple grand as a second car. An atomic bit of electronic charge chose that very instant to arc from an old water heater and ignite the pool of highly flammable gasoline, causing the spontaneous explosion and fire that burnt him to a proverbial crisp. The arson report had mentioned that the fellow who sold Jerry Shaw the Sunfire was adamant in his statement to one of their investigators that the car he had sold to Jerry Shaw had never leaked gasoline. Fox's eyebrows had raised upon reading that and he jotted down the name and address of the former owner of the Sunfire for a possible interview.

Not two minutes into Fox's surveillance, a pickup truck with ladders along both sides with the name "Bandario's Construction" blazoned along the driver and passenger doors pulled up in front of the house. Then Fox finally saw her, the grieving and potentially rich widow, Holly Shaw.

She had sauntered out of the front door in a long, securely fastened bathrobe to greet a crew of three leather-tanned workers in greasy coveralls with disheveled hair under ancient, dirty baseball caps. She pointed to the garage and they nodded dumbly. *They must be there to clean it out and fix it up.* Not a minute later another Ford pickup truck came rumbling down Northview pulling a long, dented dumpster. The dumpster was backed all the way up the small driveway of the house to what used to be the garage door but was now simply a section of fiberboard.

Fox quickly aimed the digital camera at Mrs. Shaw, zoomed in and immediately started snapping pictures as she watched the construction crew get started. She was a lovely blonde, with a slim, sexy body even under her thick, velvety white bathrobe, and she seemed amused by the almost comical banter among the crew as they shuffled around the back of the truck pulling out whatever equipment they needed to tear down walls and remove burned out gunk from the irreparably damaged garage. Finally, she left them to do their jobs and walked back to the front door and into the house. All the while, Fox kept snapping photographs. He even caught every one of the five or six workmen giving

Mrs. Shaw's slender behind a glance before she had safely gone back into the house.

Whatever potential evidence of arson and murder that had remained in the garage after the fire would soon be lost forever. Fox cringed as he watched, for the next hour or so, needing only a single trip to the Noco public restroom, as Bandario's crew tore out the remains of the inside of the garage and tossed the melted, warped walls, charred two-by-fours, and other blackened, unrecognizable stuff into the dumpster. Finally, at around ten thirty, Fox decided that there was nothing else worth watching. He snapped his binoculars into a case and tossed the digital camera onto the passenger seat. With a sigh, he started the car and drove away, returning to the hotel. The plan was to get a few hours shut-eye, then return that evening to see if what the widow was up to, if anything.

For some reason, Fox was confident there'd be something. Back at the hotel, he was more sure of it than ever as he picked up the digital camera from the desk at the far corner of the room and examined the photographs he had taken that morning of Holly Shaw outside the house. By the look of her, by the way the grieving widow sashayed within eyesight of the construction crew, Fox sensed this one was up to no good. Or maybe he was just imagining something that wasn't there. A sashaying widow is hardly proof of murder. He sighed, set the camera on the desk, and thought about finally doing what his wife had been telling him he should do after Dick Reynolds had called him and pleaded that he take the job with Global—retire and spend some time travelling with her, visiting his daughter in

Seattle, finally seeing Europe, before the Grim Reaper paid him an inevitable visit. But he craved the craft of investigation, working up a case. It was more than a job; it was an addiction.

With a yawn, Fox decided he wasn't ready to retire. Not just yet. Not in the middle of this case. No, it was more than a widow's sashay that bothered him. Dick Reynolds was right. There was something just too neat about this case. An electron arcing from a hot water heater and igniting a pool of gasoline right where the insured was laying was just too damned neat. There had to be more.

After another yawn, Fox stripped to his skivvies, lifted the covers off the bed and slid under them onto the crisp, cold sheets. He closed his eyes and allowed himself the pleasure of being overwhelmed by the wallowing security of sleep. Despite the hard bed and bad pillows, Fox could not recall ever falling asleep so fast. Perhaps, that was another sign of his age.

Six hours later, he woke with a start. After a moment of consciousness, he started cursing. He tossed off the covers and jumped out of bed and quickly showered and dressed and rushed back to set up another stakeout of the insured's house at 320 Northview Lane. This time, he parked several houses down from the target address because after dark it would have been foolish to conduct the surveillance parked along the deserted access road. For one thing, he'd stand out like a sore thumb at this hour of the night and might become a prime interest for a sheriff's patrol, not to mention that it would be next to impossible to see anything going on in the Shaw residence from that vantage point. But parked where he was just a few houses down on Northview from the Shaw residence, far enough away from the closest street lamp to keep the car bathed in darkness, all Fox had to do was slink down below the steering wheel and the car would look empty, just like the three or four others parked on this or the other side of the wide, otherwise deserted street.

But within an hour after resuming the stakeout, Fox began to doubt his certainty that the Shaw woman was up to no good. She was home, somewhere in the living room, watching television. Through the closed curtains of the wide picture window, Fox observed her shadow move about every now and then, walking somewhere, likely into the kitchen for a snack. The alternating glow of whatever she was watching on the television changed from scene to scene. It surprised Fox that Mrs. Shaw had remained at the house this close to the disaster, with her husband's horrible demise so close at hand. Perhaps, thought Fox, she treasured this time alone. That she truly was grieving.

And then Jeff Flaherty arrived.

Fox was nearly snoozing when, at about eight that night, a silver Lexus turned onto Northview and slowed as it passed the target residence. Fox came alert just in time and ducked his squat frame and head low and then laid sideways across the front seat, completely below the steering wheel. He held his breath as the Lexus finally sped up and passed, continued down Northview. But then the Lexus turned around in a driveway several houses down, came back in his direction, and pulled into a parking space just ahead of his along the curb in front of the house next door to 320 Northview.

A tall, athletic-looking young man, in his late twenties or early thirties or so, exited the Lexus. He was wearing tight blue jeans and a jean jacket. He stood outside the car a moment and used the driver's side window as a mirror to comb his right hand through a thick wave of dark brown hair. After some moments, satisfied with his appearance, he strode confidently up the driveway and onto a short walkway to the front door of the target residence. After smoothing his hair, then rolling his neck, the young man knocked on the front door.

Fox edged up in his seat and peered through the spokes of the steering wheel. He lifted his digital camera binoculars from the passenger seat onto his lap as he waited for someone, Mrs. Shaw, no doubt, to answer the door. Finally, the door opened and light flooded the porch.

Fox lifted the camera and started shooting. He caught everything—the way the Shaw woman raised up on her toes to wrap her arms around the unknown man's shoulders; the way she then lifted her left leg and nuzzled his right thigh; and, finally, the long, deep kiss she pressed onto his lips. The camera also caught the way, after a moment, the man resisted her advances and turned to look across the front yard worrying over someone like Fox catching sight of her display of passion. But it was too late. He—and they—had not been careful enough.

The man did not see Fox, hunched low behind the steering wheel in the front seat of his inconspicuous sedan in the shadows of the streetlights. After another moment, the man edged with Mrs. Shaw into the house. He remained there for the next two hours.

Fox didn't move for fifteen minutes after the silver Lexus with the unknown man drove out of the subdivision. He memorized the license plate, of course, and after hurrying back to his hotel room, he immediately tapped into Global's database and soon learned that the Lexus was registered to one Jeffrey David Flaherty. After a few more keystrokes and mouse clicks, Fox learned that Flaherty was a lawyer and that he was an associate at Curtis and Rowe, the same firm where Holly Shaw, the grieving widow, had worked the past five years.

Bingo! thought Fox. But bingo for what prize? He wasn't quite sure.

He called Chief Reynolds' cell phone right away. It was ten forty-two. The Chief would likely be up watching some old, schlock detective movie starring Humphrey Bogart or Robert Mitchum.

"Yeah?" the Chief answered.

"Chief?"

"Yeah. Fox?"

"Yeah."

"Whatcha got?"

"The grieving widow has a boyfriend," he said.

They both knew what that meant—now, at least, there was a possible motive.

The Chief was munching on potato chips as he listened to Fox tell him what he had seen. Jeff Flaherty visiting the grieving widow.

"Got that all the first night?" Reynolds said. "You sure are one slick operator, Jack."

"You want me to stay up here, Chief?" Fox asked. "Watch her another night?"

"Yeah, sure," the Chief said. "It'll be like a vacation, up there in beautiful Buffalo. Is it snowing yet?"

Fox laughed. "Hey, Chief, what you watching tonight?"

"Watching?"

"Yeah. What old movie?"

The Chief kept quiet a moment, knowing that his staff of four investigators secretly laughed about his interest in old detective movies.

"*Double Indemnity*," he said. "You know, the one with Barbara Stanwyck at her foxy and sultry best, and Ed McMurray before *My Three Sons* ruined a decent acting career. And best of all, Edward G. Robinson as the insurance investigator. Ever see that one, Jack?"

"Sure have, Chief. Sure have."

Chapter Ten

In early May, five months before they faked his death, Jerry drove down to Binghamton to buy a house in one of the nondescript, old residential neighborhoods in the town of Endicott just west of it. With a population now dwindled to around thirty thousand, Endicott constituted one part of the so-called Tri-Cities—Endicott, Johnson City, and Binghamton. More importantly, as far as Jerry, Holly, and Jeff were concerned, it was only a three and half hour ride down from Buffalo.

At one time, the Tri-Cities had been an economic hub, a vibrant metropolis with industries like Endicott Shoes and IBM, among others, providing decent wages to mostly lower middle and working class stiffs to spend in supermarkets and department stores and on mortgages for now outdated, oversized clapboard houses. But like so many other northeastern rust belt towns in the latter half of the twentieth century, the Tri-Cities had lost its manufacturing base and fell into a long, numbing, slumbering decline. The sons and daughters of its once proud and prosperous citizenry, themselves sons and daughters of proud eastern and southern European parents and grandparents, had abandoned family and friends to join the grand exodus of the U.S. masses to the more promising environs in the sun belt or out west, to boom towns like Charlotte, Orlando, Atlanta, Phoenix, Houston, or Las Vegas.

In the last decade or so, Endicott's most famous and largest employer, the iconic IBM, had sold off its manufacturing plant to Endicott Technologies resulting in yet another round of devastating layoffs. A few years before that, the longstanding Endicott-Johnson Shoes, which had employed thousands for nearly seventy years, had gone under. On and on it went, bad economic news followed by more bad economic news, as the old companies went bankrupt, closed down and boarded up or left town for better tax breaks and cheaper labor until there didn't appear to be a reason for the existence of the Tri-Cities anymore except to house the stragglers who didn't have the wherewithal or gumption to pack up and leave town.

The conspirators had selected Endicott as Jerry's initial hiding place because, first of all, it was far enough away from Buffalo to avoid the likelihood that anyone presently living there would know Jerry or Holly, yet close enough so it wasn't a hassle to make a morning or afternoon drive. Second, Jerry and Holly knew the area from their college days. They also knew that it was a quiet, nondescript community in which Jerry and later Holly could blend into until they made their ultimate move to a warmer and happier clime—say, Charlotte, Orlando, Atlanta, Phoenix or Las Vegas.

Once safely ensconced in Endicott, they would begin their new lives in earnest, with all the money they would ever need, and, according to their plan, live happily ever after. By then, Jeff would have gone his own way, out of their lives forever as strangely and expectantly as he had entered it. He would have bought that ranch in Montana or wherever he really intended to go and be living happily ever after himself in his own distinctive, filthy rich way. On occasion, they discussed missing each other once Jerry's death was faked and the insurance money paid, but mostly they avoided the topic.

Once Jerry had found a house that seemed right for them, he was to confer with Jeff. If they agreed that the place was a good fit, all he had to do was call the realtor and make an acceptable bid on behalf of a limited liability company, or "LLC," they had formed under the laws of New Mexico. Establishing the New Mexico LLC had been Jeff's idea. He had read about it after doing some research on his home computer on becoming anonymous, or invisible. He even found a website written by some former CIA agent explaining how one could fairly easily do so, becoming hidden from even the most determined law enforcement authorities.

Actually, it was quite simple. New Mexico offered the legal means of incorporating an LLC *without* identifying its members or requiring annual reports. All one needed to do was designate the name for the LLC, an address, its duration (December 31, 2099, was acceptable) and, a resident agent, —that is, an individual who resided at a real street address in New Mexico who was then authorized to receive communication and accept service of legal process. Sharp New Mexicans offered their services as resident agents for a reasonable fee, then filed the incorporation papers which, importantly, under New Mexico law, did not require the actual members, or owners, to be identified. Ever. For an additional fee, the New Mexican resident agent service offered to obtain a "ghost" address someplace for the owners of the LLC, usually in the Canary Islands.

According to Jeff, ownership of such an LLC was completely untraceable. They could use it to purchase cars, real estate, and importantly, they could open an account in the name of the LLC in an obscure local bank or credit union outside New York, where they could stash their respective shares of the life insurance money. The paper trail would lead, eventually, to an LLC that had no identifiable members. Thus, it was the rare paper trail that led nowhere and to no one, making it impossible, should they be inclined to try, for the fraud investigators to trace where the life insurance money had gone. Once it was paid, the insurance money itself would become invisible. At least, that was how Jeff explained it.

Jerry could still remember that Tuesday-with-Jeff-dinner-night in January just after the Christmas Holidays, a few weeks after they had first concocted what had seemed a cockamamie conspiracy to fake Jerry's death, when Jeff told them about the New Mexican LLC deal. He had burst into the house out of breath, laughing, proclaiming that he had found a perfect way for Jerry to become anonymous.

With his wide, handsome grin, he told them, "This is

better, much better, and safer and easier, than establishing a new identity for Jerry or setting up an offshore bank account where we could stash the insurance money." Then he had let out a whoop and danced around the kitchen with Holly in his arms.

The name selected for the LLC, at Jerry's suggestion and insistence, was "Anonymous Incorporated, LLC."

Mostly college kids attending the University of Binghamton rented in the Endicott neighborhood where Jerry had found a house that he considered acceptable for purchase by Anonymous Incorporated. In fact, Jerry and his two closest buddies from his college years had rented a flat in one of these monstrous doubles just a few blocks away. Not much had changed about the neighborhood in the ten years or so since Jerry had lived there. Or in the fifty years before that.

"The place is perfect," Jerry had told Jeff.

As instructed, Jerry was calling Jeff's cell phone from a pay phone, perhaps one of the last in existence, near the entrance of the convenience store of some self-serve gas station.

"An upper and lower flat, right now occupied by college kids who'll vacate by the end of the semester. I can move into the lower flat and keep the upstairs empty. The rest of the houses in the neighborhood are doubles, renting to college kids. I won't hardly be noticed. "

"Sounds good," Jeff said. He sighed, annoyed, as he was a lot these final weeks as they prepared to actually pull off the fraud.

"So, okay," he said after a moment, "make a bid. Lowball, but not too low. I'll handle the closing. It's a cash deal—my cash, so it should close quickly. Shouldn't arouse any suspicion. Looks like Anonymous Incorporated is about to own a house."

The bid was accepted for only two thousand dollars more than Jerry's initial offer. Less than a month after the bid had been accepted, the house was deeded to Anonymous Incorporated, LLC. It would remain empty the rest of that summer and into the fall until Jerry needed it in late October, when they planned to implement the conspiracy.

Now that they had a safe house for Jerry to spend his first anonymous days, they could move on to phase two of their plan: faking his death.

Chapter Eleven

It had been decided that Jeff would sleep over the night before they faked Jerry's death. Before going to bed, Jeff and Jerry had gone downstairs and pulled the cadaver out of the freezer so that it would be defrosted by morning. It had been stuffed into a dark blue body bag with a zipper along the side. As they lifted the body from the freezer that night, it struck Jerry funny that they were defrosting the body of a dead human being so that they could, in effect, cook it in the morning and he let out a laugh.

"What's so funny, Jer?" Jeff had asked as they lowered the body bag onto the basement floor.

"This," Jerry had said and pointed at his feet. Then, he shrugged, not seeing the humor in it anymore. "Nothing."

The alarm went off way too early the next morning, a Saturday. The plan called for them to start the fire a few minutes before eight, even as early as seven thirty. This, they believed, would ensure that most of Jerry and Holly's neighbors would still be fast asleep.

Each of them was a little hung over that morning, and Jeff was especially ornery. He insulted Jerry every now and then, barking at him to hurry it up and that he better get his "fat ass" in gear. Jeff got especially abusive as he and Jerry lifted the still quite cold and stiff cadaver off the basement floor and carried it upstairs through the kitchen and out into the attached garage.

Jerry recalled that Holly had been pretty much useless that morning, seeming more hung over and out of it than either him or Jeff. She slunk around the kitchen table with her robe half open, a coffee cup dangling in her hand, advising them to take it slow, that haste makes waste. Just take your time and do it right, she kept saying.

Jeff was first to unzip the body bag. He immediately backed away from it, gagging.

"Jesus fucking Christ," he said, wobbling, making a "gack" sound, seeming about to retch.

Jerry stepped forward and looked down at the cadaver and did likewise. The corpse was markedly decomposed, and, despite the refrigeration and still half-frozen state, it reeked. The face, what little Jerry could make of it, was badly mangled, hardly recognizable as human. Still, it was a human cadaver, formerly a man, approximately Jerry's height, if not weight.

Holly entered the garage from the kitchen carrying a supermarket paper bag containing old sweatpants that Jerry had worn out, together with a pair of his old boxers, used tee-shirt, socks, and sneakers. As she handed the bag to Jerry, she looked down at the naked cadaver.

"Ew!" she said and stepped back into the kitchen.

Jerry and Jeff looked at each other a long moment.

"Now we got to somehow dress this motherfucker," Jeff said. Jerry sighed. "Dress it? It's still stiff as a board."

So that was their first blunder and it almost soured them to the whole scam. They had totally underestimated how long it would take for the cadaver to defrost sufficiently during the night so it could be dressed with Jerry's old clothes before it was deposited under the car. Because of that, they had to wait forty-five minutes in the kitchen drinking coffee and reading the morning paper for the body to thaw to enable them to pull Jerry's boxer shorts and sweatpants up its legs, slip an old one of his tee shirts over its head, and then shove onto its feet a pair of Jerry's old sneakers. Jeff wondered how they could have overlooked that important detail and fretted about what else had been overlooked. He must have said, "Goddamn it," and "stupid fucking idiots," a hundred times.

This waiting made them commence the scam almost an hour after they had planned. Even though it was almost nine by the time they started dressing the cadaver, they decided it was still early enough to do the job. And anyway, there was no way Holly and Jerry were going to tolerate that cadaver in the house another night.

When Jerry took the initiative and tried to slip the boxer shorts up the cadaver's gummy legs. He started to retch, then he actually bent over and dry-heaved, "Jesus, Jer," Jeff said, laughing. "Get a grip."

Jerry backed off to stop from throwing up outright and with a frown, Jeff took over the job. And despite swearing the whole time, and stopping to dry-heave himself several times along the way, Jeff got it done in about ten minutes. The cadaver, laying there now on the cold cement floor of the garage fully clothed, looking somewhat like a sleeping zombie, was ready to be shoved under the car. Jerry came over and helped Jeff push the body to a spot almost directly under the old clunker's ten-gallon gas tank which Jerry had filled last night at the Noco station around the corner. Both Jerry and Jeff retched again at some point in the process and had to stop a few moments. After a breath, they got back to it. With the body in place, Jeff used an oil can to squirt a sizeable enough puddle of gasoline next to the cadaver. All they had to do now was light it.

"Ready?" Jeff turned and asked Jerry. "Guess we're at the point of no return, huh, Jer?"

Jerry shrugged.

"I wonder what the guy's name was?" Jerry asked as he and Jeff stared down at the sneakered feet of the dead body sticking out from underneath the Sunfire. The cadaver had settled in a most unnatural position, with its legs twisted around the wrong way and its sneakered feet pointing in opposite directions. But that didn't matter. In a few minutes, the thing would be a lump of ash, even more unidentifiable as a human being.

"Dumb shit," Jeff said, "like you."

"Fuck off," Jerry said and thought a moment of slugging Jeff.

Holly had entered the garage and focused her gaze on what they were looking at.

"Are we a go?" she asked.

"Yep," Jeff said. "We are a go. T-minus one minute

and counting."

Three days later, at just after five on the afternoon of his fake funeral, Jerry arrived at the house in Endicott. He opened the front door and stepped into a musty, stale smell, half-expecting a couple of sharp-edged detectives from the Endicott Police Department or mirthless Special Agents from the FBI to be waiting for him with an arrest warrant and Miranda rights. But the kitchen was empty, and the place was silent.

During his ride down from Buffalo, Jerry had been consumed by the thrill of escape. They had pulled it off, a major crime. The only thing that worried Jerry during the ride down to Binghamton was doing something stupid, like speeding or getting into an accident, that would draw the attention of a state trooper or county sheriff's deputy to himself. But nothing had happened, and here he was.

Jerry had questioned Jeff about his ability to drive once he was deemed a dead man. Jeff had assured him, and Holly as well, that he didn't have to worry.

"The DMV won't know you're dead until someone tells them you're dead," he said. "There's no death certificate database that refers that kind of information to the Department of Motor Vehicles, resulting in your license being canceled. Nobody ever thought that something like that would be necessary. They didn't imagine this situation. So, rest assured, my little chubby buddy, even after you die, you'll be able to drive. And your license doesn't expire, what did you tell me, for six years?" Then, he added with that silly grin that made him go instantaneously from serious to silly,

"You'll be is a ghost driver."

Jeff summed it up by assuring Jerry that if a state trooper, or any cop for that matter, stopped him, Jerry could flash his license and they'd accept it without ever realizing that the driver they had stopped, Jerry Shaw, was listed as deceased by the records of the County of Erie.

The lower flat was partially furnished with an old living room set including banged up end tables and a crooked wooden coffee table. It also included a gas stove and refrigerator. During a subsequent trip down to Binghamton only three weeks before his death, Jerry used cash to buy a plain bedroom set from an anonymous thrift store, together with a love seat and assorted bric-a-brac to complete the living room and satisfy his need for some semblance of comfort and homeyness during the period when he would be exiled down there alone, waiting for the proverbial dust to settle so that Holly could join him. Then she would start filling her role as the front for his anonymity. She would be just like Albert, Batman's front, or Beavis, the front Jerry had invented for his comic book hero, the Anonymous Man, after his first front, Karen, left him in Issue #2.

Jerry stood at the wide archway leading into the living room for a moment and took a deep breath. To the world, he was dead. He no longer existed. He was completely and utterly free.

But in the next moment, once this wave of initial exuberance had faded, it hit him that he was completely and utterly alone. Wifeless, friendless, family-less. Lifeless, for that matter. Literally. A person completely and irrevocably shut off from the rest of humanity. There was no one who knew him, no one who loved him. Not here, not in this house in Endicott. Holly was more than three hundred miles away. And Jeff, well, he didn't think that Jeff really cared about him. All Jeff cared about was getting the insurance money so that he could make his escape to the wide open, deserted lands of Wyoming, Utah, Montana or whatever desolate fucking place he wanted to go.

Jeff had softened the troubling prospect of becoming an invisible man this way: Jerry didn't need or want a new identity because he had Holly. Once the insurance company paid off the policy, Holly would join him and take care of all his needs forever after. The cost to Jerry, if he could call it that, was that he would have to live under Holly's yoke and whim the rest of his life. But she'd certainly have to comply with her part of the deal, Jeff assured him, and interact with the world on his behalf, in order to satisfy his needs. If she didn't, she risked losing everything she had as well. Jerry could simply turn her in, and blow the cover off their crime. By bringing them in and cooperating with law enforcement and the insurance companies, his lawyer could probably convince the DA to give him a favorable plea. But for his sudden awakening of conscience, his lawyer would undoubtedly argue, the DA and the victims in this case, Global Life and Casualty Insurance Company and all their policy-holders and the people who owned shares in their company, would have remained none the wiser and would have suffered a loss of four million dollars. He might even walk away with probation and maybe even a little money in his pocket.

Not that he would ever need to make such a deal, Jeff had added with a laugh. After all, Holly loved him, and he loved Holly, and that was all the motivation in the world she required to take care of his needs.

Jeff also reminded Jerry that going anonymous meant exactly that: he must become truly dead. There could be no contact with anyone from his former life.

Now, alone in the house, thinking about all that, the certainty of his situation hit Jerry full force, making him a little light-headed, woozy. He was a little shaky on his feet as he returned to the kitchen after exploring the rest of the house to assure himself that he was alone. Jerry stood there for a time, considering his predicament. He was unable to shake the reality of what he and Holly and Jeff had just pulled off. It rode over him like a wave of grief and continued to oppress and overwhelm him. At the time, they had planned the scheme, and even during his fake funeral, the consequences hadn't seemed all that important. But now that it had come to pass, Jerry felt horrible that he had so callously tossed aside all connection to family, friends, and the memories of his former life. He wondered if this was what gangsters went through after ratting out their colleagues entering the federal witness protection.

But even those rats retained their identities.

Now that he was anonymous, without an identity or a name, like George Bailey in *It's A Wonderful Life,* it was as if he had never been born.

But that thought didn't make Jerry feel so good. He sat at the kitchen table and stared out the window looking across a gloomy, narrow driveway at the clapboard house next door.

He felt alone, alone as he had ever felt.

Anonymity, he thought, was something like being dead.

Chapter Twelve

Fifteen minutes later, Jerry was still sitting at the kitchen table ruminating upon his situation in the glare from the old-fashioned light fixture in the center of the ceiling. And finally, he considered what had been truly nagging at him for the last couple of years, if not longer: did Holly love him anymore?

In raising the question, he had to consider a possible answer—that she didn't. That possibility made Jerry dizzy with grief and longing. After a time, still suffering and sick, he reached into the front pocket of his jacket and felt for the pre-paid cell phone.

Jeff had initially refused Jerry's request for it. There'd be too much temptation to use it, he had argued. But Jerry stood his ground and insisted that he needed some easy and ready way to communicate with them, just in case. After mulling it over for a day or two, Jeff relented with strict instructions that it could only be used in an absolute fucking emergency, as an absolute last fucking resort.

Despite Jeff's admonition, it took every ounce of

Jerry's resolve not to take out the cell phone right then and there and call Holly and tell her how sorry he was for letting their love dwindle and forgetting how special she had made him feel. But realizing that at bottom, Jeff's warning was sound, that it could endanger their ultimate plan, Jerry managed to take a few deep breaths to gather his strength and refrain from calling Holly despite how badly he needed to hear her voice, and despite how badly he needed to say hello to her followed by the inevitable, I love you.

What she would say in response, Jerry had no idea. It had been so long since he had confronted his fear that their love was over, had left it to fester like an unclean wound, he didn't care what she might say. He simply needed an answer. Bringing it up and putting it on the agenda for discussion seemed just plain necessary. Inexorable.

Finally, with trembling fingers, Jerry removed the cell phone from the pocket of his jacket and placed it on the kitchen table. He stood, took the jacket off and hung it on the back of the old, rickety wooden chair, then walked over to the refrigerator. Opening it, Jerry saw three lonely bottles of Beck's Ale on the center rack from a six pack left over from three weekends ago when he had returned to the apartment with a suitcase and two boxes of clothes and various toiletry and kitchen utensils. Jerry removed one of the bottles, opened it with a can opener on his key chain, took a sniff of the dry, "skunky" smell of the ale, then took a long swig. It was cold and felt good going down his throat.

For a moment, he forgot his disorientation and loneliness. Just what the doctor ordered. He suddenly decided that everything was going to be alright, that they had done it, pulled it off, and were going to fool the insurance companies into handing over four million dollars, enough money for a lifetime. There would always be the fear of getting caught, but that fear, Jeff had assured them, would diminish to next to nothing over time. Until, one day, it would be completely forgotten.

And he felt good about being anonymous, totally invisible, a literal nonentity in the rat race of mankind. Off the grid, as it had been termed in a book he had read some years ago, the title of which he could not recall, but had intrigued him because it concerned a guy who had escaped the human illusion that life had meaning.

Jerry shook off the thought and after resisting another urge to call Holly, he lifted his suitcase and carried it and the bottle of Beck's back into the bedroom. He switched on a glaring ceiling light and, after tossing the suitcase on top of the bed, sat on the edge of it with a glum feeling returning to his gut as he took another swallow of beer. It was dreadfully quiet in the house, and that only enhanced his loneliness. He needed a cat or dog or something to keep him company over the next long weeks; but Holly didn't like animals, so pets of any kind, even tropical fish, had always been taboo. She had explained in a long tearful soliloquy one night years ago not long after they had first met, when they were still at Harpur College, that her alcoholic father had stomped her pet beagle, Sammy, to death upon returning home after a several day's binge and tripping over the hapless creature.

After a few moments remembering that odd talk about her murdered beagle, and how it explained somewhat the person Holly had become, Jerry took off the shirt and pants and underwear he'd been wearing for two straight days and walked naked into the bathroom. After a long, hot shower, he pulled out some fresh underwear from the dresser and a brand new sweatsuit and ripped off the tags. As he slipped into them, Jerry was disgusted by their sheer size and volume, large swaths of cloth that were required to cover, as Jeff had aptly put it, his fat haunches and ass. Then he vowed, in the next days and weeks before Holly came down to join him, to do something about that. To slim down, to become desirable again.

Jerry returned to the small, square living room just off the kitchen and found the remote on top of the old, nineteen-inch color TV he had taken from the guest room of the house in Buffalo. Jerry sat on the sofa facing the TV stand, stretched out his stubby legs, and, after another swallow of beer, pointed the remote at the TV and clicked the power button. The application for cable service would have required that Jerry reveal a name, bank account, job, and credit card, none of which he had or would ever have again. And it seemed ridiculous, if not risky, to attempt to put a personal item like that in the name of Anonymous, LLC. So it was agreed he'd have to be content watching local stations until Holly came down.

It was a couple minutes past six by then, just in time for the local news. On the first leg of careers which they hoped would land them in some bigger market someday soon, two young anchors, an attractive and chirpy male and female duet, reported the news of the day, the typical assortment of house fires, car accidents, a drug-related gang killing in Binghamton's inner city, a plant closing in Johnson City laying off fifteen more workers, and some farcical local political intrigue.

Every now and then, Jerry glanced across the room into the kitchen, at his jacket hanging lopsided on the back of the chair, and thought of the cell phone on the table. He could easily get up, walk over there, grab the cell phone then press in Holly's cell number. When she answered, he would apologize for calling, for putting them at risk, but tell her that he simply had to call and tell her how desperate everything seemed without her now, that he feared she didn't love him anymore, that he was truly and irrevocably lost without her. That he loved her, would always love her. That he needed to hear her musky laugh as she assured him that he was being foolish in a tenor and tone that demonstrated she was being truthful, genuine. That she truly loved him. Wasn't that what their love-making the other night had meant?

But then, Jerry worried that if he placed that call, she wouldn't say any such thing, but instead be angry at him and scold him, tell him that he was being a stupid fool. And then, hang up on him.

Jerry fell asleep on the living room couch with the TV a low mumble in the background while still considering using the cell phone. He woke up with a start, oblivious, sometime during Double Jeopardy. But he quickly remembered where he was, his predicament. Holly was over three hundred miles away, and he had no idea what she was up to.

Just then, the cell phone let out the chime he had

programmed into it: *Take Me Out to the Ball Game.* His heart thumped and he lost his breath. Who the fuck could that be? He jumped off the sofa and scurried into the kitchen and grabbed the phone. Finally, he opened the lid and looked down at the number blazing up at him, starting with a strange area code and seven digits Jerry didn't recognize. Despite that, he clicked the "talk" button.

"Hello?"

On the other end, a woman's voice whispered, "Joe?"

"Hello?"

In the next moment, the caller hung up.

After a time, Jerry snapped the cell phone shut. He placed it on the kitchen table in the cold, silent apartment and stared at it for a time waiting for it to ring again. The light from the ceiling fixture glared down at him. It was a bright, unnatural, cold as moonlight. Who was that woman? He hadn't recognized the voice, and she had asked for Joe. But the phone didn't ring, and the apartment remained silent, lonely.

It had been a false alarm. A wrong number.

Jerry walked back into the living room and found that he was trembling, like a boy afraid of an empty house, full of ghosts.

After a time, he fell to his knees and wept.

Chapter Thirteen

Once the wrong number incident wore off, Jerry spent the next hour or so of his first night in the house in Endicott in restless agitation, trying to stave off incessant doses of fear and loneliness. Finally, tired of feeling miserable, he squeezed into a pair of jeans (and got pissed that they didn't fit, too tight, a 42 waist, and still too tight!) and a dark navy blue Michigan sweatshirt, and decided he needed to get out of the house. That despite all the self-loathing over his weight, he was starving and needed to find a decent restaurant for a chicken Caesar salad or even something more substantial. And being around other people might do him some good. Anything was better than being cooped up alone and miserable in this house.

Half way up Vestal Parkway on the way to SUNY Binghamton, he found a family diner that looked clean and appetizing. Instead of a salad, at least on his first night alone, he rewarded himself by ordering a thick, juicy burger and a chocolate shake. While waiting for the food, he began to feel better about his predicament. What was he fretting about anyway? They had pulled it off, the perfect crime and his exile to Binghamton was only temporary. Holly would be joining him soon and he resolved, at least after this meal, that he would slim down by the time she got down there. Tomorrow, he'd stock up on some healthy food from a local supermarket, vegetables, fruits, and low carb foods, and finally follow that diet in a book he had bought a few days before they had faked his death. Part of the change, his new life as an anonymous man, was to slim down, get healthy. Like Jeff challenged, dramatically change himself. Not to mention that cooking would save him money so that he would not spend the entire five-thousand-dollar allowance Jeff had given him on expensive fattening dinners at local diners, national chains, or fast food restaurants, no matter how good the food tasted.

"You gotta work on making that cash last a few weeks," Jeff had scolded. "Spend frugally, avoid going out too much to restaurants, and certainly stay away from bars and things like that. Keep a low profile. The last thing we need is you getting yourself arrested for DWI." Jeff had leaned forward, and after looking around to confirm that Holly was out of earshot, added this advice in a low, secretive voice: "Keep indoors as much as you can. Buy yourself some decent porno movies and jerk off until your dick starts bleeding." Jeff hadn't been smiling while giving him this advice, but glared at Jerry as if he had grave concerns about his co-conspirator's ability to hack it alone on the lamb.

Waiting for his milkshake, Jerry assured himself that Jeff had nothing to worry about. He'd get used to living alone, without Holly, without the prospect of any regular companionship in the short term at least. He simply needed to find something to occupy his time. He should get back into drawing storyboards for his comic book. He vowed to start reading again, sci-fi being his favorite genre, or maybe even learn how to play the guitar which was something he had always wanted to do after giving it a short try in his sophomore year of college. Jerry also vowed to spend some of his time exercising. Buy a set of barbells and set them up in the living room. Do some running around the neighborhood; get in shape.

The waitress, a pretty, thirty-something brunette, with a husky voice and narrow, intense eyes, finally delivered his burger and chocolate shake, and Jerry felt disgusted with himself. He pushed them away, but after a minute or so, he could not help himself. He drew the straw sticking out of the shake near and sucked in the sweet, thick, cool liquid. Fuck it, he thought, tonight I deserve a treat to celebrate my death. Tomorrow will be the first day of the rest of my life. He took another sip of the deliciously creamy and fattening milkshake.

During the rest of that dinner, Jerry's mood continued to brighten and he began to feel downright good about his prospects.

What was he complaining or worrying about? In this present state of anonymous existence, he was without a care in the world, totally free. How could that be bad? By the time the waitress brought Jerry his check, he smiled up at her.

"You win the lottery or something, bud?" the waitress

asked, scowling down at his happy face. "Or you just happy to see me?"

"A little bit of both," Jerry said, knowing that his flirting was all too obvious.

She left him with a wink and a cock-eyed grin as she went off to serve other customers.

On his way out of the restaurant, Jerry picked up a free weekly newspaper off the counter by the register, the *Tri-Cities Arts & Leisure*, and started leafing through it as he waited to pay his check. It published the usual assortment of *avant-garde* liberal shtick, articles about global warming, demonizing the Republican right, attacking the war on terror and reviewing the newest alternative rock releases as well as local community theater productions.

But what Jerry spotted on the back pages immediately drew his interest. There was a separate section several pages long printing line after line of advertisements for sex talk with 800 and 900 numbers, local numbers for gays or bisexuals or swinging couples, plus several columns of short escort/hooker advertisements in concise little boxes, some of them including photographs of the girls offering these services.

Jerry took the weekly out with him to the Malibu and continued studying the back sex ads section. The idea of meeting some professional stranger for sex that night, instead of walking the mall in search of a guitar or some boring book, was instantly appealing. He needed something to take his mind his loneliness, especially this first night alone. He dreaded the thought of being alone in that house, entirely separated from everyone. Anonymous and invisible to everyone. What harm could there be in filling this time with paid sex except the couple hundred dollars it would cost him? Of course, there was the ever-present problem of contracting an STD, but if he wore a condom, and stuck to kissing and screwing, he assured himself he'd be okay.

After reading through several of the escort ads, Jerry focused on this one:

"Exotic, exciting, pleasurable, call Jade.

Locally, outcalls only 24/7, 200, no tips 333-8112.

There was a small, blurry photograph next to the ad depicting "Jade" and Jerry was immediately intrigued. Jade looked just like Holly. In fact, she could have easily passed for her sister, or even twin, straight down to her short, blonde hair, and the slant of her eyes as she looked out aggressively at whoever had taken the photo.

Jerry swallowed. With her so closely resembling Holly, meeting her seemed something meant to be and that he needed to do. And arranging it seemed so easy. All he had to do was call the number in the ad, set up an appointment, an "outcall," at the house. *Exotic, exciting, pleasurable. Jade.* No one would ever have to know, not Jeff, and certainly not Holly. Jerry got hard just thinking about it.

He had brought the pre-paid cell phone to the restaurant, but using it for such a call would be dangerous, stupid. In the lobby of the diner, he had noticed a phone stall, perhaps one of the few left in existence. He had plenty of quarters, and could place the call from there. See if he could reach her directly or simply leave a message giving out his address and inviting "Jade" to come over that night. It was Thursday, so how busy could she be.

After several moments of indecision sitting in the car, Jerry finally decided to just go ahead and do it. He opened the driver's door and hurried back into the lobby of the family diner. He stood for a time at the pay phone with the *Tri-Cities Arts and Leisure* under his right arm, immobilized again with indecision. What if the ad was a fake and Jade was a cop? That would be the end of everything. All over the prospect of a night of cheap sex with a sleazy whore.

A departing customer edged past Jerry as he opened the weekly and flipped to Jade's ad. He dug some quarters out of his jacket pocket, splashed them onto the sill of the phone stall, picked one up and placed it the coin slot. After another sigh, he punched in the number given by the ad. Jerry sucked in his stomach as the phone rang four times before a voice mail message clicked on – a slow, sultry voice: "Hello, can't take the call right now. At the tone, leave a number where I can reach you." There was a beep, then silence. Jerry was caught unprepared and quickly hung up the receiver, losing the quarter.

"Shit," he muttered and looked up inside the diner. The bird skinny old hag of a waitress standing at the cash register gave him a scowl wondering why a customer who left fifteen minutes ago was loitering in the cramped lobby like a homeless panhandler. Jerry ignored her and stood there for a time considering a decent message to leave for Jade—a name ("Tom"), that he'd be free for a date any time after nine that night, and, then give the address of his apartment in Endicott since, of course, he didn't dare leave a number. He'd also tell her he had just moved in and didn't have a phone turned on as of yet, and she would just have to trust him and show up if she wanted some action that night. Or something like that. Then, after another breath, he punched in Jade's number again.

This time, someone answered.

"Hello?" said the voice, a sultry whisper, like the voice mail message only this time, it was real, live. When Jerry didn't respond right away, the voice chided, "Hell—Low?"

"I, um," he mumbled, "I—I was calling about the ad. The ad for Jade."

"Yeah?"

"Is—is this Jade?"

"Yes, hon, you got Jade."

Jerry looked down at the ad, saw the word "hiring." "You, ah, hiring?"

"What?"

"You know. Available?"

"Sure. When, hon?"

"Huh?"

The operator came on and stated his thirty seconds were up, he needed to deposit another fifty cents.

"You calling from a pay phone?"

"Yes," Jerry said, and fumbled with some difficulty and panic to pick up two more quarters and placed them into the slot. "Yes."

"What time you need me?" she asked when the line was free again.

"Tonight?" he said. "Around nine?"

"Where?"

"My house." Jerry gave the address.

She paused a moment, maybe she was writing it down. "Okay," she said. "See you at nine. Put your donation in an envelope on your kitchen table so I can see it when I walk in. Two hundred."

Jerry gulped. He was actually doing this and thought momentarily of Holly. Cheating on her. Nevertheless, he found himself saying: "Oh–oh–okay."

"See you at nine, hon," she said with an expectant attitude.

"Yeah," Jerry said. "Nine."

And she hung up.

Chapter Fourteen

At about eight o'clock, after a long hot shower, Jerry put on one of his brand new extra-large sweat suits that would hide the blubber around his waist. He went over to the dresser and pulled out the manila envelope stuck under his white athletic socks containing the fifty-one hundred dollar bills Jeff had given him that was supposed to tide him over until the insurance money came in. He took out two of the bills for the fee Jade had quoted for her services and slid them into a small white envelope which he then placed on the kitchen table, as she had directed.

For the next hour or so after that, he alternated between sitting and watching TV and pacing the apartment, driven to distraction in anticipation of Jade's arrival. Of course, there were feelings of guilt muddling his resolve and urging him to call it off. But his biological yearnings won out and, despite the guilt, he could not resist letting it happen. A woman was coming over to his lonely house for the sole purpose of giving him sexual pleasure. A woman who looked uncannily like Holly, the woman he loved, or thought he loved. And with Jade, there were no strings attached, just the exchange of a two crisp one-hundred dollar bills. At long last, he decided to just go with the flow. Let it happen.

Finally, at nine, at least according to the cheap battery-operated clock he had hung some weeks ago on the wall of the kitchen, Jerry went to the kitchen window and tried to look out at the street, but it was dark and the angle was bad so he had no idea whether this or that car that passed was her.

At ten minutes after nine, a car pulled up and parked in front of the house. After another minute, out she came, a girl looking to be in her early twenties, of medium height and slim build, attractive, with short dirty blonde hair. The advertised Jade. She was wearing gaudy pumps that made it difficult for her to walk. A moment later, the doorbell rang and Jerry went over to it to let her in. The car remained parked in front of the house on the narrow street.

Jerry opened the front door and looked at Jade, then just stood there, gawking.

"You, Tom?" she asked in that sultry voice. "You called for me?"

Jerry stuttered a moment but was finally able to admit yes, he was "Tom."

"What you looking at, hon?" she asked. Jade gave him a wide, friendly smile. "You gonna let me in?"

Jade didn't know, of course, that what was distracting Jerry was how closely she resembled Holly. Her photograph in the escort ad of the *Tri-Cities Art and Leisure* had not done that resemblance justice. Not only could she be Holly's twin, but it also appeared she really was. She had Holly's same short blonde hair, small, Scandinavian features, pert little nose, smallish forehead, and those intense, determined brown eyes.

"Y–y–you look like someone," Jerry said. "A–a girl I know."

"Well, I hope a girl," Jade laughed. "Your wife? Girlfriend?" Jerry shrugged then stepped aside and let her in.

"No," he said. "Just, just some girl."

She followed him into the living room. Jerry turned and stepped toward Jade in the darkness. Seeing his wife in her eyes, Jerry found himself kissing Jade long and deep. She let him, of course, casually and completely, letting it last, giving back to him a full measure of her wet and active tongue in the process, as if she was Holly, as if she had known him for many years, as if she was his wife. Then, her right hand went down to his crotch and rubbed him there.

Jerry backed off, gasping, suddenly unsure, and looked at her.

Her grin was as seductive and sweet as Holly's had been the first time they had kissed, and Jerry was caught up in the memory of that night as if it was only yesterday. Jade paused a few moments, letting whatever dream he was into dissolve into the reality of just her, an escort, standing before him.

Then, looking around, she asked, "You got the donation, hon?"

Jerry nodded to the kitchen. "It's in there," he said. "On the kitchen table."

She walked to the doorway and looked into the kitchen, saw the envelope on the table.

"Two hundred?"

"Yes."

She nodded. "You got a bedroom, hon," she asked, "or you wanna do it right here on the floor?"

"I thought you'd want to count it first."

"I trust you, honey," she said. "You look sincere."

Smiling, Jerry took her by the hand and led her to down a short, narrow hallway to the back of the apartment, to his bedroom. Jade completely took over, which was not unlike Holly. She pushed him onto the bed and went about expertly stripping off Jerry's sweat suit and underwear. But Jade didn't seem to mind the mound of his belly nor the frumpy roll of his shoulders and arms.

"You like getting sucked?"

"S–sure," he stuttered.

She smiled, then knelt down and leaned forward and started. After bringing him close to orgasm several times in the next five minutes or so, she pushed him onto the bed and ended up on top of him. In the next indeterminable minutes, Jerry got all his two hundred dollars' worth and then some.

Afterward, Jade rolled over and cuddled close next to him. "That okay, hon?" she asked.

"It was great," he gasped. She laughed.

"Was it okay for you?" Jerry asked, meaning it.

"Sure, hon."

They laid in silence for a time staring up at the grimy white ceiling. Finally, he turned onto his side and facing her, put his arm around her shoulders and pulled her to him, seeing Holly in her every gesture and expression. Jade didn't resist the display of tenderness on his part. Even whores had feelings, he guessed. He wondered if they ever fell in love with their tricks.

"How old are you?" he asked.

"Twenty-three," she said, and though she looked younger, Jerry had no reason to doubt it.

"You?"

"Thirty," he said.

"You want to do this again sometime, hon?" Jade asked. "Become one of my regulars?"

She let him move his hand down to her crotch. But after about half a minute, she moved his hand away.

"I could handle that," he told her. "When you gonna be free again?"

"Not until the week after next," Jade said. "I'm meeting a friend up in Albany. We do some tricks up there sometimes." She shrugged. "Then, from there, me and my friend are flying down to Florida." She laughed momentarily. "Taking a vacation in Orlando – Disney World."

"Nice," Jerry said, thinking that even whores deserved vacations.

"It's my favorite place in the world," she added.

Suddenly the girl wiggled out of his arms and jumped out of bed, got dressed. Only forty minutes of the hour had been used up, but Jerry didn't protest. He was spent physically and emotionally from the sex and the shock of seeing so much of Holly in her.

Fully dressed and looking sexy in her tight jeans and low cut top, Jade glanced down at him laying helplessly before her in his bed and asked why he spent so much time looking funny at her. Did he have a problem with her face or something?

He laughed and assured her it was only because she reminded him of somebody.

"Must be your ex."

"Huh?"

"Your ex-wife."

He shrugged, unsure how to answer that. Instead, he asked, "You really got to go?"

She gave him an odd look.

"How much for you to stay the night?" he asked. "Be my bed-mate?"

"The night?" Jade asked. "You mean as in a sleep over?"

"Yeah," he said and rubbed his flabby belly under the sheets.

"A sleep over."

She had to think a minute. No one had ever proposed such a thing before.

"Another four hundred," she said flatly, though the figure was certainly arbitrary. In the next moment, she blurted: "No, four-fifty."

Jerry told her it was a deal. He would have paid even more for the privilege of having Holly's look-a-like sleep next to him that night, and maybe screw her again sometime in the middle of it, just like he and Holly used to do way back when in the first few months of their love affair, back in college, and even the first few months after they were married.

"You gotta show me the money before I can go down and tell Luke that he can leave," she said. "Another four-fifty."

Jerry got out of bed and fished around his dresser for the money, found five crisp hundreds and showed them to her. The thought popped in the back of his mind that Jeff would be furious with him for wasting his money this way on a whore.

Smirking in that crooked, suggestive way that so reminded Jerry of Holly, Jade sat on the edge of the bed and counted out the bills herself—one, two, three, four, five.

"Hey, there's five hundred here. I said four-fifty." Jerry smiled at her and stroked her back.

"I got no fifties," he said. "And to have you overnight, like my wife or something, is worth five."

Jade smiled back at him. He was so different from most of the other gruff johns, who couldn't be rid of her fast enough after they came or sometimes tried to beat her up.

"Okay, I have to go down and tell Luke. Be right back. Why don't you get back into bed and keep it warm for me; okay?"

Jerry nodded and let her go. He did as she asked and got back into bed, pulling the covers on top of him. For the next minute or so, he feared she wouldn't return, that he'd been scammed. But then he heard her let herself back into the house. Jerry almost burst with happiness when she entered and started stripping off her clothes.

In bed, after cuddling up next to him, she asked: "You got a real name?"

"No," he told her flatly, leaving that issue non-negotiable.

That made Jade pause, but she did not press him on it. In the next moment, he was gently snoring next to her. Jade decided to let him sleep for a while. She was tired too, but it was only just past ten o'clock, the time of night she was first going out to meet her johns. Now, she was going to sleep early just like a married woman.

But she only let him sleep for a little while. After about ten minutes, she woke him up and gave him a nice surprise.

Certainly, not like any wife he ever had, or ever would, she laughed to herself. But after a moment, she frowned, wondering why she was thinking about being somebody's wife.

Chapter Fifteen

Fox saw much of the same the second night of his stakeout of Jerry Shaw's former residence. This time, he brought a zoom digital recorder to record the event.

Just like yesterday evening, the slick Jeffrey Flaherty arrived in his silver Lexus at around eight. He parked it in almost the same location on the street as the night before, a couple houses down from the Shaw residence. After inspecting his wavy hair framing a square-jawed face and bedroom eyes in the rear-view mirror, Flaherty strode straight up to the front door. This time, after opening the door a foot or so, Fox saw through the lens of the digital recorder the insured's widow greeting Flaherty wearing a skimpy lavender negligee and flashing a crooked, suggestive smile. Flaherty stepped into the house and the door shut.

If there was any doubt what the two-hour visit last night was all about, tonight's meeting resolved that. Simply put, Flaherty was banging Mrs. Shaw. However, Fox had no way of knowing how long he had been doing so—before or since Jerry Shaw's unfortunate demise? Should he be able to find out that it had been going on for a time before Mr. Shaw's death, that might lead to some other conclusions. It would, if nothing else, provide a potential motive for his murder. Thus, it became important to find out how long Jeff Flaherty and Mrs. Shaw had been carrying on. Fox knew that they worked at the same law firm, and therefore, there existed at very least the opportunity for their affair to have blossomed long before Jerry Shaw's death. But Fox also knew that he was getting way ahead of himself in proving that an affair between Jeff Flaherty and Holly Shaw had been the catalyst for Jerry Shaw's death. Still, the idea intrigued him. It fit all too well his idea of human treachery.

The obvious hypothesis, of course, without a single, corroborative shred of proof to back it up, as Fox freely acknowledged at the time—except for the posthumous affair between Flaherty and the widow Shaw—was that they had conspired to kill the insured for the life insurance money and either fell in love before, during or after hatching the plot. No shit. You didn't have to be Sherlock Holmes to deduce that. What Global Life needed was for him, as their Mr. Holmes, to come up with incriminating evidence of it, a statement, something. But for the moment, Fox had nothing but conjecture, or "bare speculation," as Chief Reynolds would have called it with a disapproving scowl.

Toward nine o'clock that night, about an hour or so after Flaherty's arrival, Fox left the homey and safe comfort of his rental car and snuck around to the back of the Shaw house for the purpose of eavesdropping on whatever Flaherty and the widow Shaw were up to in the master bedroom on the second floor (to where they surely had retired). But after standing directly beneath the darkened window of that bedroom for at least half an hour, shivering in the chilly late October night, just a few days short of Halloween, and hearing nothing save an occasional exchange of muffled voices, and with a growing ache in his kidneys from having to take a wicked piss, Fox decided to abandon the effort. He needed a better vantage point anyway, somewhere he could overhear more than incriminating grunts. He needed statements out of their respective mouths about the deed he suspected them of committing.

Fox finally retraced his steps to the car. He gently closed the driver's side door and held himself a moment to regain his warmth. He started the car and drove off to the Noco station and took a long, delightful piss in the public bathroom. On the way out, he bought a Kit-Kat bar and returned to Northview Drive. Flaherty's Lexus was still there. Fox decided to take a new spot, three houses down. Finally, an hour and a half later, just past eleven, Flaherty emerged from the Shaw house and sauntered to his Lexus and drove off.

Fox waited a few minutes after Flaherty's departure to make sure he had gone for the night and wasn't returning after a trip to the store. Finally, at around eleven forty-five, convinced that Flaherty would not be back, Fox drove back to the hotel.

After a couple shots of bourbon over ice in a plastic hotel cup, Fox nodded off on top of the bed still fully dressed, his head cranked awkwardly on a couple of too small and too fluffy hotel pillows with the TV turned down to a mere thump in the background. He woke up half an hour later with a splitting headache and an aching neck and pushed himself off the bed to get an aspirin out of the bottle of the bottle he had brought with him. After swallowing a couple pills, he took his final leak of the day.

As the trail of his piss crackled into the toilet, Fox wondered what the fuck he was doing sequestered here in some lonely hotel room in Buffalo and cursed himself for not having retired to Florida long ago. He was sixty-five years old and had spent thirty-two of them investigating human dishonesty and greed and violence as a member of the Philadelphia Police Department.

Years ago, he had grown tired of observing the transgressions of his fellow man while powerless to do much of anything about it. Most of the thousands of investigations he had worked up over those many years had failed to result in meaningful justice. Criminals got light sentences or nothing at all because of overcrowded jails, incompetent prosecutors, and crooked or stupid juries and judges. His part-time work as a private investigator while a full-time cop had done little to resolve problems among people—in fact, what he found usually exacerbated them. Wives confirmed that their husbands had grown tired of them, or vice versa; employers found out that even their most trusted employees were thieves and cheats or malingerers. And now, at the end of his career, the only justice derived from his work on behalf of this life insurance company over the past two years was to save a rich conglomerate from paying out claims to unworthy, and sometimes, cheating or murderous beneficiaries. Who won in that? Where was the honor in what he had done, and what he was doing?

What had resonated in Fox's mind after all the years in the investigation business was that people were selfish bastards, and would do just about anything to gratify themselves, whether it be for love or money or lust or just plain cruelty. They would lie and cheat and commit murder for an extra few bucks or a piece of ass. The more bucks that were involved, or the sweeter the ass, the more likely that murder and deceit would follow. Still, the idea of letting the crime go undetected and walking away from it without at least attempting to procure a measure of justice seemed a far worse thing. Fox had not yet grown so discouraged that he had completely lost all hope that earthly justice was possible.

Not yet.

After another bad night's sleep, Fox got a red-eye out of Buffalo and arrived back at Global's main office in downtown Philly shortly before noon after being stuck in another seemingly endless series of traffic jams from the airport to downtown. Chief Reynolds was waiting for him, his office looking especially cramped and glum that morning, reflecting his dour mood.

Fox made his report, quick and to the point.

"That's it?" the Chief said. "She's screwing some guy three days after the insured's funeral?" He shrugged. "Hardly enough to recommend a denial, let alone demonstrate a murder plot."

"We need more time," said Fox.

"More time?" The Chief had opened a folder and started reading a new report. After a few moments, he looked up. "To find what? You got nothing, no witnesses. Only the wife of the insured screwing around."

There was no answer to that. That's all Fox had. All he knew was that it didn't feel right. Jerry Shaw had <u>not</u> accidentally burned to death. The claim should not be paid. That would be unjust. And justice would be a denied. Again.

"More time?" Chief Reynolds was chuckling to himself now. "I don't know what to tell ya, Chief."

"You've been watching too many movies, Jack, like the one I watched last night. But life isn't like the movies. And it certainly isn't like *Double Indemnity*. The crimes we investigate usually go unsolved and the crooks remain free.

"And anyway," the Chief continued, "the arson guys really killed this one for us."

"The arson guys are full of crap. And they didn't know about the affair, a motive."

The Chief leaned forward and scribbled something on the inside flap of the Shaw case folder.

"It's a moot point," the Chief said. "Kline doesn't want to do battle on this one. Even for four mil. I told him yesterday afternoon what you found, and he told me this morning unless you found something else, he was going to authorize payment." The Chief shrugged. "Says the unit's got cases up the ying-yang. Its resources can be spent on better places."

"Better places? Four million bucks isn't a good enough place?"

Chief Reynolds shrugged. "Easy come, easy go. Lucky

for you and me, it's not our money."

Fox brooded for a time. What it all ever came down to for him, what had always motivated him to action all these years in law enforcement, was what was right. But his resolve, like that of most men, though he was more stubborn than most, had been sanded down to a nub. And more and more lately, as the hours grew short, he was coming to the awful realization once and for all that right didn't matter in the real world, only in the schlock detective movies that he and Chief Reynolds liked to watch.

When Fox looked up, he saw that the Chief was grinning. "What's so funny, Chief?"

"You," he said. "So honest. So efficient. You do remind me of that insurance adjuster in *Double Indemnity*."

"Yeah," said Fox, though without much interest.

"You know," the Chief continued, "the guy played by Edward G. Robinson?"

"And I was thinking exactly the same thing about you, Dick," said Fox, and now he broke into a smile. "Edward G. Complete with the cigar."

But then his smile faded, as did the Chief's, as they both pondered the sorry state of justice in the world.

Chapter Sixteen

So this is what it feels like to be anonymous, Jerry thought. Invisible.

He had rented the old black and white version of H. G. Wells', *The Invisible Man*, the one made in the thirties with fairly non-existent special effects, and was quickly able to relate to the feelings of the main character, played by Claude Rains.

Like the invisible man from the movie, Jerry soon realized that this sense of anonymity was both a blessing and a curse. In one sense, it made him nearly invincible, daring; but in another, he felt incredibly vulnerable, isolated and alone, dependent upon and yearning for human connection that came only when Jade was writhing in his arms. But now Jade was gone, off to Albany doing more tricks, sleeping with various men, all strangers, and then she was going down to Florida with her girlfriend, Faith, on vacation and probably doing more tricks down there. She would not be back in town, Jade had told him, for at least three weeks, depending how far her money went. She loved the sun and warmth and detested the cold, damp winters of Binghamton.

Jade offered to give him a name and number of a "friend" who might help relieve his needs in her absence, but Jerry declined, telling her that he wanted to wait, that only she could satisfy him. That earned him a weak smile and off she went.

His second day in Binghamton, with Jade long gone, Jerry bought a barbell set at a Dick's Sporting Goods store for a couple hundred dollars. He was going to take Jeff's advice and change his looks, starting with his physique. Get rid once and for all of his flab and rotundity and set out to look like somebody else. Losing weight and sculpting his frame was not only healthy, it might keep him, and them, out of jail. And it might even impress Holly.

He set up the barbell set in the small, empty bedroom and after a sigh, started using it. He put on one hundred twenty-five pounds and grunted out three sets. Then, remembering back from his freshman year in college when he worked out for a few weeks with Dan Cormack at the gym, he did some curls and squats with just enough weight that he could feel a twinge of painful resistance. He finished off with sit-ups and push-ups. The next day he added to the mix a half mile jog around a local park along the Susquehanna River. He filled the fridge with some oranges and grapes and apples, as well as yogurt, and swore off McDonald's, Burger King, Wendy's, and KFC. He also vowed to stay away from donuts and cupcakes and ice cream. After mulling it over for a time, he set a goal of losing fifty pounds in six months.

Following more of Jeff's advice, Jerry stopped shaving and watched the stubble on his chin and face blossom into a decent, full-fledged jet black beard that made him look ten years older and profoundly masculine. Wearing a flannel shirt, Jerry looked more like an outdoorsman than a soft-bellied computer software salesman. He also let his hair grow out. In addition to his eyes, Holly always said he had a good head of thick black hair that made even girls envious. In a week, he impressed himself how remarkably different he already looked, almost unrecognizable. In another month, if he continued slimming down and growing his beard and hair, he doubted if even Jeff and Holly could recognize him.

Still, the nights remained unbearably lonely. There was nothing from Jeff, and Holly, of course. It was driving him nuts not knowing what was going on back home. What, for example, was the status of the insurance claim. If it wasn't paid right away, what did that signify? Mistrust? A full-blown investigation? Four million dollars was a lot of money to hand over.

During the planning stages for the scam, Jeff had no clue how long it would take. No doubt the size of the policy would give the insurance company a reason to doubt and launch an investigation. Jerry cursed Holly for being so goddamn greedy and cursed himself for not paying better attention, for not being in better control of her. His lack of assertiveness, his lack of confidence, could cost them everything.

What was now equally maddening for Jerry was that no provision had been made for a direct and immediate line of communication between himself and Jeff and Holly as the need arose. How could they not see that was a problem? Being in the dark like this only made his mind race, imagining all kinds of problems. And on top of that, he started imagining that Holly had become unfaithful to him. After all, hadn't he become unfaithful to her in short order, only a day out of town?

But there was nothing that could be done about these concerns except to fret and wait, and toss and turn in bed during his often sleepless nights waiting for something to break.

Ten long days passed like this without news from Jeff. The silence was killing Jerry. But Jeff had cautioned him that it could be weeks, even months before the claim was paid. And for most of that time, they would not be able to connect.

Each one of those ten days, around noon, Jerry got out of the house and jogged at least a couple miles. After eating a salad or a bowl of soup for lunch, he'd take a drive to the local mall and simply walk around, stare at people, the women especially. Upon his return to the house by mid to late afternoon, he'd slink off to the bedroom, turn on his laptop and masturbate to free porn. And that was pretty much his day. He'd also worry about his relationship with Holly. It had taken this separation for Jerry to fully realize what a woman she was, that she was irreplaceable. It also made him furious that he has let his insecurity come between what should have blossomed into a legendary love affair.

It was seven o'clock on the morning of the fourteenth

day after his fake funeral, while standing in the kitchen sipping strong, dark coffee, when Jerry decided, to hell with all the mind-numbing waiting that was literally killing him. It was time to be daring. It was time to act like the Anonymous Man, to throw caution to the wind. It was time to be the superhero that he meant the Anonymous Man to be.

Jerry decided right then and there that he was going home. He took another long sip of coffee to solidify his resolve. He would sneak into his own home, barge in on Holly, then fuck her in the silent darkness of his own bed. He was still grossly overweight, even after losing ten pounds, but she would notice a profound change in him beyond that. She would notice the change of attitude, a renewal of confidence and purpose. A resurrection of his masculinity.

Yes, that was it. He needed to go home and put on a reckless display for the benefit of the woman he still loved.

This would be the year of the Anonymous Man.

Chapter Seventeen

Jerry decided he would surprise Holly that very night. If he didn't do it right away, he might lose his resolve and slip into a kind of numb brooding, a bad habit he had developed over the years.

It would be easy. The worst part would be the three-hour drive. Once there, he could use his key to sneak into the house then jump her in bed. Initially, she'd likely be pissed. But, he hoped, after a time in the secure and private darkness of their bedroom, she'd relent, deciding that what he had done was gallant and brave and romantic—and that doing so represented a significant positive change in him. This was what a man should be, like Jeff, someone who took initiative, who took risks in order to live life to the fullest, not the dull couch potato he had become in the seven years of their marriage. And then she'd lay back and let him have his way with her.

All the rest of that long afternoon, Jerry mentally prepared for the trip. At around three, he gave in to exhaustion after last night's insomnia and took a nap. He woke up at around six, treated himself to a low calorie, low cholesterol, low salt microwave dinner and a cup of yogurt. By the time he had showered and dressed and gassed up the car, it was already almost eight-thirty. If he kept to the speed limit, he'd manage to make it back to his house by around midnight.

And it was exactly midnight, to the minute, when he pulled onto Northview Lane. The street was dark and silent, as was expected for that hour on a weeknight. Every single house was dark, still, asleep. Except for his, no car came or went.

Jerry parked along the curb a few houses down from what had once been his official residence the last seven years. Outside, he drew in a deep drag of crisp, autumn air. It was mid-November, and around these parts, snow could come at any time. All that was needed for a big snowstorm was a cold front from northern Canada to cross Lake Erie to produce two or three feet of snow. In that event, he might be really fucked, holed up where he shouldn't be.

But this night, no cold front had moved in, just the normal chill of winter coming on. Still, it was damp and cold enough for each of his exhalations to produce tiny puffs of gray, smoky mist.

Jerry hurried past the vinyl siding of the garage's outer wall and edged his way to the backyard. He stopped for a time, hidden in the complete black shadow of the house directly under the master bedroom where he imagined Holly was at this hour of night fast asleep. He missed the nights sleeping next to her, listening to her quiet breathing and wondered why he had failed to appreciate her being there, next to him all those many nights. Why such a simple thing as being privy to someone's sleeping habits was so easily taken for granted.

In the next moment, Jerry started shivering, a mixture of nerves and the chilly air. The previous owner had attached a decent sized deck to the back door leading directly out from the kitchen. As he stood there shivering, Jerry again began to wonder whether he should turn around, abandon this reckless plan, and find some cheap motel for the night, then slink back to Binghamton in the morning, leaving Jeff and Holly none the wiser.

But that was the old Jerry, he told himself. He narrowed his eyes and re-affirmed that it was time to live recklessly; that he needed to be with Holly, his wife, smell her, taste her; that this was the year of the Anonymous Man. What the fuck, he told himself, then took a deep breath and stepped onto the bottom rung of the short staircase leading onto the deck.

At the back door, he nervously sucked in another crisp mouthful of air before taking out his key. But as he was about to insert it into the lock, it slipped from his fingers, clanged on the deck and fell through a crack onto the gravel below.

"Fuck," he whispered.

It took Jerry ten frantic minutes crawling along the slimy gravel in utter darkness beneath the deck to find the key. Returning to the back door, he didn't waste another moment thinking over things. He firmly inserted the key into the lock and turned the knob, but when he pushed open the door, the aggravating low whistle of an alarm greeted him. The fucking alarm! He had completely forgotten about it because, for some reason, over the years, he and Holly had stopped arming it whenever they went out. But now, for whatever reason, with him gone, Holly had done just that, armed it.

Jerry hustled to the small keypad on the wall just inside the back door entrance and quickly punched in the code. The alarm let out two short beeps then went silent. Jerry stood motionless for a time staring at the code box, hoping and praying that, having sounded so briefly, the alarm had not awakened Holly and caused her, in a panic, to dial 911, and turn his impulsive trip home into a disaster dooming them.

Jerry waited, churning inside, his heart beating fast, waiting, for what seemed forever. But no one and nothing stirred. Finally, after about a minute, he began to relax as it appeared that the alarm had not awakened Holly. By then Jerry's eyes had adjusted to the darkness, and he began to creep forward through the spacious kitchen, avoiding the center island, then passed through a doorway into a wide living room. He lingered there a moment, inspecting the shadows of familiar furniture: the thick couch with the flowery pattern, the loveseat where night after night having coming home from work he had planted his ass and read *The Buffalo News* cover to cover; the brand new fifty-five inch HDVD flat screen television they had charged fifteen hundred dollars for on their credit card six months ago.

And then, above the mantel of the fireplace across from where they had sat so many nights early in their marriage, sipping wine and having late night cheese and cracker picnics, he saw it. The urn. Containing the ashes of some poor sap who had donated his body to science and had instead become part of a thrilling scheme.

Jerry looked away from the urn and started moving again, around a wall to his right to the staircase that led to the three bedrooms upstairs. They had bought the house with the idea of creating the model, happy two-kid family. But the other two bedrooms had remained childless, a guestroom and his den. Crouching, Jerry crept upstairs, step-by-step, and despite his deliberate exercise of care, he was unable to avoid an occasional creak. With each one he winced, and moved forward, his heart beating so fast and hard he could feel it.

At last, he reached the landing at the top of the stairs. To the right were the guest bedroom and his den, across from a rather large bathroom. To the left was the master bedroom.

For the past seven years, he and Holly had slept in that very room, in the wide king bed that took up a large chunk of it. Seven years. From as far back as he could remember, they hardly ever went to sleep together anymore.

Holly always went up first, at around ten, to read one of her glamor or entertainment magazines, sometimes even some cheap tabloid she had picked up in the supermarket check-out line, occasionally a romance novel. Jerry remained downstairs clicking the remote changing channels on the TV before sneaking upstairs to his den, his man cave, where he had lately spent too much time deep into the night surfing porn on the Internet.

Turning to the master bedroom, he could see that the

door was ajar and the room dark. Holly was in there, so close, sound asleep. But at the threshold he stopped and listened for the sound of Holly sleeping. Soft, gentle breathing, whimpering, or talking in her sleep, moving, wrestling in a dream under the covers. But he heard nothing. Jerry stepped forward and pushed open the door. The bed was made, empty. Holly wasn't home. All that worrying about the alarm going off and sneaking up the stairs was for nothing. Where the fuck was she? Out with friends? Sleeping over at her brother Ray's because she hated being alone in a big, dark house? Jerry sighed, completely disappointed and disheartened. He had come home to an empty house.

Chapter Eighteen

After a few moments, Jerry heard something, a commotion, some fumbling, the front door opening and people walking in. Jerry stood his ground in the shadows of the master bedroom, a couple of steps inside the room. Voices rose up from downstairs. One of them was Holly's. Then it occurred to him that the other was Jeff's. What the fuck was he doing here at this hour, alone with Holly, in his house?

Jerry heard them coming up the stairs, giggling about something. Panic gripped him as he realized that there was no escape. There was no going down; they were coming up, already near the landing. Trapped, he backed further into the darkness of the master bedroom until he found himself against the door of the deep walk-in closet. He slid open the door, stepped inside, and after closing it almost all the way, pushed back as far as he could among a thick swath of Holly's dresses and blouses hanging in there, smelling in them her usual perfume, a musk of bitter sweetness. There were some boxes pushed against the far wall stuffed with

Holly's old sweaters and other clothes providing a ready seat for Jerry's ass.

An instant later, Jeff and Holly entered the dark bedroom. One of them flipped on the switch to the ceiling fan and light and Jerry held his breath for a time worrying that the simple act of breathing might give himself away. He thought of how silly it was for him to be hiding in his own house and thought of coming out and confronting them. See what the fuck was really going on. Were they lovers? As the dizzying, immobilizing shock of the thought wore off a bit after a minute or so, Jerry decided to keep his cool, stay put, and, as if it wasn't already patently clear, learn the full extent of what was going on.

And then Jerry heard the unmistakable sound of kissing. But after a moment, it stopped.

"Hey," Holly said. "The alarm didn't go off." More kissing.

"What?"

"The alarm."

"What about it?"

"It didn't go off."

"Well, did you arm the fucking thing?" Jeff asked.

"I was sure I had."

The discussion was interrupted by the soft barely audible squishy-ness of lips touching, tongues licking, penetrating, probing, and the hushed, exciting exhalations of breath.

"I think, anyway," Holly said, and then a rush of air emitted from her. "I don't know."

They kissed again, longer this time, and Jerry imagined

Jeff's hands caressing Holly's ass, her back, her breasts.

"You ever get tired of this?" Holly joked during a lull. Jeff chuckled.

"No, my love," he said. "I don't. Your body endlessly excites me."

"I bet you say that to all the girls," she laughed.

"Ah, I do," he laughed back. "But for now, only you."

They fell silent, kissing again, long and deep in the quiet bedroom. Jerry tried desperately not to breathe. To be caught now would be the height of humiliation.

But the kissing persisted.

What Jeff and Holly were up to soon became obvious and real, and Jerry had to use every ounce of his resolve to remain still. Restrain his anger. He must remain anonymous, he told himself, and find out the full extent of what was going on, how bad it was. Was it only sex (and that was bad enough), or more? Was it something that threatened the plan for Holly to come down to Binghamton and become his front?

Okay, Jeff and Holly were having an affair. That much was clear. But after a moment's thought, Jerry wasn't surprised. Hadn't he seen it coming? They were a natural pair. It may have started out as a fantasy, a passionate daydream, a private admission of their respective mutual attraction. It was perhaps inevitable that it had culminated in what they were now doing.

And why not? Jeff was much more the kind of man Holly needed and deserved. He was slim, strong, virile. He was decisive, opinionated, brave and bold. Not overweight, not weak, not insignificant, not indecisive.

Jerry resolved to remain among the safe perfume of Holly's dresses, sitting comfortably, though fretfully, on a crushed box of her old sweaters, and listen with kind of masochistic alarm as they continued kissing.

The bedroom light went off, and Jerry listened as Jeff and Holly undressed, kissing all the while, their clothes landing upon the carpeted floor with a muffled plop. After several moments, Jerry slowly and carefully edged forward, off his ass and onto his knees, careful not to make a peep. He crawled gingerly forward a couple of feet in the complete darkness of the closet until he was kneeling, bent slightly forward, at the small crack of the sliding door. Looking out into the bedroom in a narrow scope of vision from that vantage point, his thighs aching, he nevertheless had a surprisingly unobstructed view of their treachery.

By then they were naked, in bed, under the covers, kissing and groping, oblivious of Jerry's voyeurism. He watched the performance, transfixed, as their bodies writhed under the covers, moaning, churning in lustful play and evident passion.

For the next twenty minutes Jerry observed all this in rapt silence as Jeff finally mounted Holly and thrust forward, grunting, while Holly softly growled, like some kind of small, wild animal, as she always did out of carnal delight, a sound Jerry had not coaxed out of her in months, or years perhaps. Jerry continued watching them, unable to shut his eyes, as Jeff pumped harder and harder and harder, until he finally blasted his load inside her.

Wide-eyed, breathless, and, Jerry dreaded to admit, thrilled, he watched as Jeff rolled off Holly, let out a kind of soft laugh, and said something like, "Woo!" Holly, for her part, remained still, spent, on her back.

"That was fucking great," moaned Jeff.

Holly gave no answer. Jerry was never sure if she had ever had an orgasm. Women, he knew from what others told him, and from his few sexual experiences (two, to be exact) before Holly came into his life (and now a total of four, with Jade), were like that. You never knew for sure if they had an orgasm. It was the one significant advantage they held over men, that they could fake an orgasm, and often did. (Though Jerry genuinely believed that Jade had not faked her orgasm with him that night now a long ten days ago.)

Jerry closed his eyes and slowly retreated to the recesses of the closet, careful not to rustle any of Holly's dresses until he came to the box with the old sweaters and sat on it again. All Jerry could do was restrain his emotions, his tears, and listen. Try not to think about what he had just witnessed.

"Did you take care of that guy?" Holly suddenly asked out of the darkness. "Pay him?"

Jerry felt a rush seize his lungs, and a cry almost burst out of him.

"The body guy?" Jeff asked.

"Yeah," she said. "Him."

"Unfortunately, yes," Jeff said.

The "body guy" they were talking about was Willie Robinson, the "Anatomical Preparator," a state position, Grade 13, who was employed by the University of Buffalo Medical School. Some months before they staged Jerry's death, Jeff had Googled the term, "human cadaver,' and found that it was not unusual for people to leave their bodies to medical schools for dissection by students. Further research had led Jeff to the occupation of "anatomical preparator," the person who had the grisly job of accepting possession of the donated cadavers, cleaning them up for dissection, and disposing of them by cremation after there was essentially nothing left to dissect. Jeff also found that there was such an anatomical preparator working at the University of Buffalo School of Medicine making around thirty thousand dollars a year. He was a black guy in his late thirties, or early forties, named Willie Robinson. Jeff then made a deal with Robinson to provide them with a cadaver that they could substitute for Jerry's body and burn to a crisp in the planned garage fire.

Before approaching him, Jeff followed Robinson around for a few days and learned that he lived with a woman and a school age kid in the ghetto, and liked to stop off every Tuesday and Thursday at a seedy looking bar on Fillmore Avenue called "The Adams Lounge." Finally, one Tuesday night, Jeff followed Robinson into the bar, sidled up to him and struck up a conversation. After three or four beers, some laughs, and finding out what the other did, Jeff finally asked Robinson what it would take to obtain an already dissected cadaver.

"Why would someone need one?" Robinson wanted to know. "I'm just asking," Jeff said. "If I need a body, could you get it to me and not get caught? I mean for a reasonable, well, fee?" Robinson had given him a cold, hard stare. "For ten grand,"

He said, "maybe it's possible."

That was it, Robinson became the body guy. And now, the body guy wanted more of the take.

The sheets rustled as Jeff sat up, the magic of their sex completely worn off now that she has raised this topic.

"But I don't think this is ever gonna stop."

"No?" Holly asked.

"He sees us as an endless supply of cash, his goddamn personal ATM machine." Jeff sighed. "He told me he'd be getting back in touch with me—next month. Cost us another couple grand." Another sigh. "I think he's got a heroin problem."

"We already paid him what, ten thousand?"

"Yeah, ten. I think he's figured out our scam," said Jeff. "Knows we'll be making a lot of money, that what he gave us was worth more than he got."

"But what's his leverage?" Holly asked after a time. "Why should we pay him? If he tells on us, doesn't he give himself up, too?"

"Can we take that chance? He's desperate. Says he needs the money. For a gambling debt or something. Or maybe he's got a dope problem. I don't know. He's an accomplice for sure, but like he told me, he did the scam, just like us, and he wants more of a take."

Jeff mulled it over for a time.

"Or, maybe he figured out a way to do it without implicating himself." He sighed. "I don't know. It's just so goddamned worrisome. And we are *this* close to pulling it off."

Jeff suddenly flicked off the covers and sat on the

edge of the bed biting his nails, thinking. After a time, he stood, picked up his jeans from the floor and pulled them on.

"Where you going, huns?"

Jeff didn't respond. He walked over to the long dresser against the side wall and, staring into the mirror on top of it, started combing his sex-tousled hair with one of Jerry's old brushes.

"Huns?"

Satisfied with the way his hair looked, Jeff gave himself one last long look in the mirror before turning around and leaning against the dresser.

"The bottom line," Jeff said, looking at Holly stretched out under the covers, "is that the body guy is a problem that probably isn't going away."

"Yeah?" Holly asked. "Where you going with this?"

"Where I'm going with this, is this. We have to do away with him."

"Do away?" She laughed. "As in-"

"Yeah, that." Jeff reached down and picked up his sweater off the floor. "Well, what else do you propose we do? Keep paying him and hope he ends up satisfied and keeps his mouth shut? Or maybe he gets arrested someday for shoplifting or robbing a convenience store, whatever, and to beat the rap, maybe he decides to become a snitch, trade us in for a plea deal. He's no Einstein but he's as street smart as they come," Jeff frowned. "Like I said, he's never going away. He'll be a mortgage payment for us to the day we die."

"Jeff," Holly said. "Jesus. Once we get the money and

leave here, how's he gonna find us?"

"That's the other problem," Jeff said. "Irrespective of the blackmail, he's a witness. He's someone—whether he does it voluntarily, or because they figure out he lost a body from whatever audit they might do over there someday— he's someone who can tell the authorities who he gave the body to. And they can then figure out the rest. That ole Jerry Shaw wasn't burned alive, that he ain't dead, and never was, just anonymous in some anonymous shit hole. The problem is, you and me, we won't be anonymous. We can be found."

"So," said Holly, turning to her side, and propping herself up on an elbow. She looked at Jeff, who was now fully dressed and looked ready to leave. "We kill him?" There was genuine alarm in Holly's voice. "To fake a death is one thing, killing someone and getting away with it, another."

"Yeah, we kill him," Jeff said. He shrugged, then turned and looked at himself in the mirror. He smoothed down his hair and sighed. "You haven't met this other human being," Jeff said. "We'd probably be doing society a big fucking favor. Fucking cokehead, heroin addict, degenerate gambler, whatever. Probably beats his wife, and no doubt he'll screw up that fucking nigger kid he's trying to get out of the ghetto."

"Still, Jeff," she said, then dropping onto her back again.

"Murder." After another moment, she asked, "How, how would you do it? Hire someone?"

"Hire someone? Don't we have enough witnesses? No, I'd do it myself. I've been following him. He usually stops off at the bar I met him at a couple nights a week. When he does that, he gets home around nine or so. Nice and dark on his ghetto street. Nobody around. I could wait for him on one of those nights. I could bring out a knife in a flash and cut his throat before he ever had a chance to think about it. Half the lights don't work on the street he lives. It gets so dark out there, he'll never see me coming."

"Sounds like you've thought about this? Actually doing it?" Jeff came over and sat on the edge of the bed.

"That, and the other problem," he said. "The other problem?"

"You know," Jeff said. "The eight-hundred-pound gorilla in the room. Literally. Your fucking ex."

Jerry shuddered as he listened to himself being described like that. He began to tremble with rage. He wanted to leap out and jump on Jeff and beat his brains out.

"Why is Jerry a problem?" Holly asked.

"I have my doubts that he can hack it. Don't you? Especially if you're not really gonna join him, be his eyes and ears while he remains in some anonymous state of being. Like his fucking stupid cartoon superhero. I had my doubts from the beginning he could hack it even waiting for you to get down there."

"You really think he'll crack? Blow us in when I don't show?"

"Maybe not deliberately," he said. "But left to his own devices, given time, he's sure to slip up, give himself away, and give us away in the process. What we're doing is committing class C felonies, hun. We get caught, we'll spend time in jail. Maybe a lot of time. Our lives will definitely be over, fucking ruined. And the thought of jail…"

"So, what are you going to do, kill him, too?"

The question, stated so simply, so directly, hung in the room for a time. From the other side of the sliding doors of the walk-in closet, Jerry felt as if someone had punched him in the gut. He fought another impulse to surprise them silly by blasting out of that closet and busting Jeff, then Holly, in the chops. Instead, he pursed his lips and stiffened a moment, desperate to remain silent and still. In the ramble of those moments, Jerry let his head clear and came to the bleak conclusion that giving himself away right then was not the wise thing to do. That it was, in fact, stupid. He had the upper hand. He knew what they were planning. Why give that up?

And anyway, though Jerry was loath to admit it to himself right then, he seriously doubted his ability to best Jeff in a physical confrontation, even with the element of surprise on his side. He had no other weapon than his fists, and he had to take into account that Jeff was certainly a better athlete than him, quicker to begin with, and worked out on a regular basis, lifting weights at some club and running in Delaware Park two, three times a week. Jeff had also mentioned somewhere along the way that he had taken tae kwon do lessons from an authentic samurai a few years back, and had attained a green belt or something, and still practiced the art.

"I just need to think," was all Jeff said after that long moment had passed. "Try and find some solution. Hopefully, that doesn't involve that."

"Like I said," said Holly, "sounds like you've already

given it a lot of thought," She added, "Is there one?"

"What?"

Jerry tensed up again—they were talking about him, about possibly murdering him. His life was in the balance. Despite his fear, he moved off the box of sweaters, got onto his knees and started to inching forward again to the opening in the sliding door so he could watch Holly and Jeff engage in this conversation.

From the crack in the doorway, he observed Jeff's shadow dance upon the far wall as he paced around the bedroom. Then, his physical self suddenly emerged into Jerry's field of view and Jerry let out a short gasp. Jeff stopped pacing and looked back, toward the closet, staring, it seemed in that indeterminable instant, straight into Jerry's eyes. But in the next moment, he looked away and stood sideways to Jerry with a hand to his chin. He was deep in thought, pondering the situation while glaring at the far wall.

"A solution," said Holly. "Other than that, killing him. Is there one?"

It was as if Holly was goading Jeff into the obvious answer, that killing Jerry was not only a solution, but their only solution. Jeff lowered his hand and looked at her. "No, I haven't come up with one yet," he said. "But, like you said, murder is not something I really ever thought of getting into. Especially as it pertains to Jerry."

Jeff went back over and sat on the edge of the bed.

While Jeff and Holly gazed into each other's eyes, their fingers intertwined tenderly, she said to him, "I have to agree with you, though. Jerry may not be able to hack it.

He'd slip up down the line. Certainly without me there watching him."

"That's what I fear."

"So, maybe we have no choice in the matter," she said, just above a whisper.

Jeff leaned forward and started kissing her again, their passion renewed perhaps by the thought of her complicity in the murder of her husband. The thought of killing him with her encouragement was the ultimate aphrodisiac. The brutal murder of a cuckold by the cuckold's rival.

"I think you have to do it," she moaned with passion in her every breath, as he kissed her lips and face. "I think that you must do it."

"Yes," Jeff said breathlessly, himself wrapped up in the fantasy. "Yes!"

He was tearing off his clothes again and reaching under the covers for her body.

"I'm gonna shoot that motherfucker right between the eyes," Jeff said as he thrust forward, hard, deep.

Jerry watched dispassionately this time, shocked, alone there in the dark closet.

They meant to murder him.

Chapter Nineteen

Back at the cheap motel, the same one out by Ralph Wilson Stadium, fifteen minutes outside of Buffalo, where he had stayed during his fake funeral, Jerry spent the rest of that night, and early into the next morning, pacing the small, claustrophobic room, taking swigs out of a bottle of cheap whiskey. Every now and then he'd stop and sit on the edge of the bed and simply stare for a time at the grimy, smoke-stained cinder block walls or the coffee-colored blank TV screen propped up on an old, cheap dresser. His world had just crumbled. The worst of everything had come to pass, crashing down upon him. He had lost Holly to Jeff, who had now become his arch- nemesis and his prospective assassin. And Holly had participated willfully, even gleefully, in the ultimate betrayal.

The whiskey enhanced Jerry's deep sorrow and desperate loneliness following the shock of this revelation. Still, what was he to do? Where was he to run? He thought of calling his sister Joan and confessing the whole sordid mess, and turning himself into the cops the following morning with a lawyer and Joan by his side. But Jerry soon gave up on that idea. He and Joan had never been close, and she had enough problems with his alcoholic, abusive brother-in-law, and her boorish teenage boys constantly causing her grief. And his father was certainly not an option. Big Pete was old and worn out and the last thing he needed was for Jerry, the wrong son, to come back from the dead. Furthermore, Jerry would be the laughing stock of the local news, his family and friends once the story got out that he was the ultimate cuckold and had turned himself in out of cowardice and shame.

At some point, Jerry got up and wobbled over to the small radio alarm clock on the table next to the bed, clicked it on, hoping some decent music might break his dire mood and give him cause for hope. It was already tuned to some oldies FM station and, ironically enough, the old Jethro Tull song, *Locomotive Breath,* was playing the following verse:

In the shuffling madness of the locomotive breath, runs the all-time loser, headlong to his death.

He feels the piston scraping—steam breaking on his brow—

old Charlie stole the handle and the train won't stop going—

no way to slow down.

He sees his children jumping off at the stations— one by one.

His woman and his best friend— in bed and having fun.

He's crawling down the corridor on his hands and knees—

old Charlie stole the handle and the train won't stop going—

no way to slow down.

He hears the silence howling— catches angels as they fall.

And the all-time winner has got him by the balls.

He picks up Gideon's Bible— open at page one—

old Charlie stole the handle and the train won't stop going—

no way to slow down.

After Jeff had finally left his house, Jerry had to wait deep in the recesses of the closet until Holly got off the bed and shuffled into the master bathroom and proceeded through her nightly ritual in preparation for bed. After seven years of living with her, Jerry knew all that it entailed. All in the same order, she would methodically remove her makeup, then comb out her shoulder length, wheat-blonde hair, and finally, brush her teeth before gargling a mouthful of Listerine. Jerry had always laughed at the unsexy sound of her gargling.

So when Jerry heard her brushing her teeth, he knew he had to move fast. But first, he had to restrain himself from jumping out of his hiding place and rushing into the bathroom to confront her with what she had done and with what she had said that night, the full depth of her betrayal. Then he might slap her around before raping her and strangling her to death. The wonder of that plan was that he couldn't possibly become suspected of her murder, that he could indeed get away with it. To the authorities, he was dust.

But deep down, Jerry knew he couldn't kill Holly, despite how easily and savagely she had betrayed him. The problem was that he still had feelings for her, genuine feelings, and he couldn't accept that her betrayal, no matter how bad it seemed, was complete. Furthermore, to confront her now would gain nothing, but rather give away his secret advantage. Knowledge is power, and he had certainly obtained the upper hand in that respect that night over Holly and Jeff.

So after a deep breath, Jerry clambered to his feet and negotiated his way through Holly's dresses and blouses, taking a deep breath of the sweet perfume wafting through them before gingerly opening the sliding door and peeking out. He took a single step into the bedroom and heard Holly spit into the bathroom sink. In the next moment, she was gargling.

Jerry hustled to the open door of the master bedroom out into the dark hallway leading to the staircase. At the top stair, he stopped and listened. Holly had not yet switched off the bathroom light. That gave him all the time he needed to get downstairs and out of the house.

He had escaped, and like the invisible man he was, had not been seen. He went out the way he had come, through the kitchen door leading out to the deck. When Jeff had left the house, he had set the alarm, so Jerry had to remember to disarm it before arming it again on his way out.

"Mother-fucking bitch!" Jerry shouted as he fell back onto the lumpy bed of his motel room after the Tull song ended and some late night DJ, in a soft and pleasant voice identified the song and artist for the benefit of his few listeners, the year it first broadcast on the album *Aqualung* in 1971.

"Mother-fucking bastards!"

But after a minute or so of disgorging his drunken anger and sorrow, there was a part of Jerry that felt fairly good right then. Emboldened suddenly by the alcohol buzzing through his veins and brain after a long tiring day that included driving three and a half hours and watching his wife and best friend in bed having fun screwing and plotting his murder. By some favor granted by the gods, he had found out the lying fuckers that Jeff and Holly had turned out to be. Still better, he knew that they had a plan and what it was.

All he had to do was think up a suitable revenge, a betrayal all his own.

Chapter Twenty

Jerry decided that the first thing he needed to do was contact the body guy.

Jeff had told him about his encounter with the body guy, and so Jerry knew his name and where he worked. For the better part of two days, Jerry watched Willie Robinson come and go from his job at the medical school. During those two days, Jerry didn't learn that much about Robinson, except that he drove a rusty, beat-up old dark green Ford Taurus and that he was punctual to a fault, arriving in his parking space at 8:55 each morning.

Robinson was a slight built, diminutive, dark-skinned black man in his late thirties. His hair was greased straight back and the first time Jerry saw him he thought of Sammy Davis Jr. He carried a small paper bag, undoubtedly his lunch, and walked briskly from the old Taurus up the long, narrow sidewalk from the parking lot to the entrance of the basement where Willie Robinson spent his long eight-hour shift in the glaring light scrubbing newly arrived bodies, making sure they were ready for the future doctors of

America.

At exactly 5:05 both days, the body guy left the building, shuffled unenthusiastically down the long sidewalk to his parking space, and drove home. Jerry could only guess what could be on the body guy's mind. Perhaps he was thinking of his next payment from Jeff and what he was going to blow it on.

Home was on the east side of Buffalo, on the fringes of a rough, black neighborhood that didn't look safe for anyone at any time. His house was well-kept, however, a massive clapboard not unlike so many others along the street of that old, tired neighborhood.

Robinson arrived home around six the first day of Jerry's surveillance and shuffled toward it like a man who really desired to be someplace else. But on the second day, a Tuesday, just as Jeff had said, Robinson stopped off at a rundown tavern, Adams Lounge, on Fillmore Avenue a few blocks from his home. It was the bar where Jeff had met Robinson and first broached the idea of buying a cadaver. If Jeff had been correct in his observations, he'd remain at Adams' Lounge until about eight thirty, nine o'clock and then slunker home to his big-ass wife and kid.

Jerry watched Robinson another day but finally, on the fourth day of watching him, at 5:09 P.M., Jerry strode out between a couple cars across from Robinson's parking spot and approached him at the driver's side door of his Taurus.

"Mister Robinson? Willie Robinson?" Robinson turned and squinted at Jerry.

"Who wants to know?" he asked.

"Ah, me," said Jerry. "A friend."

Robinson's squint hardened into a scowl. "I know you?"

"No," Jerry said, "but I think you should."

"Say what?"

"Let's just say, I'm an acquaintance of Jeff Flaherty. You sold him a body a few weeks back."

Jerry had practiced these lines, this approach. "I don't know nothing about it."

"Look, man, "Jerry said. "I'm Flaherty's accomplice."

"Accomplice?"

"The body you gave him," said Jerry, "became me." After a moment, Robinson nodded.

"So what you want?"

"To talk."

"'Bout what?"

"Let's go someplace."

They settled on a quiet tavern in a strip mall not far from the university. There were only two other customers in the place that Thursday evening, both of whom occupied stools at the far corner of the bar. They gave Jerry and Willie Robinson passing glances as they settled into a dark back booth. Jerry went up to the bar and ordered two cold Miller drafts and brought them back to the table.

After taking a sip, Robinson asked, "So what you got to tell me?"

Jerry launched into it, starting from beginning to end. How he and Holly had met Jeff Flaherty at the law firm Christmas Party now almost two years ago. Almost a year to the day later, they hatched a plot to defraud Global insurance out of four million dollars. Now the plan had been executed, and they were waiting for the claim to be paid.

"Four million?" interrupted Robinson. He had not realized until that moment the magnitude of the crime.

And then Jerry told Willie Robinson about the betrayal of Jeff and Holly.

"Shit man," Willie said. "That be cruel."

"Yeah. Cruel. But that's not the half of it." After another swallow of beer, Jerry told Willie Robinson how his blackmailing had forced Jeff Flaherty to consider murdering him.

"Kill me?" Robinson laughed.

"And then after you," Jerry added, "me."

Robinson mulled all this over for a time, then said, "So they double-crossing me, and you."

"Yep," Jerry said. "Looks that way."

"That's bad shit," Robinson said.

"Plenty bad," said Jerry.

They sipped their beers in silence for a time until Jerry said, "So that's why we got to help each other. Scare the living shit out of them, not to mention take some of their money. A lot of their money."

Willie Robinson nodded and gave Jerry a kindly, friendly look, then Jerry asked, "So why'd you get mixed up in our little scam?"

"Well," he said with a laugh, "being honest and good don't always pay the bills." He sighed, straightened up, started tapping his fingers on the table. "You really want to know? I got involved in something before this that I shouldn't have. I like to play the numbers. And sometimes, the numbers like to play me. I ended up owing this guy, Stevie, a lot of money.

"So when that yuppie dude, your accomplice and all that, stopped by the Adams Lounge and started talking to me about needing a body, I thought, what the hell, let me think about it. I knew there's almost no way for anyone to find out I sold one. Who the hell would want a body, anyway? Plus, I burn them up afterward, and ash is ash, you know what I mean? Anyway, I thought about it a day, then I called him up and said, let's play.

"He gave me the ten grand, and I got him the body," Robinson went on. "But then, afterward, I got to thinking, what the hell he do with that body? And I figured, shit man, I got underpaid. The ten grand was just enough to pay off Stevie, I had nothing left. So I thought, what the hell, if I can get a few thousand more, maybe I can get the hell out of this place and find a nice place for my wife and kid."

He let Jerry buy him another round.

"So what's next?" Robinson asked. "What's your deal?"

"I call Jeff and tell him what I know," Jerry said. "That I know their plan to kill you, then me, and so when the insurance money comes, I get a cut, and so do you."

"How much?" Willie asked, a hard edge to his look. "A cool mil, okay?"

Robinson's eyes boggled. A million dollars! He laughed and shook his head. "You kidding me?"

"No man," Jerry said. "A million. That's a million for each of us."

Robinson nodded. "Shit man, let's fucking drink on it."

They toasted to their good fortune and coming riches and shook hands and laughed at how marvelously things were going to turn out. And then they followed that beer with another. And another after that. They drank to knowledge. They drank to revenge. They drank to money. They drank to big ass mamas and cheating sluts. They drank to rotting cadavers waiting to be carved open by smart-ass medical students. They drank to big, long, safe master bedroom closets full of dresses and sweaters and women's smelly shoes.

When Robinson finally left the bar, Jerry knew he was more than a little drunk and implored him to be careful. The last thing either of them needed was a DWI. He even suggested that he drive Robinson home.

But Robinson found his keys and waved him off. "I be fine. Plus, what's Sondra gonna say if a white boy drive me home drunk? Like I say, I be fine." Unbeknownst to Jerry, Robinson wasn't going straight home. He was stopping off at the Adams Lounge first for his usual Thursday night boozing.

Jerry stayed behind in the bar and ordered a hamburger and fries. He drank two glasses of water, no more beer. Stupid, he said to himself. Getting drunk was the last thing he needed.

He left the bar at around nine feeling pretty much sober and made it back to his motel without incident. He laid down on the bed and stretched out. After a minute or so, he started laughing. Sometimes there was justice in the world. This had certainly turned out to be Willie Robinson's lucky day. He had fallen into unexpected riches and freedom from the awful job as an Anatomical Preparator, a body guy, toiling in the lonely morgue washing and disposing of cadavers in the dark basement of the medical school lab. Never again would Willie Robinson have to go home smelling like formaldehyde.

Jerry closed his eyes and tried to get his bearings. It had been a long last few days and all the stress and running around was finally getting to him. And the five or six beers with the body guy that evening hadn't helped.

The plan had been for him to call Jeff that night and tell him that he knew everything and that he wanted two million dollars, one for himself, and one for the body guy. And if he didn't get it, he'd turn himself in and cop a decent plea for himself and Willie Robinson.

But before Jerry ever got a chance to make that call, he fell asleep.

Chapter Twenty-One

At around ten the following morning, Jerry was awakened by the ringtone of his cell phone. After a moment, he sat up and stared at it on the small, cheap night table by the bed. His immediate thought as he shook off a dreamless sleep was that it must be another wrong number.

With his head aching from the night before, Jerry grabbed for the cell phone. It slipped out of his grasp and fell to the carpet below.

"Fuck."

He reached down and picked up the phone, now on its fourth ring.

"H-hello?"

"Where the fuck were you?" came Jeff's voice. "On the pooper?"

Jerry held his breath for a long moment desperately trying to keep his cool.

"You there?"

"Yeah," Jerry said, "Just got up."

Jeff laughed. "It's quarter past ten, dude," he said.

"But I forgot, you are no longer a resident of the world of the living."

"What's up?"

"It's a done deal," he said, and Jerry could feel the glee in Jeff's voice. "The check is in the mail."

That was the code Jeff had agreed to use to notify Jerry that Global had paid the claim. That they had pulled it off! Four million dollars was being, or had already been, wire-transferred into the LLC checking account which Holly had opened for that purpose. In the next couple of days, they would transfer the money into several other accounts set up in obscure, out of state banks, in the names of the several other LLCs. The paper chase would be daunting and difficult if it was ever pursued, something, of course, they hoped would never happen. Eventually, after two or three months, the four million would be divided two ways – two-thirds to be shared by Holly and Jerry, and the other third for Jeff.

Jerry knew that with the money now in their laps, Jeff and Holly would have to make a final decision concerning the killings.

"Once the money is deposited, she'll travel down there," Jeff promised. Of course, he was thinking that Jerry was still waiting for her in Binghamton. "You holding up okay?"

"Yeah, sure," Jerry said. "I'm fine."

"Just a couple more days," Jeff said. "Hold tight."

Jerry knew more than ever what they intended to do. First, Jeff would kill the body guy. Then, Holly would come down to Binghamton once the insurance money was deposited, but not to act as his front. Instead, she was going to help set him up for murder.

But Jerry held the cards now. He started to say something, but for some reason, he couldn't bring himself to tell Jeff that he was on to their murderous plots and that the body guy had been forewarned and was now his partner. The old conspiracy was over and a new one was beginning. And he was going to make a new life without Holly. With Jade, perhaps.

"What?" Jeff asked.

"No-nothing," he said. "I – I didn't say anything."

"Alright," Jeff said. "You sure you're okay?"

"Yeah, sure," Jerry said. "Just a couple more days."

Jerry felt refreshed and alive with purpose as he paid the grim-faced, nodding Arab motel owner for yet another night, then stopped for breakfast at a nearby diner. Right after a cup of coffee and some eggs, bacon and home fries, he'd pull out his cell phone and tell Jeff and Holly that they could go to fucking hell. That the conspiracy was over. That a new day had dawned, and he had demands.

In the foyer on his way into the restaurant, Jerry found a *Buffalo News* box, dropped three-quarters into the slot, and pulled out a paper. After being shown a booth in the mostly empty, post-breakfast/pre-lunch rush, a waitress came over and filled a cup in front of him to the brim with steaming black coffee. With professional efficiency and indifference, she took his order.

While sipping the coffee, Jerry spread the newspaper out on the table and, as always, went straight to the sports pages. He was pulling out the local news section just as the waitress was bringing his breakfast platter.

After shoveling a fork-full of over-salted, over-buttered scrambled eggs into his mouth, swallowing them down with more coffee, Jerry was immediately drawn to a headline in the far right column of the local section:

Med School Worker Stabbed To Death -- City police found William Robinson, 38, stabbed to death near his home on Box Avenue. Robinson's body was found in an alley between two houses by a man walking his dog shortly after midnight. According to Robinson's wife, he had not returned home that evening from his job at the University of Buffalo Medical School where he cared for cadavers donated for dissection. Police suspect that he was killed earlier and that robbery was a possible motive for the slaying in that high crime neighborhood.

Jerry could not move. He just sat there for a time staring at the headline.

Stabbed to death.

He put down the fork, his appetite gone. Jeff and Holly had acted more swiftly than he had anticipated.

The waitress came over and filled his cup.

"Something the matter with your eggs, honey?" she asked.

Jerry couldn't think of what to say as he looked up at her with a weak smile.

"N-no," he said. "Just not so hungry all of a sudden."

She smirked at him and quickly walked away. Jerry picked up the paper and re-read the article.

Med School Worker... Stabbed to Death... William Robinson... 38.

He crumpled the paper and tossed it aside on the booth next to him. Goddammit, he thought. So Jeff really had it in him. Jerry's next thought was doubly disturbing.

He was next.

Part Two - Second Betrayal

Chapter Twenty-Two

When Jerry returned to Binghamton two weeks after the body guy's murder, he decided that he could no longer stay at the house in Endicott. Jeff knew where he lived and could readily find him.

So his first night back, Jerry found a cheap motel off State Route 11 and booked a room. Then he called Jade. She had returned from her "vacations" to Albany and Florida, and Jerry was glad to hear her voice. And he was doubly glad that she unhesitatingly agreed to meet him.

"Why you staying there?" she had asked.

"I'll tell you when you get here."

Upon her arrival, Jerry gave her a long embrace.

"You're shaking, hon," she said and, knowing something bad was bothering Jerry, let his embrace linger.

Jerry took her to the bed and they laid down together. "What's the matter?" she asked, stroking his hair as he lay, balled up, in her bosom.

Then, after a deep breath, he told her. everything. Ending with how the body guy had paid with his life and he was next. And how without Holly, he needed a "front." After telling Jade all this, Jerry admitted that most of all, he was just plain scared.

Jade remained silent for a time. There was a lot to digest.

And most of it was fantastical. Like a cheap crime novel.

"You did that?" she asked. "Faked your death. Stole four million dollars?" She laughed at him with an amazed look.

"Yes."

"That took fucking balls, hon." Jerry laughed. "I guess."

Then they kissed for a time while lying on the bed, deeply and passionately, not as whore and customer, but as friends, lovers perhaps. She called Luke's cell phone and told him to go home. She was staying the night. They made love and afterward, Jade held Jerry in her arms and soothed his trepidation and despair deep into the night.

Later that night, holding Jade securely in his arms, Jerry revealed how he intended to exact his revenge.

"I already set them up," Jerry told her with a sigh. Jade snuggled even deeper into Jerry's arms.

"You set them up? How?"

"After the shock wore off over the body guy's murder, I formulated a plan."

"So what's your plan?"

"Well, first I thought about just giving up and turning myself in. Snitch on Jeff and Holly and work out a deal. Spend a couple of years in jail and have the satisfaction of getting back at them that way. But, what is the saying? That would be cutting off my nose to spite my face. Plus, I'd be looked at, mocked, for what I was, a goddamn weak cuckold. I'd never be able to look myself in the mirror, have any self-respect. So that was out."

Jade had started playing with Jerry's chest hairs and though it tickled, he let her do it. Clearly, she was growing a little fond of him. "So what did you do?"

"Well, first of all, I planted two emails messages, fake emails," Jerry said, "emails that incriminated both of them for my murder. For one of them, I used an email address I set up under Holly's name and sent it over our old home computer. The message will show up on the hard drive of that computer and link her solidly to the crime. She had access to it, only her, and whatever message was sent from it would be linked to her and only her.

"I snuck in the house during the lunch hour one afternoon while Holly was at work and sent an email from that computer to Jeff's email address on his computer at work. Then, I hustled my ass downtown and slipped into Jeff's office at the law firm toward the end of that same lunch hour and sent the response to Holly's computer at home." Jerry snapped his fingers. "And, just like that, both of them are incriminated in my murder."

"How'd you pull that off? The emails. You had to do it pretty quick. I mean simultaneous, right?"

Jade had finished playing with his chest hairs and had moved her hand to his crotch and was massaging it. A moment later, Jerry laughed.

"Don't you ever stop?"

"Tell me about how you did it — the emails. It's making me excited."

"Everything makes you excited," Jerry laughed.

Then she was sliding down him, licking his chest and upper belly, then belly, as she went.

"Jesus," he sighed.

"Tell me," she whispered, her mouth up against his lower belly, licking him just above his crotch.

"I can't tell you anything when you're doing that."

"Then don't. Wait til I'm finished."

She was finished in about ten minutes and moved back up to snuggle into his arms again. Jerry was spent. He felt himself drifting off to sleep.

"No, you can't. Don't go to sleep," she said. "Tell me."

"Geez, you're killing me, girl."

The emails.

"Yes, the emails."

"How did you plant them? Sounds like spy stuff. Like James Bond or something."

Jerry laughed and took a deep breath as he sat up to tell her. Jade turned toward him and started playing with his chest hairs again.

"Stop that a minute and listen," he said and sighed. She giggled and leaned back in his arms.

"The first thing I had to do was break into my own house. Well, not break in. I had a key, the same key from the night I snuck in and found them out, and I knew the security code. So that was easy."

"Well, let me back up a minute," he said. "The first

thing I did actually was sneak up to the law firm where Jeff and Holly worked, to case out Jeff's office. See if he ever left his computer unattended, and when and all that. I wasn't well known up there, hadn't been up to Holly's workspace too often, just a handful of times in five years. And she works in a totally different department than Jeff anyway. It's such a large firm, a lot of employees don't even know each other.

"Plus, I had this beard going–" he fingered his chin "– that acted as somewhat of a disguise. But to be on the safe side, I picked up a decent looking wig at one of those spy stores, and a maintenance man outfit they used at the building. I asked and without thinking twice about it, some building maintenance guy told me the store they got them from."

"Sounds neat so far," Jade said. "CIA stuff, like I said."

"Anyway, I went up to the law office toward the end of the lunch hour, around one or so, and found Jeff's office empty. Just as important as that, he had left his office door wide open and his computer was still on, despite whatever memos I knew from Holly that the firm had sent about turning it off for security reasons or whatever.

"So the plan was set. I'd break into my house around noon the next day and send Jeff the email message from the old PC in my den, using the email address I had set up for Holly, and then hurry downtown to the law firm before lunch ended, sneak into Jeff's office and use his computer to answer it.

"Anyway, this cockamamie plan worked somehow,"

Jerry said with a laugh. "I generated two emails that can incriminate both of them for my murder."

Jerry gently moved Jade out of his arms, jumped off the bed and switched on the lamp on the night table next to it. Jade squinted in the harsh, sudden light as she sat up and watched Jerry pull his suitcase out from under the bed. After a few moments, he found what he was looking for – an envelope containing the incriminating emails.

Standing naked before her, he started reading from the top one:

Dearest Jeff:

It's hard to believe that we pulled it off. In a few short days, we will have everything we need, money, each other, time. I miss you so much but I agree that we have to wait to change our patterns. I thought I would feel guilty, but I don't. I just don't. I am amazed at my lack of guilt; how giddy I feel. I miss you so these evenings when I come home to an empty house. I am glad you agreed that it wouldn't be suspicious if you started visiting me some evenings.

That is what I live for now. I need you here. And it's so hard at work playing the part of a grieving widow and resisting going up to you, hugging you, kissing you, laughing out loud over what we pulled off.

All My Love, Holly

"Sounds just like her," Jerry lamented, staring off for a moment, hearing her saying those things.

"So what does Jeff's response say?" Jade asked. "What did you write back?"

"Only two lines," he told her, and lifted the copy of the email from under the fake one from Holly. "There's no greeting, of course, just this: 'Don't write stuff like that to me here.' It's all in caps. Then, I added: 'It could ruin everything,' and repeated, 'Everything' again. The beauty of it was that it implicated him in the whole plot, especially the "ruin everything,' in caps part."

"But what did Holly do when she got that message?" Jade asked.

"She didn't do anything," Jerry said. "The beauty of it is that she never uses that email address. She doesn't even know it exists. But it was her address, and it would be linked to her through the computer in my old house."

Jerry stuck the copies of the incriminating email messages back in the envelope, returned it to the suitcase, and shoved it under the bed. Then, he got back in bed and snuggled next Jade.

"And that's it," he said. "The first part of the plan."

"What's the second?" Jade asked.

"I call them."

"Who? Call who?"

"Them," Jerry said. "Well, him – Jeff."

"Why?"

"I tell him I know everything," Jerry said. "I tell him I know they are lying, cheating murderers. And then I blackmail them. Once they pay me the money, I wait some time, five, six months, and then send the incriminating emails to the cops."

Jade laughed. She was twirling his chest hairs again.

"You're awesome," she said, and down she went to

give him his reward.

Chapter Twenty-Three

For six months after planting the emails, Jerry lived anonymously with Jade with her acting as his front. Jerry worked out a lot, made love often to Jade, and they shopped and cooked dinners together and generally acted like the happy newlywed couple they often pretended in public to be.

Still, Jerry wasn't going to be satisfied until his plan for getting back at Holly and Jeff was fully realized.

The first part involved obtaining his share of the insurance money, $1.33 million, had gone off as planned. A week after he had returned to Binghamton, Jerry had called Jeff and told him that he knew about his affair with Holly that he had killed the body guy, and that if Jeff didn't wire his share of the insurance money within three days, he'd turn himself into the police. Two days later, the money was safely wired into various accounts in obscure banks around the country under the names of the various LLCs which Jerry had filed in New Mexico before placing the call to Jeff.

And just yesterday morning, six months after

receiving his share of the insurance money, the second part of Jerry's plan was irrevocably put into motion. He drove the hour or so up Interstate 81 to Syracuse and found the downtown post office. He parked in a surface lot and entered the squat, ugly building. He slid the stamped envelope containing the emails he had created now over six months ago, incriminating Holly and Jeff for his murder, into the opening of a first class mail drop. The envelope was addressed to Global Insurance's Philadelphia headquarters office.

For a paranoid moment, Jerry worried about video surveillance cameras outside and inside the building capturing him walking in and mailing the letter while wearing latex gloves, but soon enough, he laughed off how farfetched that worry was. Except for the postmark which would reveal that the emails were mailed from this post office in Syracuse, no one would ever figure out a way, if there even was one, to determine who had mailed them. The primary concern, initially at least, would be with the content of the emails. Only later might the focus change to who had sent them and why. But by then, months would have passed and whatever surveillance video that may have existed, if any existed at all, would long ago have been erased. Furthermore, there was no way of knowing, from the video, if one existed, who had mailed the letter. Hundreds of people probably walked in the post office on a daily basis.

Tomorrow or the next day at the latest, Global's fraud unit guys would be salivating over the incriminating emails. Some old, crusty insurance company investigator would grumble that the arson investigators had been wrong. Jerry Shaw had been murdered, burned alive. Once that connection was made, they would be after Jeff and Holly like flies on shit.

The best part of the Jerry's plan was he was no longer recognizable as the old Jerry Shaw. Even Holly and Jeff probably wouldn't recognize him. His beard was neatly trimmed, giving him an academic look, like a college professor. Even more impressive, he had lost *fifty* pounds, slimming down to a svelte two hundred, his lowest weight since high school, and he had gone from a size 44 to 38 waist. The act of losing weight and toning his body had remarkably changed the shape of his face as well. His chubby jowls had transformed into a gaunt, sharp countenance, and his eyes had narrowed into a determined, distinguished scowl. Somehow he looked older, more mature, a serious guy. Jade was amazed at the transformation but added that she liked it. She liked the new Jerry Shaw.

Jerry's dramatic loss of blubber around his mid-section was attributed, first of all, to a radical change of eating habits. He had sworn off burgers and shakes and fries from any fast food chain and instead ate healthy doses of salads and fresh fruit and vegetables. In his regimen of reclaiming his manhood and self-confidence, he worked out regularly and with sincerity at a local Gold's Gym, and he joined a Tae Kwon Do class where he learned how to respect his mind and body.

From these sustained efforts, Jerry had not merely excised his flab, but he had become downright ripped. His mental attitude had also changed for the better. He believed in himself for the first time in his life and his thinking had become positive and confident. He no longer saw himself as weak and unfortunate, but instead as strong and opportune. Jerry now sometimes found himself admiring his pectorals in the mirror, and how his good-looking, boyishly square features had returned after so many years hidden by fleshy, unappealing jowls. In short, after only six months as an anonymous man, through sheer discipline and dedication and hard work, and with Jade's help, Jerry had a developed a whole new sense of well-being, confidence and determination that would mark the rest of his life.

Jerry's biggest regret was that he was unable to show the new him to Holly and see her reaction. He spent too much time fantasizing over that, imagining her goggling eyes, and the way she might throw herself at him.

But more importantly, as Jerry had changed over the months, transforming himself, he sensed that Jade saw in him more than a means to riches. At some point, Jerry believed that she may have fallen in love with the man he had become.

Chapter Twenty-Four

The typed address for Global Life & Casualty Insurance was blazoned across the center of the envelope in bold, crisp black capital letters. But the upper left-hand corner of the envelope was blank – there was no return address.

Three weeks after the letter had been delivered, Jack Fox found it one morning in the in-basket on the squat desk in the small cubicle assigned to him at Global's headquarters offices in downtown Philadelphia. There appeared to have been no good reason, except bureaucratic sloth or negligence, for the letter to have taken so long to find its way to him.

Later that same afternoon, Fox found himself sitting in Chief Reynolds office. He watched with some impatience as the Chief meticulously inspected the envelope, then the two emails. Wearing rubber gloves, the Chief turned the emails over in his hands several times before finally reading them. Fox thought the gloves were unnecessary in light of the fact that the envelope and emails had been handled by at least two secretaries and himself since their arrival.

Chief Reynolds settled into an intense scowl as he continued reading. He lingered over them a few minutes more, his mouth moving to the words at times, before again turning them over and over again in his hands, inspecting every last millimeter of them. Fox suspected that the Chief was trying to find fingerprints, hair follicles, skin scrapings, DNA, something to link them to Holly and Jeff.

Finally, Chief Reynolds looked up.

"These are confessions," he said. "Or pretty damn close. At the very least, highly incriminating."

Though his expression remained deadpanned, the Chief seemed genuinely surprised and just about as happy as Fox had ever seen his old friend. Then, after letting a few moments pass, he sighed. "We've confirmed these email addresses belong to her, him?"

"Yep," Fox said. "Our computer forensic geeks did. It's conclusive, they said." Fox waved a piece of paper. "Here's their report. The address is registered to Holly Shaw. And the other one belongs to Jeff Flaherty, his work email. And Flaherty's the guy I saw at the house after the insured's funeral. Of course, we still need the computers they were typed on to confirm that the emails were prepared and sent on them. But short of that, looks like we got a break in this case. The proverbial gift horse."

The Chief nodded. "Hard being right all the time, hey Jack?" Then asked his old friend, "So how did they end up in our lap? Who sent them?"

"That's what I mean by gift horse, Chief. I haven't a clue why I got them," said Fox with a shrug. "I suppose

Mrs. Shaw and, or, Flaherty, have an arch-nemesis out there. All we know is that they were mailed from Syracuse in upstate New York."

"Syracuse?" Reynolds rubbed his chin and thought a moment. There was something too neat about this. Too gift-wrapped. Finally, he looked up.

"Fingerprints?"

"Nada," said Fox.

"Anything else? Hair, skin. Saliva on the envelope? For a DNA check."

"Did all that," Fox said. "The envelope is one of the modern ones, with the seal security strip or whatever. The lab found nothing else – no hair follicles, skin particles, spit. They put it under electro-violet light and all that. It's clean. So, like I said, we still need to link them to Holly Shaw's and Flaherty's computers."

Chief Reynolds mulled over the situation for a time.

"Think this will convince the DA down in Buffalo to reopen the case, get a warrant?" he asked. "Grab her computer, his. Find out what other incriminating emails or other stuff we can find. Maybe grab enough evidence to charge them both with murder?"

Fox shrugged. "All we can do is ask," he said.

Early the next morning Fox was on a flight back to Buffalo. He had an appointment at eleven with the deputy chiefs of the homicide and white collar crime bureaus of the Erie County District Attorney's Office. By 12:15, having read the emails and discussing the case for a time, the deputy chiefs were downright enthusiastic. They told Fox they didn't foresee a problem getting a judge to sign a search warrant. In fact, they expected to be executing one at the Shaw home, seizing her computer, by the end of the week, or early next week at the latest. Flaherty's might be more complicated, since it could contain client confidences wholly unrelated to his communications with Holly Shaw. But they promised to do the research on that and hopefully be in a position to simultaneously execute both warrants.

"During the search, I suggest we come down hard on the widow Shaw," chimed in Inspector Dan Miller, an investigator with the DA's office. "See if we can make her come clean. Snitch out her lover on the hope of getting a plea deal."

It was just short of 1:30 by the time the meeting ended. As Fox was shaking hands with the deputies and Inspector Miller, Miller offered to take Fox to lunch at a diner out by the airport then drive him to his departure gate.

At the diner, while chewing his burger, Fox told the inspector that his instincts had been right all along.

"I knew something was up when I saw Flaherty at the house Friday after the funeral," Fox told Miller. "Still, this turn of events has left me less than satisfied. Those emails plopping down in our laps from Heaven. As if our insured, Shaw sent them." He took another bite of his hamburger and looked off mulling over the whole case.

Inspector Miller frowned as he twirled a spoon around inside his cup of coffee. He was a wizened old cop himself, having served a long and honorable career, now close to retirement. He understood completely about hunches, and could tell right off that Fox's had been right on more often than not.

"Sometimes you don't look a gift horse in the mouth," Miller said. "Sounds like your company may have just saved itself four million bucks; or, whatever the perpetrators haven't spent or hidden."

"Yeah," said Fox, "I know. But this only created another, maybe more interesting mystery."

After chewing his burger for a time, Miller said, "As in, who sent those emails?"

"Exactly," Fox said. "And how did we get them?" Miller set the burger down on a plate.

"Sounds like that one might be even harder to solve," he said, "than the murder we are about to."

Hard or not, it seemed to Fox that it might be worth solving. Something wasn't quite right about the whole damned thing. Incriminating evidence just didn't plop out of thin air. Whoever had sent those emails incriminating Holly Shaw was deeply involved in this caper as well.

And Fox desperately meant to learn who that person was.

Chapter Twenty-Five

The Erie County Sheriff's Department executed a search warrant at Holly Shaw's house that afternoon and seized the old personal computer from the small desk in what used to be Jerry's den. On the computer hard drive, the Department's forensic computer guys would subsequently find evidence that the email message Jerry had planted had been transmitted from the machine to Jeff's work computer. Of course, because Jerry was presumed dead, and no one else had access to his old computer except Holly, they would naturally conclude that Holly had typed and sent it. Who else could have? They would also find the purported reply message from Jeff, sent by Jerry from Jeff's work computer.

That same afternoon, the managing partner of Carlton and Rowe voluntarily handed over to the Sheriff Department's investigator, Inspector Dan Miller, the hard-drive of what used to be Jeff's work computer. It seemed that about three or four months ago, Jeff had abruptly left the firm. Inspector Miller had learned just that week that

Jeff was still living in Buffalo, in a three-bedroom apartment on Anderson Street just off Elmwood Avenue. However, during an interview with the apartment's landlord, he found that Jeff had given notice of lease termination and was in the process of buying a large chunk of property, a ranch or something, out in Montana. Lastly, during surveillance conducted on Wednesday night, Inspector Miller learned that Jeff was still seeing Holly Shaw.

The Department forensic geeks were quickly able to find the incriminating email message on Jeff's hard-drive in answer to Holly Shaw's received message. The managing partner of Carlton and Rowe confirmed that no one in the firm except Jeff Flaherty had access to that particular computer on the day in question. The password used to access the computer and e-mail was known only by Jeff. In short, no one except Jeff Flaherty could have sent the email message.

And better yet, during their subsequent analysis of Jeff's computer hard drive the following week, they discovered more incriminating evidence. Someone, presumably Jeff, had been surfing the Internet for information about garage fires in the weeks before the purported and now questionable accidental fire; and, that someone had saved a newspaper article about some poor schlep who had been burned in a garage fire while working under his used car.

At around ten that same morning, Holly was home when Inspector Miller arrived to confront her about the incriminating emails found on the computer in her upstairs den. He handed her crisp copies and watched as she read them over for a time. Finally, she looked up and surprised him by remaining cool, aloof, and silent. Still, he noticed that her hands were shaking as she handed the emails back to him.

"I didn't send this," she said. "They're fake."

"Well," Inspector Miller said, taking them back from her, "they sure look real to me. And my computer guy tells me this one was written on the very computer we took out of here yesterday."

"I have no idea how that happened," Holly said, keeping calm. She remembered what Jeff had told her if the time ever came when she was confronted by police or insurance investigators. Keep your mouth shut. Say nothing. Don't even deny anything, or try to defend yourself in any way. Assert your right to remain silent, he had told her, and more importantly, your right to a lawyer.

Holly's stare hardened. "And that's all I got to say to you, Inspector," she said. "I don't have to talk to you. I have the right to remain silent."

"That's right," Inspector Miller said, his demeanor hardening as well. But if you won't explain the meaning of those emails, I have to be wondering, why not?"

"I don't care what you're wondering," Holly said. "I'm not answering any questions. I stand by my rights."

But she kept talking anyway.

"That was Jerry's computer," she said. "I never used it."

"Well, someone used it," Inspector Miller said. "And Jerry's dead.

She cursed herself for saying that. "I said, I'm done

talking to you. I want a lawyer."

"Look, I'm just trying to help you," Miller said, trying now to play the good cop, become her confident. "These e-mails make it seem you got yourself involved in maybe something you shouldn't have. Maybe someone forced you into it. I'm just trying to get you out of trouble."

"I said, I want my lawyer," Holly told Miller.

"Sure, sure," Miller said. Then, he looked to one of the police officers assisting in the search. "Take her in."

They took her to an Erie County Sheriff's Department substation near the town hall and sat her on a hard plastic chair in a small conference room used exclusively for interrogations. But Miller didn't let anyone ask her a single question while waiting for the lawyer she had called, a guy by the name of Dan Morgan from Carlton and Rowe.

"Never heard of him," she heard Miller whisper to another cop.

While waiting for Morgan to arrive, Miller returned to the conference room. He told her he didn't want her to say a thing, just listen. Then he filled her head with all kinds of devastating scenarios if she persisted in keeping quiet and protecting Flaherty. He told her she was going to jail for life all because she was protecting her dumb ass lover who'd probably blow her in the first chance he got. The young detective with Miller, whose name she never quite got, Detective Orson, Olson or something, started playing the good cop, chiming in that the judge would certainly consider her cooperation in coming clean and helping them to convict Flaherty, who surely must have been the real brains behind the murder plot.

But Holly kept her poise, staring forward trying not to listen.

Finally, Miller said, "Go ahead, keep your mouth shut. Doesn't matter anyway. With these emails, we don't even need you to talk." He flipped the two emails out in front of himself. "We got your own words. Your own treasonous words. You and that asshole murderous boyfriend of yours are as good as cooked. You cruel, murderous bitch."

Holly remained stoic. Once or twice, she smirked, seemingly pleased with herself.

Finally, Dan Morgan arrived and demanded to speak with Holly alone.

"What the hell is this about, Hol?" All the cops had told him that his client had become a suspect in the murder of her husband.

Holly had worked for Morgan from time to time at Carlton and Rowe. Morgan had ended up in the commercial litigation department primarily making sure that commercial contracts didn't screw the firm's clients. Conversing in the firm kitchen, they had talked about their lives at times and she had even told him how unhappy she was with the way things had turned out for her and Jerry. Morgan said his life had pretty much the same humdrum feel. He had married his college sweetheart and they quickly had two kids. He was making a good living at the firm but the rest of his life seemed laid out for him. He had told Holly that he and his wife rarely made love anymore. And for a time, before Jeff came into their lives, Holly had fantasized going to bed with Morgan.

Now, looking at him across the conference table, she

thanked God she hadn't. He was balding with a perpetually worried frown, a clone of all the other junior partners and associates in the firm. All of them, comfortably numb.

"I need to call Jeff," Holly said.

"Jeff?" he asked. "As in Jeff Flaherty?"

"Yeah," she said, "that Jeff Flaherty."

Morgan handed Holly his cell phone and watched while she punched in the number.

"Yeah, speak." It was Jeff, the brusque way he always answered, as if the last thing he wanted to do right then was talk to whoever was calling.

"It's me," Holly said and had to hold back from whimpering.

"What's wrong?"

In the next minute or so, Holly told him what was going on as coherently as she possibly could with Dan Morgan standing there, watching her.

"You kept your mouth shut, right?"

"Of course. Like you told me to, I kept quiet."

"Emails?" Jeff said, mulling it over with himself. "Where the hell did they come from?"

He drew in a breath, suddenly concerned. "Listen, we better watch what we say. This call could be tapped, you know. If they got a search warrant, they might have gotten a wire-tap order. I'm not even sure they need one for a cell phone call. I'm surprised they are letting you call me in the first place."

"They're not letting me. I called Dan Morgan, it's his phone I'm using."

"That idiot?"

"Yes." Holly sighed. "Jeff, listen. Maybe…maybe we should tell them. The truth."

"Shut the fuck up!" he snapped. "Just shut the fuck up and keep your cool. They aren't going to prove anything on the strength of a couple ambiguous emails."

"But you haven't seen them," she said, still whispering with her back to Morgan. "They make it sound pretty bad. Like I was involved in Jerry's death. And you, too."

"Look," he said, softer. "Enough. Just keep quiet. This conversation is getting us nowhere except perhaps in trouble. And that goes for Dan Morgan, too. Don't tell that asshole a goddamn thing."

Half an hour later, they released Holly and she left the sub-station with Morgan hurrying behind her. She wasn't going to be arrested, was all he had been told, but otherwise, they didn't have to tell him squat.

In the car driving Holly back to the house on Northview Lane, Morgan wanted to know what this what all about. "You guys do something you shouldn't have?"

Holly stared out the passenger side window, trying desperately not to tell Dan everything, release herself from all the guilt and shame that had been boiling up within herself over the past six months especially now that the cops were involved.

"Holly," said Morgan. "Is there something going on here?" He sighed. "You know the police came by the office today. They grabbed Jeff's old computer." Still nothing. "So tell me the truth – is something going on that I should know about? As your lawyer?"

She finally turned and glared at Morgan. "No," she

said flatly. "Nothing is going on. It's all one big misunderstanding."

Chapter Twenty-Six

That night, Jeff was pacing around Holly's bedroom in his boxer shorts.

"You didn't tell them anything?" he asked, for what seemed like the hundredth time. He stopped his pacing to wait for an answer. "Right?"

"I told you," Holly said, lying on her side on the bed, "I didn't say a thing."

"Not even to Morgan? You told that dumb shit nothing?"

"Nothing," she said. "Although I don't see why not. He's my lawyer."

"He's an ass," Jeff said nastily. "I don't want that stupid fool or anyone from that firm knowing anything. He isn't who I'd hire in case you, or we, get charged with something. He's not a criminal lawyer anyway, just some schlep stuck in the commercial litigation department re-wording contracts. No, something bad happens, we need to go for someone good, the best, like Dan Stauber, or Pete Dobson."

"So why haven't they approached you?" She asked. "The cops. Dan said they came and took your computer, too."

"I have no idea," Jeff said. But how the fuck? He must have set us up somehow."

"Who?" she asked, looking up at him. "Jerry?"

"Yeah," he said. "That dumb fuck Jerry. Maybe, he isn't so dumb and ball-less after all. I think we underestimated him, big time." Jeff started pacing again. "He didn't disappear because he was scared, like we thought. He concocted a nice little plot of his own to get rid of us. Fat fucker must have set it up even before he called me and told me he knew everything."

Jeff remembered that call. Verbatim.

"So you think this is all part of the set-up," Holly said, rubbing her temples. "His getting even with us. But can you blame him? Can you?"

"No," Jeff said after a time. "But I'd still like to wring the fat fucker's neck."

He sat on the bed next to Holly. "Jesus Christ," he said, "I wish I had closed the deal on the ranch already. We were supposed to be leaving town next week."

"Why don't we just go anyway?"

"It's too fucking late," Jeff said. "We have to stand pat. See what happens."

"But shouldn't Jerry be worried, too? If we go down, he does too?"

"No," Jeff said with a sour laugh. "It's perfect, what he did. Perfect. First of all, the money I sent him is certainly gone by now, lost in bank account cyberspace. Then he plops the emails in the laps of the police, knowing we'd be stuck between a rock and hard place no matter how we played it out. If we confess what really happened, they could either believe us, and throw us in jail for insurance fraud and grand larceny, or, if they chose not to believe us, they could still try you and probably me for murder." Jeff sighed. "Worse yet, if we confess to what really happened, and that Jerry is simply setting us up, that would probably lead them to the body guy. And we get arrested for that murder."

"It was you who did that, Jeff," Holly said. "You killed him. You."

Jeff looked sharply at Holly.

"You were in on it, honey," he snapped. "You're an accomplice. Just like in everything else. It was my idea, but you approved it. If I go down for it, you go down for it too."

Jeff suddenly stopped pacing, seeming to have reached a momentous decision of some kind.

"Our only option," he said, "is to fight this tooth and nail. Proclaim innocence on all counts. Go to trial."

Holly grimaced. There could be nothing good coming from being the defendant in what promised to be a scandalous, highly publicized murder trial, a regular eyewitness news media circus extravaganza. She'd have to sit there in the courtroom day in and day out hearing all the sordid details that would surely come out regarding her affair with Jeff and all the implications of that. Not to mention the expense of hiring high-class lawyers to help them win an acquittal, no doubt whittling their remaining share of the insurance money down considerably. After paying Jerry the two million, they had two left. But with this going on, it was going to be damned hard to get their hands on it.

"How the hell did he do it?" she demanded, aching for an answer.

"Do what?" "The emails."

Jeff thought a moment and shrugged.

"Snuck in, I guess," he said. "The one that was sent from his old PC, in his den, that was easy. He must have done it while you were at work. Then, somehow, he got the balls to sneak into my office."

Jeff sighed. "I think we really fucking underestimated him."

"No," Holly said, shaking her head. "*You* underestimated him."

In truth, however, she had to admit, she had underestimated Jerry as well.

"So now what?" Holly asked after a long, heavy silence between them.

"Now what?" Jeff said. "Now we wait."

Chapter Twenty-Seven

"I wanted to give you an update," said Inspector Miller on the phone with Fox. "Flaherty sent the return message. At least, that's what our computer geeks say."

Fox punched his arm into the air, a private victory salute. He couldn't wait to tell Chief Reynolds.

"And they found some incriminating other stuff on Flaherty's computer. Some stuff about arson and garage fires. What people won't do for money."

"You tell the DA boys what you found?" Fox asked.

"Yep," Miller said. "Just got off the phone with them. They're mulling it over. But I don't see how they don't go forward with it. Strong arm the woman, first of all, the poor, rich widow Shaw. See if she'll flip. We could even offer her something to give up her lover. Close this case. If not, so what? The DA likes these kind of trials. Lots of publicity. White collar cases, especially with the spice of murder, always generate more press interest than the killing of some gangster drug dealer from the inner city."

After the call, Fox went down to Reynolds' office. The

Chief was on the phone, discussing some case with a senior claims adjuster. When he hung up, he squinted at Fox. This time, Fox let him wait. He sat heavily in the chair before the Chief's desk and grinned.

"So what you got, Jack?" Reynolds finally asked.

"Looks like that Shaw case took a turn in our favor," Fox told him. "They found the incriminating email on Flaherty's computer. He sent the return message. Also, some research into arson fires."

Reynolds leaned back and allowed himself to return a small smile.

"Maybe the perfect crime wasn't so perfect after all," he said. "Never is," said Fox, "right Chief?"

"Maybe they know something about it," Reynolds suggested, out of left field.

"About what, Chief?"

"How we got the e-mails. The perpetrators. Mrs. Shaw and Flaherty."

Fox nodded. "Yeah. I thought about that," he said.

"Why do we assume that only the wife and her boyfriend were involved in the murder?" Reynolds went on. "Maybe they needed someone else, a third party or something, to help them do it, and now that third party just stabbed them in the back. He got paid a wad of cash and disappeared. Maybe this was his way of getting rid of them."

"Maybe when the wife rats out the boyfriend," Fox suggested, sure that was going to eventually happen, "she'll rat out the double-crosser as well."

"Why wouldn't she?" Reynolds asked. "Might buy her an even better plea."

After a time, Reynolds turned his mind to another matter. "The boys upstairs want to know if we were able to find the money."

Fox sighed. He had been so preoccupied with the arrest, and the mystery of the emails miraculously dumped in his lap, that he had not given much thought to the money.

"Not yet," he told Reynolds. "We haven't found a cent of it. Wherever it went, they've kept it secret."

"Honestly," Chief Reynolds said with some level of exasperation rising in his voice, "that's the only justice Global cares about."

Chapter Twenty-Eight

Jerry learned about the arrests over the Internet. It was five weeks after he had mailed the phony emails to Global's fraud unit, sitting in Jade's apartment reading the *Buffalo News* on her laptop, when he spotted the headline that he had been waiting for on the lower right-hand side column of the front page of paper.

Pair Accused in Murder Plot
The sub-heading stated: Gruesome Slaying Tied to Husband's Life Insurance

Jerry knew this was it, the fruits of his daring plan. He punched out his arm with a triumphant "Yeah!" before reading the article:

A man and woman were arrested late yesterday afternoon and charged with murder for allegedly burning the woman's husband alive in a plot to collect the victim's four-million-dollar insurance policy. Erie County District

Attorney Jack Connors released a statement saying that Holly Shaw, 30, and Jeffrey Flaherty, 31, concocted the plot during an affair which started at the prominent local law firm, Carlton and Rowe, where Flaherty was formerly employed as an associate attorney and Shaw had been a secretary for several years.

Just then, Jade walked into the guest bedroom of her cramped, two-bedroom apartment which had been converted into Jerry's den.

"What you shouting for, hon?" she asked, still sleepy-eyed and yawning. It was a little past nine in the morning, and Jade wasn't used to being an early riser. The fact that she woke up much later than Jerry every morning, sometimes around noon, gave him some quiet time which he had come to appreciate. Sometimes he surfed the internet, but mostly he worked on his comic book superheroes, especially stories about the Anonymous Man.

"They arrested them," Jerry told her, still excited as he pointed to the computer screen. "They're finally getting what they deserve."

Yawning, Jade sauntered over to the side of his chair. Her silk robe came open as she leaned over, allowing her breast to rub against his shoulder as she squinted at the article on the computer screen. As she bent over, her tired, sexy attitude and unique, sensual aroma had the desired effect on Jerry. He turned in his chair and grabbed Jade around the waist, pulled her to him.

"That's wonderful, hon," she said. "You did it."

She stooped down and kissed Jerry on the lips. It

turned deep and passionate. He moved her hand down to his crotch to show his erection. Jade grinned mischievously and Jerry got to thinking that life had never been so good.

"You do it to me every time," he said.

"Well, come back to bed," she said and tugged at the sleeve of his sweatshirt.

"Let me just finish this," he said. "I want to read the rest." She let go of his sleeve and, pouting, started out of the den.

At the doorway, she said, "Well, you better hurry up, hon. If I fall back asleep, you'll be pleasing yourself this morning."

There really wasn't much left to read. Holly and Jeff had been indicted for Murder in the First Degree, which, if convicted, could get them life in prison without the possibility of parole. Each of them had retained prominent attorneys who indignantly proclaimed the innocence of their respective clients outside the courtroom where they had just been arraigned. Each attorney went on to inform the press, and public, that this was nothing more than a weak attempt on the part of a greedy insurance company to take back the money to which Mrs. Shaw was rightfully entitled through the terrible, tragic death of her husband, to whom she had always been faithful. Jeff's lawyer added it was a terrible shame that the District Attorney saw fit to assist in the greedy insurance company's effort against a helpless citizen of his county.

Jerry laughed to himself. The article was juicy enough as it was, but if they only knew the truth, the real story. Now that would make some real news.

Jade was asleep by the time Jerry returned to bed. He slid under the covers next to her and tried to wake her up by nuzzling against her. No good. All she did was groan. Jerry closed his eyes, and soon enough, he was sleeping, too.

It was Jade who woke him an hour later. She was nibbling on his ear, stroking his crotch, laughing to herself.

"C'mon, Mister," she said in her best, husky dominatrix voice, "time to wake up and serve the master."

He turned to her and they made fast, furious love. Afterward, with her lying in his arms, content and relaxed, she blurted out, "When we gonna get out of this town?"

"Huh?"

"Go down south," she said. "Florida. Disney World. Like you promised. Buy a house somewhere down there. What was the place called, with that funny name? Kiss-me?"

"Kissimmee." He paused and then decided to go ahead and ask. "What's the big deal with Disney World, anyway?"

"It's just somewhere I feel right. When I was a kid, that's where my parents took me during Easter vacations. I always thought it was like being in heaven. Then we stopped going."

"Why?"

"My real father died," Jade said, then she told Jerry about how her step-father started crawling into her bed with her, feeling her up and making her kiss him. Do other things she couldn't even talk about, not even now, years later. She told Jerry how she had run away not long after turning sixteen because her mother wouldn't listen and her stepfather wouldn't stop.

Jerry kept quiet while he listened, almost sorry he had brought it up. At least now he knew.

Jerry reached over and squeezed her hand. "Yeah, hon," he said, "sure, we can go down there. Anytime you want. Florida it is."

Jerry meant it. Going south at some point had always been part of the plan. Binghamton was no good, too cold and ugly for his tastes. And it was too close to his real life. He could be truly and completely anonymous down in Kissimmee.

"Really?" she said. "We're going?"

"Sure Jade," he said. "Let's pack up the car and leave first thing tomorrow. It'll take us two days to get down there. We'll rent an apartment, then buy a house. Something small, with a pool. Right on the outskirts of Disney so you can go there every day."

She rose to her knees and started jumping on the bed like a little kid. Jerry smiled. She was so full of energy and innocence. And still in that moment, he saw Holly in her. The way Holly had been when they had first met. Full of promise and hope with Hollywood and stardom ahead of her.

"But when the time comes," he added as Jade celebrated on the bed, "I'm gonna head back north to watch the trial. Watch Jeff and Holly squirm at the defense table while the jury eyes them up and down like the trash they are. Watch them fry."

"Watch their trial?" Jade asked. She stopped celebrating and her smile faded to an incredulous look.

"Yeah," he said. "Why not? Nobody will recognize me, with my beard and all, my hair different, a totally different color and longer than it used to be. And, most of all, all the weight I lost. I'm a hundred pounds lighter." Jerry slapped his gut, flat and rippled from his daily doses of crunches, amazed that he looked that way. Sexy.

"But what for?" she asked. "What's the point?"

Jerry really didn't have a decent answer for that except it would be great theater watching Jeff and Holly twist and turn in the wind. Holly especially.

What was just as likely, Jerry feared, as his revelry soured, was that they would beat the charges and walked away free and clear, with unfettered access to all the rest of the insurance money.

If that happened, the thought had crossed Jerry's mind on his most dismal nights, when even Jade's best blow job couldn't mollify his anger at being so terribly betrayed by Holly, that he would step forward and ruin the celebration of their dual acquittals by revealing who he was, and their plot – and that Jeff had murdered the body guy.

"I just need to do it," Jerry finally stated in a voice so low she hardly heard him.

They settled back down into the bed, holding each other. "So we really going down to Disney?" Jade asked.

"Sure, I said it, didn't I? Tomorrow morning. We'll move next door to Mickey and Minnie. Buy a decent house, with a pool and everything. Permanently."

As Jade relished the idea of leaving the bad memory of a life she had led in Binghamton for the sunny future promised by the purchase of a Florida home, with tile floors, a yard lined with palm trees, a pool and all, Jerry relished the thought of what he was putting Holly and Jeff through.

"But, like I said, "Jerry said as Jade snuggled close under his arms, "when the time comes, I'm heading north to watch Jeff and Holly fry."

Chapter Twenty-Nine

"She won't budge," Inspector Miller told Fox.

He had called Fox to update him on the Holly Shaw/Jeff Flaherty case. It had finally been set for trial, in a month.

The Assistant District Attorney prosecuting the case, Joe McGraw, had asked Miller to make arrangements to bring Fox up to testify. McGraw was a veteran prosecutor, trial-tested at every level, and arrogant as one gets after all those trials, especially when one routinely wins. He had not lost a murder trial in four years.

"Having you testify will plant the idea that Global was suspicious from the get-go," McGraw had told Fox not long after Holly and Jeff had been indicted a few months back. "Not to mention the actual visual image that will be burned into the jurors' collective brains when we show them your surveillance video. They'll get a bird's eyes view of the merry widow dry-humping her accomplice on the front stoop of the murder victim's own house while her husband was fresh in the grave."

"He was cremated," said Fox, "the insured."

"Well, she was screwing Flaherty while her dead husband's ashes were still hot." McGraw laughed to himself. "I have to write that line down. I think I'm going to use it in my opening statement." For his bluster and arrogance, Fox got the impression that McGraw was also a true believer in such now passé thing called justice.

"In truth," Miller told Fox, "the DA isn't offering much. But I don't think she'd take even a disorderly conduct if it meant putting her lover, that Flaherty guy, away. I guess she loves him that much."

"Well," said Fox, "she loved him enough to kill her husband. And while I guess it'd be for the best if we could get her to testify against Flaherty, make the case a lock, I guess there's part of me that's glad she's being stupid. For me, she's worse than Flaherty. She committed the ultimate betrayal, don't you think?"

After a moment, Miller asked, "You still looking into that other thing?"

Fox shrugged to himself.

"What? Who sent the emails to Global?"

"Yeah, that."

"No time," he told Miller. "Too busy these last few weeks busting one of those fake car accident rings on Long Island. Involves lawyers, doctors, and the mob. Russian mafia, too. A regular dream team of criminal scum."

"I bet," said Miller. "So you got no more ideas who blew them in?"

"No," sighed Fox. "You?"

"Nada."

Fox scowled. That was still bothering him, like a stone in his shoe. He regretted that Miller had brought it up, reminding him.

"It's probably what you thought—just some friend or relative or someone who got into Holly's email somehow and found the message," Miller said. "Maybe Holly forgot to shut her computer off and this someone happened to start fishing around. I don't know. Wherever it came from, all you need to know is that it came."

"Think the defense will make anything out of it?" Fox asked. "McGraw doubts it," Miller said. "Where do they go with it? The computer guys will give lock solid testimony linking the messages to his and her computers. And some other folks will lock each of them as the only users of those email servers. That's what Joe McGraw is good at— highlighting the good parts of his proof, while diminishing the negative impacts of the bad. It's a goddamn game to him, and truth be damned. But it's the same game the best defense lawyers play. Only this time, McGraw is just as good at that game as they are."

"Maybe someone planted them," Fox said. "That's what I would argue."

"And then what?" asked Miller. "Maybe there are little green men on Mars."

"So you think we really got a chance to win this one?" asked Fox.

"With McGraw in the game," Miller said, "I wouldn't bet against it."

Miller told Fox he'd make arrangements for his trip to Buffalo, get him the flight information and reserve a hotel room. At the Marriot downtown, he promised, nice, clean place, near the theater district.

After a moment, Fox asked, "Any luck finding the money?"

"The insurance money?" Miller said. "No, not yet. And the defendants obviously aren't talking about that."

"But how the hell can you hide four million dollars?" Miller added. "It's gotta show up somewhere."

Fox had done enough investigating scam artists over the years to know that a person and their money could become invisible.

"Not necessarily," Fox said. "Not necessarily at all."

Chapter Thirty

Holly's lawyer, Pete Dobson, laid it out for her while Jeff and his lawyer met in another conference room down the hall. Dobson was a bright kid with an easy demeanor, though a little too boyish looking perhaps to be totally convincing to the old men on a jury. But his good looks, supplemented by a square, athletic build and intense blue eyes, didn't hurt with the soccer moms, and maybe even some of the old ladies, if he used it right, and certainly would sell to the white trash housewives. Dobson had been practicing out in the real world only five years but already had a solid reputation and, after a string of surprising not guilty verdicts in recent months, he certainly was a budding star.

"They're offering Voluntary Manslaughter," Dobson told Holly. "Sentence range is an indeterminate, seven to fifteen years. Most likely, you'll serve seven. The other part of this deal is revealing where the money is."

Holly turned away, frowning. The deal meant, of course, that she would have to betray Jeff. Just last night, he had warned her that they were going to offer her a better plea, though this one wasn't all that much better. Seven years in jail during the prime of her now accursed life. And once out of jail, she'd be broke, having to start over again as a tainted woman.

It was a bad deal, Jeff had told her, because they'd both end up in prison for a long time, and have nothing to show for it when they got out. Certainly, they would lose each other forever. And yeah, she'd be tainted. Forever known as the cruel bitch that had burned her husband to death.

Furthermore, Jeff had argued, ranting at times, the DA's case wasn't all that strong, consisting of purely circumstantial evidence, the two ambiguous emails and a two-day surveillance by some insurance company hack investigator that linked them as lovers within a couple days of Jerry's funeral. So what? On cross-examination, their attorneys would belittle the meaning of all that.

Their attorneys would also easily poke holes in the meaning of the emails. They certainly weren't confessions, just ambiguous ramblings between two close friends (and perhaps lovers, by then again, so what?).

Furthermore, there wasn't one speck of DNA or any other physical evidence linking them to the actual, purported crime. Or that even a crime had been committed. The donated cadaver had been cremated leaving only an urn full of ash and the garage had been totally washed out and rebuilt.

But that Assistant DA, McGraw, was supposed to be good, one sharp and tough-minded son-of-a-bitch, Holly had whined, never lost a case or something.

This'll be his first then, Jeff had snapped.

Holly looked at her lawyer, Dobson, that dull, dark, gray morning. He was so damned handsome, and his eyes were so blue, it was a little hard to concentrate, despite the circumstances.

"So, what do you think," she asked him, "is it a good deal?" He gave her the usual song and dance that even though he thought the prosecution case was somewhat weak, not the strongest anyway, in various particulars, you never knew what a jury was going to do. It was always a gamble – freedom if the jury acquitted her, or life in prison without the possibility of parole if they bought the prosecution's story. A guilty plea guaranteed her a specific result, not the best perhaps, but one far less bad than life in prison.

That was the risk. Ultimately, it was her decision.

"What would you do?" she asked Dobson. "If you were me."

"I'm not you," he said.

For him, the best thing that could happen was for her to refuse the plea and go to trial. The publicity was already ferocious and a trial would be an absolute circus. Dobson would be a household name by the end of it, and his phone would be ringing off the hook with calls from prospective clients.

As for Holly, thinking wasn't coming easy. The idea of spending any time locked up in prison, wearing a drab olive green prisoner's uniform, having to associate with the other women prisoners, most of them lesbians, was simply paralyzing, unreal. She thought of all the prison movies she had ever seen and decided that undertaking that life would simply be unbearable.

"Can I speak to Jeff?" she suddenly asked. "Alone?"

Dobson looked at her a moment, then shrugged. He picked up the receiver on a telephone on the table behind him. A minute later, Jeff walked into the room and, without a word, without even a glance, Holly's lawyer walked out.

Jeff sat down across from her in a heavy way in the same black chair swivel her lawyer had just been occupying. He looked pale and morose, expecting the worst. He remembered the quarrel they had last night, followed by a sleepless night tossing and turning in bed beside her. He knew she had not slept well either, he could feel her awake beside him. At one point, he wondered if making love might do them both a world of good. It had been some time since they had done so with all the stress.

When she just sat there for a time, seeming unable to speak, Jeff decided that he had to break the ice:

"Dan told me that they made you an offer," he said.

She nodded sheepishly, staring straight ahead at the top of the glossy conference table.

"Yeah, with jail," she whimpered, barely audible. "I could be out in seven years." She couldn't believe she was hearing herself saying that. Seven years in jail was perhaps the best she could hope for. She felt tears coming on but stopped herself with a deep breath. "Plus, I'd have to turn over the money."

"That's fucking worse than the jail," he said and slammed a fist on the table. "Turning over the money—

and we don't have all of it anyway." He let go of a heavy sigh. "Some deal." Jeff thought a moment then looked at her. "He tell you to take it? Dobson?"

She shook her head. "Didn't tell me either way," she said. "Said the DA's got a somewhat weak case, but you never know with a jury."

Jeff nodded. "I still say we roll the dice," he said.

Holly broke down. She started sobbing and shaking uncontrollably, and Jeff had to get up, go around the conference table, and console her by reaching down and hugging her to his bosom, thinking to himself, like any man would, that a blow job wouldn't be a bad outcome right now.

"We can beat this, hon," he whispered into her hair which smelled like fresh bubble-gum that morning. "I know we can." Finally, she settled down, drew in some deep breaths, and looked up at Jeff. He leaned down and they kissed, and the whole matter seemed settled in that instant. She was going to stay put, go to trial.

"I'll tell Pete to come back in," Jeff said. "I'll tell him what we decided. Then we can get Dan and you in here so we can meet on this together. Listen to what their tactics are for when we go to trial."

The thought of the trial got her shaking again. But she drew a breath and settled down.

When Dobson returned to the conference room, and Jeff had left, Holly asked, "Do you think there will be any possibility, if we reject the plea now, of approaching the DA again with it during the trial?"

"Could be," he said with a shrug. "Depends on how

it's going. Like I said, this case is no slam dunk. Another move would be to make a counter-offer now, Manslaughter Second, or even Involuntary Manslaughter, so you can get even less time, even though I doubt that prick McGraw will go for that."

Holly shook her head.

"No, let's just do it," she said. "Go to trial. See what happens."

Dobson reached out his hand and patted Holly's right forearm.

"Dan and I will do our best to see that you and Jeff are acquitted," he said. "I have all the confidence in your innocence."

She nodded weakly, fearing that the jury would see right through her.

Chapter Thirty-One

Jerry had been staring at himself for some time in the full-length mirror in the spacious master bathroom of the four-bedroom ranch-style house in a tidy subdivision just south of Disney World. They had purchased the place, about a month ago at the ridiculously reduced price of $135,000. Five years ago, when it was built, the house had sold for just over $300,000. Property values were certainly not what they used to be in this part of Florida, to the benefit of Jerry and Jade and a whole lot of other buyers.

Jade came in from the back pool deck where she had been working on her tan when she surprised Jerry admiring himself in the bathroom mirror. She stood there smiling a moment before asking him what he was looking at.

"Me," he unabashedly admitted and stuck his hands out at his reflection. "This handsome creature." He turned to Jade and smiled.

But in the next moment, Jade turned glum and looked away. "So how are you getting there?"

"One of the cars." They had two of them, both in the

LLC's name. He planned on taking the inconspicuous, silver Toyota Corolla, that blended in well. She could keep the newer Honda Accord.

"How long you gonna be gone?"

"However long it takes," he told her. "A week or two I guess.

He had kept tabs on the criminal proceedings through periodic telephone calls to the clerk of the judge to whom the case had been assigned. He had called at least once a week claiming to be a reporter covering the case. That morning, the clerk had told him that jury selection was scheduled to start tomorrow morning. Picking the jury should take no more than a day or so, the clerk had assured him. Then the trial would start immediately.

"And what am I supposed to do when you're gone?" Jade asked, pouting.

"What you always do," Jerry told her with a smile. "Sunbathe. Tan. Read those trashy novels."

He didn't add that sometimes it seemed to him that tanning, reading trashy novels, sleeping long hours, and fucking, were the only things in life she seemed to be good at. After almost nine months, Jerry had grown a little tired of Jade. She was basic, almost too carnal, in her desires. Not that Jerry felt this was something necessarily bad. It just may not be totally what he was looking for in a woman. He wished that she was a little more cerebral, someone with whom he could make interesting conversation, about a book or theory of life and existence. Then again, maybe all that wasn't what it was cracked up to be. Take Holly, for instance. She could do all those things, be smart as hell, even smarter than him. And where had that gotten him?

And Jade had served him very well, and loyally, up to this point, as both his front and fuck buddy. He could not have survived, or continue to survive in the world, without her cover, and her sex, and that was certainly something every anonymous man needed. He had a major soft spot in his heart for her, so dumping her certainly seemed out of the question. There was also the very real fear that if he let on to what he was thinking, his misgivings over the depth and longevity of their relationship, she'd run to the police and blow him in.

The real problem, he had come to suspect, was not Jade at all. The real problem was that he still loved Holly. And this nagging feeling was not helped one iota by Jade's uncanny resemblance to her.

He looked at his reflection again and thought, his transformation was complete.

"Hey hon," Jerry said. "What's the matter? Stop being so blue."

Jerry strolled over and put his arms around her and held her close.

"You have nothing to worry about," he whispered into her ear. Her hair smelled delicious, like strawberry bubblegum. He moved his hands to her breasts and started massaging them. Despite all his misgivings and second thoughts, Jerry had to admit that he truly did feel something for Jade.

"I love you," he whispered.

Maybe he did, and maybe he didn't. All he knew was that he wanted to fuck her right then.

Jerry led her to into the master bedroom and pushed her down onto the wide, king bed, and then crawled on top of her. She kept showing a token resistance. But as Jerry's tongue found its way into her left earlobe, then down to the back of her neck, and his hands traced a path to the small of her back, then to her ass, Jade stopped resisting and let him go and do what he wanted.

When he was finished, Jerry laid back and stared up at the ceiling feeling worse than ever. The fan whooshed around endlessly, with seeming eternal life. The sex had resolved nothing.

"When are you going?" She was laying on her side, looking sad and helpless.

"I should have left already," he told her.

"So go already." She turned over, away from him. "I don't give a fuck."

Jerry looked across at her and smiled.

She made a face, still trying to fathom what he was up to.

Her insecurity made no sense.

"I just need you to stay here. Be waiting for me when I get back." He reached out and stroked her hair.

After a long silence, she turned to him and kissed his lips. "Okay," Jade said. "I'll be here."

Chapter Thirty-Two

When the heavy wooden door to old County Courtroom 10-B squeaked open and shut with a hollow thud upon Jerry's entrance at about ten o'clock that morning, both Holly and Jeff glanced back at him. The prosecution's first witness in the trial, Dr. Glenn Nguyen, a deputy county medical examiner was on the stand testifying about the condition of Jerry's purported body upon his initial examination of it. Jerry averted his eyes and tried covering his face by rubbing his nose. He dodged into an empty space along the aisle in the second last row of the spectator gallery. Jeff's look back at him lingered a few moments longer than Holly's, but he finally shifted around and focused on the medical examiner's testimony. Jerry sighed as he settled against the back of the gallery bench, relieved that there had not appeared to have been the slightest hint of recognition in the eyes of either Jeff or Holly.

It surprised Jerry that there weren't more spectators in the ten rows of mahogany benches, like church pews, split in half by a narrow aisle, making up the spectator gallery of the ornate courtroom in the century-old, granite Erie County Courthouse Building. The trial had garnered its share of circus-like coverage from the local media but nothing like it would have been in a big city like New York, Chicago or LA.

Outside the courthouse, Jerry had noticed that the local TV stations had set up satellite transmission trailers so that their reporters could present live coverage of the day's events in the morning, before the trial was called to order, during the lunch hour, and after the trial adjourned for the day just in time for the six o'clock news. Presently, Jerry noticed four guys in sports jackets, who looked to be reporters from the local TV news and newspaper, *The Buffalo News*, had crowded into the second row behind the defense table. They were watching the testimony unfold with mild interest, jotting notes every now and then in their respective compact notebooks, while Dr. Nguyen's testimony droned on.

Jerry's sister, Joan, was in the row immediately behind the low railing separating the gallery from the prosecutor's long oak table. Jerry hadn't noticed whether or not she had glanced back upon his entrance. If she had, she too had failed to recognize him.

Jerry was wearing a dark blue sports coat, khaki dress slacks, a crisp navy blue shirt, and a nondescript striped tie. It was his plan to be mistaken for a young lawyer or reporter who had ventured inside the courtroom simply to observe one of the more interesting homicide trials going on that week in the county courthouse. As he settled into his seat to observe the testimony, Jerry chuckled to himself with the realization that the judge, the lawyers, Holly and Jeff, the bailiffs, the jurors and the other spectators, including Joan, were oblivious to the fact that the alleged victim of this murder trial— himself—had just walked in. Perhaps given a few minutes, rather than a quick glance, Holly and Jeff and his sister would have seen past his disguise. Then again, perhaps not.

Jerry's father was missing from the gallery. This worried Jerry and he wondered how the old man was holding up. Jerry felt bad about participating in a crime which had left him invisible to Joan and his father. Granted, he hadn't been all that close to Joan after leaving for college. They hadn't really had a meaningful conversation about anything in all that time, and he really wasn't sure what was going on in her life, how her kids were, how her marriage was going. But all that was behind him now, too late. Perhaps she too regretted never establishing a relationship with him. Little brothers are hard to find.

Standing at the podium conducting the direct examination was a tall, gaunt Assistant District Attorney, Matt O'Connor. He was assisting the lead prosecutor, the confident and determined, Joe McGraw, who sat stiffly with a smug, astute expression at the prosecutor's table. O'Connor's slow, stilted questioning of the deputy county medical examiner gave himself away as a rookie, Jerry thought, McGraw's shambling apprentice.

Not that the testimony of Dr. Nguyen was a substantial factor in the course of this trial. The medical examiner really had nothing important to say. It hardly took an expert to reach the conclusion that the victim had burned to death.

Still, at McGraw's direction, his protégé had Dr. Nguyen meticulously describe the lump of charred human flesh that had been found on the burnt floor of the garage after the Town of Hamburg volunteer fire unit had put out the fire. O'Connor also had Dr. Nguyen describe the manner in which a human body is decomposed by fire into a grayish, lifeless, unrecognizable pile of ash.

Then the young prosecutor stepped forward and after stopping to ask permission from the Judge, approached Dr. Nguyen with a handful of photographs, the first one of which was the lump of burnt flesh. After Dr. Nguyen had laboriously identified each photograph, and stated that they were accurate depictions of the human flesh upon which he had conducted the autopsy, ADA O'Connor asked the Judge permission to publish the photographs to the jury. The Judge nodded his consent, mumbled something, and then O'Connor handed them to the bailiff, who gave them to the jury foreman. The six men and six women jurors, most of them elderly, squinted and sighed as they observed the ghastly human remains depicted in the photographs.

The bailiff took back the photos and deposited them before the stenographer, who remained expressionless.

"Would that be painful?" O'Connor abruptly asked Dr. Nguyen, as he had been surely coached by McGraw. "Dying like that?"

"Objection!" stated Dan Stauber, Jeff's lawyer. He stood and waited.

In his mid-forties, he was an accomplished enough

criminal defense attorney who made the papers regularly by defending high- level drug dealers and the occasional homicidal maniac. What the papers didn't reveal was that most of his colleagues thought him arrogant and over-rated.

"Sustained," replied the Judge, an emphatic growl. "Irrelevant, speculative and no foundation for this witness in this particular case," he added gratuitously, as he always did to explain his decision, like an umpire locating the pitch outside, inside, high or low, to inform the pitcher why his pitched had been called a ball.

The judge was the Honorable Leonard Pratt, a trial judge of many years, a slight bodied, bald-headed, hard-nosed chap with a reputation for being tough on attorneys, prosecutors and defense counsel alike. The old codger made everyone's life miserable, even that of his confidential law clerk and secretary. It was a big mistake to be late for work or especially for a proceeding in his court or to fail to have a grasp of the law or facts in a case pending before him.

O'Connor didn't protest, but meekly thanked the judge, who grunted again, and moved on. Still, the point had been made. It was obvious that someone who had died this way suffered pain, lots of it. Asking the question highlighted the point and made the crime all the worse.

Jerry shivered and realized that the young ADA, for all his amateurish ability, had somehow pulled it off, hitting the jury over the head with the extreme cruelty of Jerry Shaw's murder and planting the seed of distaste and dislike in the minds of the jurors for the defendants, Holly and Jeff.

Dan Stauber's cross-examination of Dr. Nguyen was next. Stauber was tall and lean, wearing a crisp, dark suit, nothing flashy, but reeking of professional savvy. His brown hair was freshly barbered, and the brief gray tinges at his temples further enhanced his air of professionalism.

"Isn't it a true and accurate fact, Dr. Nguyen, that you are unable to state, based upon your medical examination, whether or not Mr. Shaw's death was accidental or the result of a homicide?"

"Correct," said the medical examiner, seemingly non-plussed, just a McGraw had told him he should be. "I am unable to state which one it was."

"So Mister Shaw's injuries were consistent with accidental death, correct?"

"Yes."

Stauber nodded, thanked the witness, and smiled at the jury. "No further questions, your Honor."

Judge Pratt looked to Holly's attorney, Paul Blake. Holly had hired Blake after Pete Dobson had suddenly quit her case, unhappy with her decision not to take a plea and just too damned busy with a major federal drug case starting at around the same time that was paying him big bucks.

Blake was an older fellow who looked about as yellowed and tattered as an old newspaper. His defiant alcoholism was destroying his liver and gave his eyes a perpetually rheumy glaze. Still, he was a rare bird, a fossil of forgotten lore, a much respected, legendary old veteran. He was noted particularly for his sly glances at the jury and his flair for the comic hyperbole. And, it was well known, he was an extremely effective and wily cross-examiner, feigning ignorance or a lack of sophistication in the manner of Detective Colombo.

"Mr. Blake, any questions?"

"After that stirring debate," Blake boomed, looking up casually from the page full of doodling on his long, yellow legal pad, "I have nothing to add, your Honor."

"Mr. O'Connor?" Judge Pratt turned to the young prosecutor. "Any redirect?"

It was McGraw who stood.

"May I ask one question, your Honor?" He asked.

"Be my guest."

McGraw stood, but before he could start, Blake piped up. "I must protest, your Honor. This is a veritable double-team."

McGraw smiled. "Now, we're even. There's two of you, and two of us."

"Gentlemen!" Judge Pratt snapped. "I will not put up with clever banter from either one of you." He glared at Blake. "Even you, Mr. Blake, will exercise decorum in my courtroom." The Judge scowled as Blake shrugged indifferently, and turned to McGraw. "You may ask, Mr. McGraw, but keep it brief."

"Of course, your Honor," said McGraw, then he faced the witness.

"Dr. Nguyen," he said. "It was your testimony that the medical examination was consistent with an accident, correct?"

"Yes, sir."

"Mr. Shaw's burning alive could have been accidental."

"Yes."

"But someone also could have intended to burn him

alive, correct?"

"Yes."

"Like the defendants, for instance, as far as you know."

"Objection!" it was Stauber.

"You made your point, counselor," interrupted Judge Pratt. "Objection sustained."

"Thank you, your Honor," said McGraw. He looked to the jury. "No further questions."

Chapter Thirty-Three

The next two witnesses that first morning of the trial were Jerry's former Northview Lane next door neighbors, a Mrs. Gladys Kovach, sixty-something, squinty-eyed, white-haired, plump, judgmental, gossipy; the other, Sandi Morgan, Holly's age, somewhat pretty in a slutty way, and certainly pert and opinionated.

The young prosecutor, O'Connor, conducted the direct examination of Gladys Kovach, a laborious, stilted process, peppered by meaningless objections from Stauber, in which, at long last, she described seeing Flaherty at the Shaw house day and night immediately after Jerry's death.

In cross-examination, Stauber again failed to make any points, except perhaps for the prosecution. After getting Mrs. Kovach to admit that she never actually saw Holly and Jeff together, she gratuitously added, and quite comically, Jerry thought, what else was he doing there? His laundry? That got a chuckle out of the two or three members of the jury who seemed to be paying attention; a smirk out of Stauber; and, left McGraw grinning.

McGraw conducted the direct examination of Sandi Morgan and seemed to thoroughly enjoy himself as he led her on a lively recitation of her observations of the Flaherty visits. How could she remember all this, McGraw asked, calling her "Sandi" at one point as if they were old friends.

"Because he's so damned good looking," she replied, nodding toward Flaherty.

"I think I looked forward to his visits as much as she did," said Ms. Morgan with a laugh as she nodded at Holly and naturally, the jury laughed along with her.

Neither Jerry nor Holly had been close to either woman, though Jerry had certainly noticed Sandi Morgan. Gladys Kovach and her husband, Stan, were quiet, lonely people who kept to themselves. Jerry didn't realize at the time, but the testimony of the busybody neighbors would serve to provide an opening for McGraw to challenge the conclusion of the arson investigators that the fire in the garage killing the victim had been caused accidentally.

Neither woman had anything specific to say about the fire itself. Gladys Kovach heard the fire engines coming from out of nowhere and suddenly stopping in front of the Shaw's house. She had looked out the picture window of her living room and watched the firemen hustling into action and spraying the garage and had worried about her house catching fire and burning down, too.

And then McGraw called Jack Fox, telling Judge Pratt that Fox would be his last witness that first morning of the trial.

Chapter Thirty-Four

"What is your occupation, Mr. Fox?" McGraw asked.

"I'm an investigator for the Special Frauds Unit of the Global Life and Casualty Insurance Company."

"How long you been so employed?"

"Three years."

"And before that, where were you employed?"

"Philadelphia Police Department."

Fox went on to chronicle his considerable law enforcement career, an impressive resume of training and experience, including several medals for bravery and outstanding achievement. He had even won a Purple Heart in Vietnam.

Then McGraw turned to the meat of Fox's testimony.

"Did there come a time when you were assigned to the claim made by the defendant, in this case, Holly Shaw, under a policy of life insurance in the name of her deceased husband, Jerry Shaw?"

"Yes."

"And do you see Mrs. Shaw in the courtroom today?"

"Yes."

"Could you please identify her for the record."

Fox pointed at Holly and indicated that she was the blonde haired, attractive lady sitting at the defense table wearing a lavender pants suit.

"I would ask the record to reflect that Investigator Fox has identified the defendant, Holly Shaw."

"Well, he pointed to her and said her name," growled Judge Pratt. "The record shall reflect that, Mister McGraw."

McGraw gave a begrudging smile. Judge Pratt, always a pip. "Thank you," he said to the judge, then to Fox, "And on what date were you assigned to the Shaw claim?" Fox gave the date.

"Do you know how the company received the claim?"

"It was Fed-Exed."

"What did you do upon being assigned to the claim, Investigator Fox?"

"Flew to Buffalo -"

"From Philly?"

"Yes, from Philadelphia."

"By the way, what was the amount of the claim, the claim that had been submitted by the defendant, Holly Shaw?"

"Four million dollars."

"Mr. Shaw had taken out a policy of insurance with Global for four million dollars?"

"No, for two," said Fox. "It was a double-indemnity policy. If Shaw was deemed to have been killed as the result of an accident, the policy doubled."

"And upon your arrival in Buffalo, could you describe

what you did in the course of your assignment?"

Fox went on to quickly outline how he set up the stake-out of the Shaw residence on Northview Lane. He then described his observations the first night of Jeff's arrival at the Shaw house, and the friendly manner in which he had been greeted by the widow Shaw. And that they had kissed.

Jerry sighed, then scanned the jury. Most of them were scowling, and two middle-aged women sitting in the front row wore hard expressions. Their faces remained the same as Fox described how Holly had finally welcomed Jeff into the house.

"By your calculation, Investigator Fox," asked McGraw, "how long did Mr. Flaherty remain in the house?"

"About three hours," said Fox.

"Three full hours?"

"Yes, sir."

Fox then narrated what he saw the next night, pretty much the same as the first, only this time with much less detail.

After eliciting this verbal testimony, McGraw asked Fox if he had videoed his observations and Fox said of course he had. He also identified the digital recorder he had used. McGraw asked permission from Judge Pratt to play the video, promising that it wasn't long. Stauber objected and he and McGraw went over to discuss the objection in a sidebar with Judge Pratt.

After an animated debate, Stauber returned to the defense table with a displeased expression. McGraw had his younger colleague, O'Connor, rolled in a table holding a flat screen television monitor directly before the jury. After some fumbling under the disagreeable, impatient scowl of Judge Pratt, he finally managed to get the DVD player that was attached to the television working.

The video displayed all that Fox had stated during his testimony and more. Jerry had to admit that the picture of it was better than a thousand of Fox's words. With several deep breaths, he managed to restrain himself from standing up, striding over to the defense table and putting a fist straight into Jeff's mouth.

When the video finished, O'Connor rolled the table away.

Then, McGraw got straight into the emails, how they surprised Fox by showing up in his in-basket one day, just about seven months after Shaw had burned to death. McGraw walked over to the defense table holding the two emails, and showed them to Stauber and Blake, who both nodded with apparent disinterest. McGraw then asked permission from Judge Pratt to approach Fox on the witness stand with the emails, and after the Judge grunted his approval, he did just that and Fox identified them as the emails he had received.

And that was it. McGraw didn't ask to publish the emails to the jury, and Jerry thought that another clever ruse. The jury frowned as he told Judge Pratt he had nothing further for this witness at this time and had concluded his direct examination. This, of course, left the jury wondering what the hell was in those emails, and that would, when the time came, magnify whatever they stated.

McGraw told the Judge he had no further questions

and Stauber rose.

"Your observations weren't enough, were they, Agent Fox, to prevent your employer, Global Insurance, from paying the claim?"

"It's not agent," Fox snapped. "What?"

"I'm not an agent," he said. "I'm an investigator."

"Yes, whatever," Stauber said. "Global paid the claim despite your observations, isn't that correct?"

"Yes," said Fox. "They paid Mrs. Shaw four million dollars despite what I saw."

"They paid it," repeated Stauber. "Yes."

Then Stauber appeared to fall into a trap laid by McGraw. "And you waited three hours in the car? Both nights?" he asked.

"No, sir," Fox said, "I did not." Stauber looked surprised.

"The second night," Fox explained, "after about a half an hour or so, I exited the car and positioned myself against the outside of the back of the house under what appeared to be the upstairs master bedroom." Stauber appeared dumbstruck as Fox continued. "From that position, I was able to hear the muffled sounds of two voices, one deep, like a man's, another softer, higher, like a woman's. I surmised from that observation that Mr. Flaherty and Ms. Fox were together in the master bedroom of the house."

Flustered, Stauber went on to commit the cardinal sin of cross-examination by asking Fox a question to which he certainly did not know the answer.

"And how could you possibly know that, Mr. Fox? That you were hearing voices coming from the master bedroom? Had you ever been in the house prior to or after that night, or ever?"

McGraw had anticipated the question and had provided Fox with a blueprint of the house in preparation for cross-examination. Fox did not hesitate to inform Stauber and the jury of that fact.

"So, yes," he added, "I knew exactly where I was standing. Under the master bedroom, where I heard the voices of both defendants."

During this segment of the cross-examination, Jerry glanced over at McGraw. It was plain that he was restraining himself from smiling. At the defense table on the other side, Paul Blake kept looking up at Stauber with a sad expression.

Stauber swallowed, paused for a moment, mulling perhaps how much damage Fox's testimony had just caused, and moved on.

But then he went on to ask, "So what you saw those two nights proved nothing to your superiors." Ten feet away from him, Paul Blake let out a barely audible groan. "Isn't that correct, Mr. Fox?"

Judge Pratt was scowling. "Is everything alright, Mr. Blake?"

"It was ten minutes ago," he told the Judge, "before my colleague's cross-examination began."

The jurors chuckled and so did Jerry Shaw.

Stauber still didn't appear to get it. When the chuckling subsided, he turned to Fox and repeated, "Isn't that correct, Mr. Fox? What you saw proved nothing to Global Insurance."

"It proved only that the insured's wife and his best

friend were screwing around. But at the time, not murder. The proof for that came later."

Stauber had been had and he knew it. He turned to Judge Pratt, was about to ask him to strike Fox's gratuitous testimony, then thought better of it.

"That is for the jury to decide," he told Fox, turned and went back to his seat.

"Anything else, Mr. Stauber?" Judge Pratt asked.

"No, no your Honor."

The judge looked tiredly at Paul Blake, who was leaning on his right elbow with his eyes closed. On the defense table in front of him was a long yellow legal pad full of doodles. "Anything, Mr. Blake?"

Blake seemed to have been roused from a nap. He sat upright and blinked at the judge.

"Just this," he said as he rose from behind the defense tabled and ambled to the podium. "Do you have any idea who sent you those emails?"

Fox grimaced. "No," he said. "No idea."

"And you have no direct knowledge, out of your own mind, who prepared them, do you?"

"No, not out of my own mind."

"You have no direct knowledge whether my client, Holly Shaw, prepared the one attributed to her, do you?"

"No. Except that –"

"Thank you, Mr. Fox. That answer is sufficient. I know you are trained to add things, etcetera, but I am not going to let you do that."

"I only add the truth, counselor."

"I'm sure you do, or what you think is the truth."

"Is this debate finished?" asked Judge Pratt. "Move it along, Mr. Blake."

"And as to what you saw the nights of your surveillance, or what is more properly referred to as a stake-out," Blake asked, "you have no direct knowledge what it means."

"No, no direct knowledge."

"And would it surprise you if two good friends got together after the death of the spouse of one of them and commiserated?"

"That's not my definition of commiseration, counselor," Fox said.

"Because it was your job when you were conducting this surveillance for Global Insurance to find something incriminating so that Global wouldn't have to pay out four million dollars."

McGraw leaned forward and thought a moment, and Fox, seeing that, waited a moment to answer. When McGraw shrugged and lowered the inch or so back down to the seat, Fox answered, "Yes, that was my job."

"And as my esteemed counsel pointed out," Blake continued, "you didn't find anything at least back at that time because Global paid the claim."

"Yes, Global paid the claim."

"And it was only later, when the emails mysteriously plopped out of the clear blue sky onto your lap that changed Global's mind."

"Yes."

"Well, how convenient for Global." Blake didn't let Fox respond to that. He turned to Judge Pratt and asked for the emails to be published to the jury and the judge agreed.

Each member of the jury took some moments to review the emails, some of them taking more time than others in reading them.

Blake told the Judge he had no further questions and McGraw indicated he had no re-direct. And that was it. Fox was finished. On his way down the narrow aisle between the gallery pews of the courtroom, Fox slowed his gait ever so briefly as he glanced over at Jerry. Something stopped him cold, and that made Jerry freeze up as well. Fox visibly scowled before finally, after an interminable moment, he started walking again and departed the courtroom. It was as if Jerry had emitted some kind of vibe that had been detected by the sixth intuitive sense with which investigators like Fox are supposedly born.

Jerry didn't emit even the slightest exhale for a time until he was certain that Fox had left the courtroom. Then he slowly turned his head to be sure, worried that he would find Fox standing there. There was no one.

Chapter Thirty-Five

The first witness of the afternoon was Inspector Vince Bancroft, the chief investigator from the county arson squad which had initially determined that arson was not the cause of the fire. In McGraw's direct examination, Inspector Bancroft was first made to describe the scene of the fire as he found it—the charred out hollow of the interior of the garage, the blackened skeleton of a barely recognizable automobile, and, under the twisted, charred metal, the lump of damp, blackened ash, the remains of poor Jerry.

Next, McGraw handed the Inspector's final report and asked him to examine it.

"Inspector Bancroft," the prosecutor finally asked, "you filed this report, did you not, which concluded that the fire in the garage at 320 Northview Lane had not been intentionally set, but was accidental?"

"I did."

"Well," continued McGraw, "could you inform the jury how the fire started."

As instructed by McGraw in their pre-trial meeting just two days ago, he turned to the jury with a serious expression. *Frown*, was what McGraw had told him to do.

"It is probable that a spark of some kind, arced from its source and ignited the pool of gasoline which had formed on the garage floor from the leaky tank under the car. At the time this report was written, we surmised that the source of the spark was the thermo-coupler of the water heater unit in the garage."

"A spark of some kind, from some source, ignited the gas under the car," said McGraw, not really a question, but a statement as he turned slowly and faced the jury panel. "Correct?"

Inspector Bancroft nodded. "Yes."

McGraw thought a moment, the fingers of his right hand tickling his chin, apparently deep in thought. After several moments, he turned abruptly to Bancroft.

"A spark from some source," he said, "which you concluded was the water heater, but which, is it not true, could have come from anywhere—"

"Objection, your Honor." It was Stauber who came to his feet, glaring.

"—from one of those hand held gas grill starters perhaps?" "Objection, your Honor! Leading! Speculative!"

From way back in the gallery, Jerry Shaw was impressed.

McGraw had figured it out exactly.

"I'll give him some latitude with this, Mister Stauber," ruled the judge. "Over-ruled. He's an expert witness."

"Could a grill starter have been the cause of the spark

that ignited that gasoline spill, Inspector Bancroft?"

He nodded. "It certainly could have."

"Your Honor," interrupted Stauber as he rose to his feet again, "so could lightning have been the cause."

"Had there been a thunderstorm in the area the morning of the fire, Inspector Bancroft?" McGraw had seized on the opening.

"Of course not," Bancroft said and grinned. "Your Honor!"

"Alright, Mr. McGraw– "the Judge started to say, his voice rising with concern that he was losing control of this examination, but McGraw wouldn't let him finish.

"Would someone who lit a hand-held starter to spark-ignite the gasoline pool have had time to back out of there before an explosion?" he asked Bancroft.

"It's possible," Bancroft answered, just as Stauber stood and angrily shouted, "Objection!" which, of course, merely highlighted the import of the answer in the minds of the jurors.

"Sustained," stated Judge Pratt. "That answer will be stricken."

"Thank you, your Honor," said McGraw, as if the judge's decision had gone in his favor. "No further questions."

As McGraw returned to his seat, Judge Pratt called to him, "Mister McGraw!"

McGraw turned with the most innocent expression he could muster. He knew a scolding was coming.

"You do that again in my court," admonished the judge. "And you will find yourself in a prison cell."

"Yes, your Honor," said McGraw. "I humbly apologize."

"Or better yet, young man," the Judge continued, seeing that McGraw was not taking him seriously, "I'll declare a mistrial. Understood?"

Now, McGraw did look concerned. That was the last thing he wanted.

"Yes, your Honor," McGraw said and even bowed. "My humble apologies. Got carried away."

Stauber stood and asked for one anyway, a mistrial for gross prosecutorial misconduct whose sole purpose was to prejudice the jury.

"Overruled, Mister Stauber," said the Judge. "Unless you want another curative instruction that will only serve to highlight the point Mister McGraw was trying to make."

"Of course not, your Honor," said Stauber.

"Well, then, your witness."

Not surprisingly, during his cross-examination of Inspector Bancroft, Stauber painstakingly highlighted the initial findings of the arson unit that the fire had been accidentally started by the spark of the water heater. He even got Bancroft to admit that garage fires often start that way. But Bancroft was allowed to blurt out, as instructed by McGraw that he do so at some point during his cross-examination, that he was no longer totally convinced of his initial assessment that the source of the fire was the garage water heater. At very least, it had been pure speculation and he had no idea how the fire had started. In looking back at it, Bancroft lamented, while Stauber protested to Judge Pratt that he was being unresponsive and cleverly coached, the conclusion may have been a rush to judgment in the crush of work which the arson unit had faced at the time.

Bravo! Jerry thought. McGraw may just have successfully neutralized the adverse arson report and had, perhaps, even turned it on its head in favor of the prosecution's position.

After Stauber sat down red-faced, seething, Holly's attorney, Paul Blake, was called upon by Judge Pratt for his cross. Blake stood and wobbled over to the podium which he held with two out-stretched arms, using it to prop himself. After a time, he peeked at the jury over his wire rim bifocals, glanced across at McGraw, then looked up at Inspector Bancroft.

"Fact of the matter is, Inspector," he said, his voice gravelly and somewhat difficult to follow, "you rendered a professional, expert opinion at some point, that the fire was accidentally started, correct?"

Bancroft could not deny that and shrugged. "Correct, sir. But, as I said—"

"And you put that opinion in writing," continued Blake, and waved a piece of paper in the air. "In an official police department report."

"Yes."

"And when you signed off on that report," said Blake, "you believed that it was correct, isn't that right?"

"But—"

Blake waved a hand at him.

"No, buts, sir, please." Blake sighed. "Just answer the question. It's a simple question. When you signed off on the official report of your department, you believed the fire had been accidentally started?"

"Why, yes."

"And now you question that."

"Yes, I do."

"Fair enough." Blake frowned. "But there have been no new physical details come to light about the fire, has there, from the date you filed the report to now?"

"No," Inspector Bancroft stated.

Blake looked at Judge Pratt and nodded. "I have nothing further, your Honor."

McGraw immediately stood. He did not return to the podium but asked the question from the prosecution table.

"What additional facts do you know today that you did not know when you wrote the report?" he asked.

Stauber rose slightly off his seat.

"Why, the emails," he said. "The incriminating emails." Now Stauber stood.

"Objection, your Honor," Stauber barked, "and I urge you to have that remark, 'incriminating,' stricken from the record. The emails if they are anything at all, are at most ambiguous. They are anything but incriminating."

Jerry frowned. The tables had suddenly turned on how the case was going. It seemed to him that McGraw had perhaps asked one question too many.

"Sustained, Mr. Stauber," Judge Pratt said. He looked to the jury and told them to ignore the remark about emails, and certainly that they were incriminating. However, the point had been made. The arson report concluding that the fire was accidental had been reached without the benefit of the emails, incriminating or not. Jerry nodded, finally getting that.

"Anything further gentlemen?" He looked first to the prosecution, then to the defense.

With that, Judge Pratt checked the large round clock above the long doorway. It was already three thirty and Judge Pratt told them he had a sentencing hearing that would take the rest of the afternoon.

He dismissed the jury, counsel, and the defendants, and Jerry quickly and inconspicuously as possible, exited the courtroom ahead of Holly and Jeff, and his sister, Joan.

Chapter Thirty-Six

Jerry found an entrance foyer to another courtroom in the spacious hallway diagonal from Courtroom 10-B. He stood in the shadows waiting for Holly and Jeff and their lawyers to exit. When they finally did, Jerry had to smile. Holly and Jeff appeared shaken by the day's testimony, although Jeff tried to smile and act unconcerned as if everything had gone just fine.

They stood in the hallway just outside the courtroom, back to back, waiting for their lawyers, Stauber and Blake, to fend off the television, radio, and newspaper reporters. If only they knew, Jerry thought, and felt a thrill course through him, that the victim was standing there, in the shadows, mere yards away, watching it all. Blake said something funny and the reporters laughed while Stauber scowled with professional aplomb. During the interview, he had tried to remain supremely confident as he demeaned the prosecution's case while on the other side of the hallway McGraw crooned and said he felt pretty good about the day's testimony.

The reporters eventually scattered, leaving Jeff and Holly alone to chat with their respective lawyers, cradled in separate corners whispering their respective concerns and strategies. Finally, Stauber and Blake let go of their clients, and Holly and Jeff, after stealing quick, desirous glances at each other, walked their separate ways out of the courthouse.

Jerry held back a few moments in the deep shadows of the foyer before he broke off in the direction Holly had gone, down the winding marble stairs to the main floor. He spotted her sauntering out the front door to Franklin Street. Jeff had gone the opposite way, down a staircase to the Delaware Avenue entrance. Now was the opportune time to catch up with her, Jerry thought, confront Holly alone, perhaps the only chance he would ever get. He had fantasized doing this almost every single day the last few weeks. Of course, that was something he had never told Jade.

There was parking garage across the street from the courthouse and Jerry followed Holly into it. The sky was steely gray, with low, ominous clouds moving quickly across the sky. And dark was coming on fast.

Jerry rushed into the garage just a few feet behind Holly and ran to the elevator she had entered just as the door was closing. He stuck an arm out to stop it and stepped inside. Holly stared forward, her mind on something else as Jerry bowed his head and settled with his back against the wall. Holly had already pressed the button for the third floor. After a moment, as the elevator started to rise, she glanced at him and frowned. Then, she looked at him again, and a moment after the elevator beeped as it passed the second floor, her eyes widened and she gasped.

"Jerry?"

He looked at her and she went totally pale.

"It is you," she said. She leaned back against the side wall as the elevator came to a stop on the third floor and the door opened.

Jerry stepped out with her into the garage. He took her right arm and led her aimlessly out among the cars lined up on a slight angle in crammed parking spaces.

"Where's your car?" he asked.

She kept turning and looking at Jerry with a dumbstruck expression as they walked on. To Jerry, it made her look vulnerable and innocent, beautiful too. He was struck by how odd it was that after all she had done to him, he still could have feelings for her. That he did still, well, love her. And now that he was within a couple of feet of her, and could smell her perfume, he could no longer deny it.

"Your car," Jerry repeated.

Holly finally seemed to have regained a measure of composure and nodded in the direction of her brand new black Mustang. Jerry looked around as they approached, worried that someone like that Investigator Fox might still be lurking about, following her.

Holly went over to the driver's side, clicked her remote key to open the doors and nodded for Jerry to get in. In the car, she kept looking over at Jerry, still mostly dumbstruck, as if Jerry had really come back from the dead.

"You look fantastic, Jerry," she said. "It's— it's

amazing. Y— you lost a ton of weight." She gave him a closer look.

Jerry smiled. The compliment seemed genuine, and he shrugged, blushed. But his mood soured a moment later as he considered asking, "Better than Jeff?" But he kept quiet. He was happy, yes happy, just to be sitting next to her again, presently the sole object of her attention.

"Jeff said it was you that set us up." She frowned. "Did you?"

That destroyed the mood. "What else could I do?" he said. "You were planning to kill me."

Holly looked down to her lap and started to cry. Jerry was suddenly torn between his feelings of affection, lust, love or whatever it was, and loathing and disgust. And although his conflict was great, he thought better of reaching over and pulling her into his arms. Instead, he sat there and watched her sob for a time, until she finally calmed down, drew a breath and looked over at him.

"It was Jeff," she said, averting her eyes. "He's a cruel, selfish bastard."

Jerry followed the line of her sight to her feet, and he became fully aware that they were encased in sexy black high heels.

"If he hadn't taken over, taken control of, of this, of everything…" She sighed, unable really to offer a justifiable excuse. "I just panicked."

"It was going to happen no matter what," Jerry said, pissed off now that she was making excuses, trying to blame Jeff for everything, and avoiding the truth, as he had heard it that night in the master bedroom closet. Not to mention, she had started having an affair with Jeff even before that.

"Just tell me one thing," Jerry said.

With red, swollen eyes, telling him she was crying real tears, Holly looked up. But Jerry remembered that she had majored in theater in college and that she had often read scripts to him requiring her to break down in tears, fake tears.

"How many times did you fuck him before we faked my death?"

She squinted hard, still wondering perhaps why he had come out of the shadows, what this visit could be about. Had he come back merely to taunt her, or win her back?

"How many days or weeks or months had you been screwing him?"

"None of it started until after that day," she said. "The day we faked your death. There was some part of me that thought it had really happened. That you had really died."

Of course, Jerry had no way of verifying this claim. And the way she was carrying on seemed slightly contrived, as if she was acting.

"Sure, we had flirted before that," Holly went on after another sniffle. "You knew that. You saw it. I think you even mentioned it once or twice that Jeff seemed to be coming on to me. But it never amounted to anything. Not back then. It was only when we had really gone through with it and faked your death, and you had left for Binghamton. When you were gone."

Jerry's thoughts suddenly turned to Jade. He wondered what she was doing right then. Probably laying on a wet blanket on the pool deck at the back of the house, soaking the sun, letting her lithe, ultra-tan body get even browner. Jerry wondered if he should reveal her existence to Holly, throw it in her face right then.

"So what is this about, Jerry?" Holly asked. "What do you want?"

"I want to tell you what to do," he said. "Sell you on a way out of the mess you're in."

She gave him a funny, helpless look.

"That DA is going to burn both of you," Jerry said. "Jeff *and you.*"

"You think?" she said. "That's not what Jeff says, not what his lawyer says."

"That Stauber guy?" Jerry laughed. "He's a fool. You saw him bumbling around today. That DA, McGraw, ran circles around him. You already lost."

When Holly put her hands to her face, close to tears again, Jerry found himself pulling her into his chest and putting his arms around her. He started patting her soft, blonde hair, sniffing it and drawing in a whiff, a long, lovely whiff of Holly's scent, the way it always had been, a lovely, intoxicating, sexy fragrance, sophisticated and so unlike the childish bubblegum aroma of Jade's perfume.

"You gotta take a plea, Holly," Jerry whispered into her right ear. He even nibbled at it, completely letting himself go. "You have to sell Jeff out. Betray him. Betray him like you betrayed me."

She was shaking in his arms.

"But, but then I'll go to prison," she said. "Maybe for years. Be slobbered over by dike inmates and dike cops. I can't do that, Jerry, I can't."

"No," he said. The idea of what to do had been ruminating in his mind in the days leading up to coming down here to observe the trial. A way to save Holly. And a way to get Jeff.

"Whatever deal you work will include jail, sure," Jerry went on, "and you'll certainly have to testify against Jeff because they need to put someone behind bars for life for my murder. But before you're ever sentenced, you leave town. With me. You become a fugitive under my cover. I become your anonymous man. Just like in my comic book."

"But this isn't a comic book, Jerry," she said. "This is real life."

"But I am anonymous, aren't I?" Jerry said. "They think I'm dead. So I can hide you however long it takes for the dust to clear. For them to stop looking for you. With Jeff in jail, who they consider the real culprit in all this, they'll forget about you. They'll move on to other things."

"Even that Fox guy?" Holly asked, and in truth, for Jerry, Fox was the one wild card.

"Let me worry about Fox," said Jerry.

Holly sighed and sunk back into the driver's seat.

"So that's it," she said and looked over at Jerry, "I plead guilty to a lesser crime."

"It won't matter anyway, since after you testify against Jeff, you are leaving town. You'll never spend a day in jail. That's the other thing, the plea has to be conditioned on no increase in bail. So you remain free until your sentencing."

Holly nodded, seeming to get all this, letting it sink in.

"Why weren't you this way before?" she asked and gave him a long, hopeful look. "Strong for both of us."

He didn't know for sure, but he meant to stay this way. Just like the quiet hero of his comic book, *The Anonymous Man*, helping other people change their lives for the better by drifting out of the bad one they had made for themselves into a new life with freedom, promise. People who needed to run away from bad marriages, failed businesses, the mob. Whatever. the Anonymous Man was there to save the day.

He had already freed Jade from her bad life, hadn't he? So why not Holly? Help her escape from the evil that Jeff had wrought. He had all that money in the LLC accounts, still over a million dollars. That should tide them over—including Jade, of course—for a considerable time, maybe a lifetime if they handled it right. He could have both of the women he loved in his life.

"Alright," Holly whispered. "I'll do it."

Then she slumped completely against him. She looked up into his eyes and Jerry kissed her long and deep, so in love with her again.

Chapter Thirty-Seven

Fox was flat on his back on the bed in his hotel room with his cell phone to his ear, speaking with Chief Reynolds back in Philadelphia.

"Looks like she's gonna cop a plea," he told Reynolds.

"No shit."

"Yep, just like that."

"What's the deal?"

"She rats Flaherty out, tells the jury it was his plan, that he did the dirty deed while she was in the shower," Fox said. "Burned our insured alive. Also, that she never really believed he was serious, but admits that she played along, didn't stop him like she should have. Even took part of the money, a few thousand, although she says Flaherty took control over all the rest of it, and that she has no idea where the rest of it is now."

"Well, that's no good," said the Chief.

"And about the emails," continued Fox, "she agrees they are solid proof of what they had done, but they only show that she had joined in after Jerry Shaw was already dead. There was no turning back, she was in too deep by then."

"Hm," said the Chief, pondering this change of events. "So what's the deal?"

"For taking a plea and testifying against Flaherty, she gets seven to fifteen in some minimum secure facility downstate. With good behavior, she gets out in something like four and a half, five years."

"Not too bad for murdering a guy," remarked Chief Reynolds. "Her own husband. And the judge, he agreed to that?"

"Yeah," said Fox half-heartedly. "Her lawyer floated some bullshit about Jerry Shaw being a wife beater, but the Judge didn't want to hear it."

"Good for him," said Reynolds. "When did this all come down?"

"Just a few minutes ago," said Fox. "Just got the call from Inspector Miller. She'll enter the plea tomorrow morning. Once that happens, they'll break the news to Flaherty's lawyer. There'll be a mistrial. They'll have to start again with the trial involving only him, now, that is, if Flaherty doesn't cop a plea of his own. But he's not in the best bargaining position. The DA is going to want to get his pound of flesh."

"Yes, I would think so," Reynolds said, almost grunting.

Fox knew Reynolds wasn't one hundred percent happy with the news. It was just after nine and Fox imagined his old friend sitting in his dark living room slurping down some scotch and rolling it around with the ice clinking against the sides of his thick, short glass. His wife Meredith, or "Merry-width" as Reynolds fondly called her, was probably upstairs in her robe and slippers already in bed reading one of her Hollywood magazines.

"How much did we recover from them?" Reynolds asked.

"Only about a hundred grand," said Fox. "What was left in a local bank account."

"A hundred grand! That's it?" Reynolds sighed. "Jesus.

Any idea what happened to the rest of it?"

"Stashed somewhere, no doubt. We're tracing it. Like I said, the widow Shaw claims Flaherty was in charge of it. I already complained to the DA's office that her plea should be conditioned on her telling us where the money went, but her lawyer insists she doesn't know. And the ADA, McGraw, told me that he'd only push for something if and when Flaherty starting talking plea which, as we know, is quite doubtful. That would definitely be a condition and, in truth, it's really the only bargaining chip Flaherty has right now."

Reynolds grunted, took a sip of his scotch. Fox could hear the ice cubes clink up against the crystal of his glass.

"Any idea why she flipped?" he asked.

"I think she's already got another boyfriend," Fox said.

"What?"

"I followed her after court let out this afternoon. She met him in the parking garage across from the courthouse. They talked in her car. It got cozy for a few minutes. Then she went back to her place while the guy drove out to some cheap motel near the football stadium where the Bills play."

"No shit," Chief Reynolds said then downed what was left of his Scotch. "You have any idea who the guy is?"

"Not yet, but I will. He may be her link to the outside world and where she intends to safeguard her end of our money while she does her time. Unless she's telling the truth and doesn't know where any of it is."

Reynolds grunted again, scoffing at the credibility of that. "Know what, Foxy?"

"What, Chief?"

"Crime does pay."

"Yeah, Chief," he said. "I learned that a long time ago."

Chapter Thirty-Eight

At nine o'clock sharp the next morning, Holly entered the courtroom with her attorney, Paul Blake. He looked ashen and sullen and was probably a little hung over while Holly kept her head down.

Moments later, after the massive, ornate door to the courtroom closed with a thud, Jerry walked in and took the same seat along the aisle he had occupied the day before. After Holly and Blake had taken their respective seats, McGraw strode in, nodded and smiled at them, and sat. Moments later, Judge Pratt entered from his chambers behind the bench and the overweight sheriff deputy who was assigned as the court's bailiff barked, "All rise!"

Judge Pratt sat down and looked over at McGraw.

"Mister McGraw," he said, all business. "You may proceed." McGraw stood and informed the Judge that Holly was changing her not guilty plea to guilty to a charge of Voluntary Manslaughter. That information got a rise out of everyone in the courtroom. Judge Pratt banged his gavel and the gallery became silent and stayed that way for the next several moments. Holly glanced back at Jerry and nodded briefly as if to let him know that their connection had truly been re-established.

Fox took a note of that. He glanced over his shoulder at Jerry and also took note that he was the same guy he had seen in the car with Holly yesterday afternoon. Her new lover or boyfriend or whatever who may have convinced her to do this. There was something familiar about the guy nagging at Fox, but he could not quite place it. Judge Pratt turned to the defense table.

"That your understanding, Mister Blake? Your client is entering a plea of guilty to the lesser charge, Voluntary Manslaughter?"

Blake stood. "Yes, your Honor."

"You understand, Mrs. Shaw," said Judge Pratt, "that I am promising nothing in terms of a sentence. And you understand that you could be sentenced to up to fifteen years for the crime to which you are apparently willing to enter a plea of guilty."

Holly looked at Blake who flashed a tight smile and brief nod. Then, she looked back at the Judge.

"Yes, Judge," she said, "I understand."

"Very well."

Holly was asked to stand and admitted to the Judge that she was guilty of helping Jeff kill Jerry. When she was finished, and had professed that she had enough time to consult with her attorney about what she was doing, and knew full well what rights she was giving up, that, more or less, she was of sound mind and knew what she was doing, the Judge accepted her guilty plea without further comment, and scheduled her sentencing for two months from that day.

"What about bail, counselors?" the Judge asked, looking at McGraw.

"The People do not request a change in bail terms."

The Judge frowned. "You have no quarrel with that I take it, Mister Blake? She's out on bail, presently free on bond, right?"

"No quarrel whatsoever, your Honor," Blake said.

Holly and Blake were excused from the courtroom and the Judge immediately called in Jeff and his lawyer, Stauber. Jerry remained behind with glad anticipation as to what was about to transpire.

Jeff looked around the courtroom for a time, wondering what had happened to Holly, worrying that she had betrayed him. Judge Pratt told Jeff and Stauber what they already suspected, that Holly had entered a plea of guilty in exchange for her cooperation and testimony against Jeff, and because of that, he had to rule a mistrial in the proceedings conducted to date. Jerry wasn't quite sure what that meant at the time, and worried that somehow Jeff had gotten a free ride on double jeopardy or something. The Judge called the jury in and told them they were dismissed, that one of the defendants had pled guilty and the trial had to be called off until a future date.

Jerry's concern was eased when, after the last jury member, an elderly white-haired woman with an arthritic gait who had to be escorted from the courtroom by one of the overweight bailiffs, the Judge scheduled Jeff's trial for a month from that day.

"Anything else, counselors?"

That's when McGraw got to his feet and asked that higher bail be set in light of the change of circumstances.

Stauber went ballistic. Regardless, Judge Pratt, without a word of explanation, promptly raised Jeff's bail to $250,000 cash, or property bond, and remanded him to the county lock-up until it was paid. Jeff had a shocked look when a couple of bailiffs grabbed him and slapped on handcuffs. They then escorted him out of the courtroom via a side door.

Jerry chuckled to himself, almost unable to restrain his glee.

His revenge was now complete.

Chapter Thirty-Nine

Jerry couldn't resist sneaking off to see Holly that night. Arriving at just after eight, he had no way of knowing that Jack Fox was sitting in an inconspicuous dark green sedan, parked in the shadow of some trees a few houses down from 320 Northview Lane.

Jerry rang the doorbell and soon enough Holly was peeking at him through the curtains that ran the length of the long, slit windows. Seeing Jerry, she quickly opened the door.

"Jerry," she said, "I thought you might come."

But then, Holly looked past him down Northview and sighed. "Hope that goddamn Fox isn't watching the house."

"So?" he asked. "I'm dead. He'll never find me."

Holly stepped aside and let Jerry into his own house. And Jerry wanted her bad right then. The idea of tasting her treachery excited him beyond all else. He lifted Holly up into his arms and carried her upstairs to what used to be, and now would be again, their bedroom.

Once there, Jerry literally tore off her clothes. He

popped off the buttons of her blouse, separated it from her back and tossed it to the floor. He slashed open the zipper of her pants and pulled them down to her ankles and off her feet before throwing himself on top of her on the bed. As they smothered themselves in wet kisses, Jerry removed her bra and ripped off her panties. He stood up then, staring down at her on the bed, naked and completely in his control. If only Jeff Flaherty could see the fat man now.

Holly gazed up at him, her lips quivering, panting, wanting more, wanting him, desperate for him to fuck her. She had never seen him looking this good, and together with his Florida tan, Jerry was every bit as desirable as Jeff Flaherty ever was.

Half an hour later, their passion was spent. The lovemaking had been their best ever. And yet, in the silent darkness right then, Jerry thought of Jade as Holly sidled up to him, breathing slowly, content. He felt a pang of guilt for cheating on Jade with Holly, his wife, as bizarre as that seemed. And he felt equally bad for thinking of Jade with Holly lying next to him. Life had suddenly become so goddamned complicated.

Still, he wondered what Jade was doing that night, that moment. He wondered if she had been fucking around while he was away or if she was waiting dutifully, like a soldier's wife, for him to return to her from battle. He had called her every night. The last two nights, the calls had been late, well past eleven, and she had sounded hurt by his forgetfulness or lack of consideration. He had not called her tonight.

"So now what?" Holly asked out of the darkness. Jerry

let the question hang there for a time.

"Now what, what?"

"What happens next?"

"Now, we wait. You keep a low profile for a month until you testify against Jeff," he said. "Then after that, we decide when it's best for you to skedaddle out of town."

"And what about us?" she asked. "Can we, well, keep seeing each other like this?"

"No. I don't think that would be wise."

He had not told Holly about Jade. But Jade offered them the perfect solution. If only he could convince her to become the front for both of them. Jerry wondered how Jade would react to that proposition. None too good, he bet. And if she really loved him, she would flatly refuse to do it.

And then Holly, seeming to guess what he was thinking, asked from the darkness, "So who's been your front with that world?"

He sighed, laughed, then blurted out everything about Jade. Holly just laid there listening and afterward, said nothing for a time. "So let me get this straight," she finally said. "You've been fucking some whore all these months. A fucking whore? What the fuck diseases did I just catch?"

"No diseases," Jerry said. "I had her checked. She's perfectly clean." Then he got pissed. "And look who's calling who a whore. You're the biggest whore of all time. A murderous fucking whore."

She launched a vicious slap but Jerry caught it and squeezed her wrist around.

"You're hurting me," she cried as she tried to wrench

out of his grasp.

"Calm the fuck down," he told her. "I…love you."

That stopped her and he let her fall onto her back and snivel for a time before leaning over her and telling her again, as sincerely and softly as he could, "I love you."

"What about her?" she asked. "That whore?"

"Don't call her that," he said. "She's come a long way from that." He sighed. "And no," he said. "I don't know what it is about her. But she was there for me when I needed someone. When you-"

Holly reached for him.

"I'm sorry, Jerry," she said. "So sorry. It was Jeff. Goddamn Jeff."

Jerry held her. The bottom line, he finally decided, was that he loved her. And after another moment, he decided that he loved Jade as well.

"And so," Jerry said, deciding for both of them, "you become my anonymous soul mate. Come down with me to Florida, and I'll put you up in a house I'll buy in the name of one of our LLCs. I'll tell her— Jade— that I bought it as an investment, a just in case place."

"So, what's she look like?" Holly asked, whining a little, and maybe worried that Jade was prettier than her.

Jerry laughed as he reached over to the night table for the cell phone. It was in Jade's name, of course. He quickly found the media app and clicked upon Jade's photograph. She was standing on the pool deck of their house in Florida in her bikini, her head cocked sideways, flashing a marvelously cocky smile. He loved that picture.

After a moment, he handed the phone over to Holly

and watched her look at Jade's photograph.

"She look familiar?"

Holly's eyes narrowed into a deep scowl as she examined Jade's picture.

"She's your twin," Jerry said. "Don't you think?"

Holly looked at Jade's picture a moment longer, huffed, then handed him back the phone.

"My twin?" she asked. "She's an ugly skank."

Jerry laughed. "She looks just like you."

Chapter Forty

Fox had to sit there until almost eleven-thirty before the new guy left Holly Shaw's house. For some reason, Fox had started referring to the new guy as "the third man." Poor, murdered Jerry Shaw was the "first man," and his murderer, Jeff Flaherty, was the "second man." Now this mysterious new fellow, contestant number three, became "third man." So Fox's current mission in life had become to find out just who this "third man" was.

Fox had a hunch that the third man was no Johnny-come-lately, but had some connection with Holly Shaw that pre-dated her husband's murder plot. And for some reason, Fox also thought the third man maybe even pre-dated Jeff Flaherty.

After calling Chief Reynolds with the Holly Shaw plea news, he used his laptop to conduct a national DMV search and learned that the Corolla being driven by the third man was registered to The Anonymity Group, LLC, a limited liability company registered a few months back in New Mexico. Because the Anonymity Group had been registered in New Mexico, the identity of the LLC's owner was secret. The other curious thing was that the car had been registered in New York, with its yellow state plates, and an address for the Anonymity Group in Johnson City, of all places, an old rust belt town bordering Binghamton in south-central New York. Fox had also learned that the Corolla had been insured by a national company and he made a mental note to try and track down how the payments were being made. Even if it was likely done electrically, at least he would find out the location of the LLC's bank account. And perhaps there'd be four million dollars in it.

Fox was able to get some geek back at Global headquarters to run a quick computer search and report to him that the Anonymity address on the Corolla's vehicle registration was to a seventy-five-year-old clapboard double owned by one Michael Donovan. He gave Fox a number and Fox called Donovan who, after some hesitation, told him that the names of the current tenants. He had never heard of the Anonymity Group. But that might not mean anything because one of the tenants could have simply used the apartment address for that of Anonymity.

Fox felt frustrated by the lack of a definitive lead from all of this computer and phone play while following the third man back to the cheap motel out by Ralph Wilson Stadium where he was staying. The best and perhaps only way to get to the bottom of the mystery of the third man was to seek it from the horse's mouth itself.

Fox pulled along the shoulder of the road and watched as Jerry parked in the mostly empty lot which wound around a squat, depressing two-story motel. Fox continued to watch through a set of binoculars as Jerry exited the car and clambered up a narrow stairwell along the side of the building to the second floor. Fox sharpened the focus of the lens until he could make out the room number, "221," as Jerry fumbled with his key card, opened the door, and stepped inside.

With Jerry inside, Fox pulled into the lot and parked a few spots down from the third man's Corolla. It was by now a few minutes past midnight. Fox had his plan and took a slow stroll around the motel, up the stairwell to the second floor, and onto the narrow walkway outside the rooms. He stopped in front of #221. The time was now or never to break the case.

He had to bang three times before the guy approached the door and asked who was it, what did he want.

"Name's Jack Fox," Fox said. "I'm an investigator with Global Life and Casualty. I was wondering if I could have a couple minutes of your time."

Jerry started hyperventilating, suddenly scared. But that was the old Jerry Shaw's way of thinking, and he was the new Jerry Shaw. A superhero. He closed his eyes and took a deep breath.

"Yeah?" Jerry asked. "Like what kind of things?"

"Well, to start," Fox said, "Holly Shaw."

"She's just an old friend," Jerry said through the door. "I knew she's been going through a tough time, with this trial and all. I wanted to give her some friendly advice."

"And you gave her that advice," Fox asked, "with a kiss?" Jerry kept quiet for a time, considering his options.

"What's that got to do with anything?" Jerry finally

asked. "The point is, or should be, that she took my advice and did the right thing in court today."

"But why the kiss?"

"Let's just say we're old friends."

"Why don't you just let me inside a few minutes so we can talk face-to-face," said Fox.

"I'm sorry, Mister Fox," Jerry said, "but I was about to go to sleep."

"Did she tire you out?"

"What?"

"At the house, did her grieving tire you out," Fox said. "I saw that you visited her tonight."

"Good night, Mister Fox," said Jerry. "And if you refuse to leave, I'll call down to the desk clerk and have him to call the police to escort you off this property."

"Look," Fox said, "just one minute is all I ask."

Jerry thought a moment, and decided there'd probably be no harm talking with Fox face to face, see what he knew. And anyway, it would be dumb to get the police involved. With a sick grin, he let Fox into his cramped motel room.

Jerry sat on the edge of the lumpy bed while Fox pulled an armless chair away from a small, cheap oak veneer desk. Jerry was wearing sweats and a t-shirt, while Fox looked uncomfortable in jeans that seemed a waist size too small and a light blue dress shirt that was also too tight for his body.

"So how do you know Holly Shaw?" Fox asked, going for the jugular straight off.

"We met in college, years ago," Jerry said. "We were boyfriend and girlfriend for a short time before she met

Jerry Shaw. But it ended almost as soon as it started, and we just became good friends. Anyway, she and I never completely lost touch." Jerry shrugged. "So when I heard what was happening up here, how she had been arrested and all that, I couldn't resist coming back here, showing my support."

"So what happened when you came back up here? I mean, you and Mrs. Shaw seemed pretty friendly in the parking garage yesterday."

"You followed us?"

"It's my job," Fox said. "So what did she tell you? In between kisses?"

"Look," Jerry said, "you got to put me on the stand if you want to know that."

"The DA just might do that," Fox said.

"Screw that," Jerry said. "She didn't say anything."

"Mind telling me your name?" Fox asked. "Name's Gordon," Jerry said. "Alan Gordon."

It was the first name that popped into Jerry's head. An old college chum. And funny thing was, Alan Gordon had really been an early boyfriend of Holly, freshman year. It wouldn't take long for Fox to discover that the real Alan Gordon was an accountant living in Queens.

While Fox sat before him with a serious frown, Jerry decided that was it. He had to stop right there. "Look, Mr. Fox, I think that's all you need to know."

Fox shrugged and looked about the room. As he was looking, he asked, "Mind telling me what the Anonymity Group is, Mr. Gordon?"

That question threw Jerry for a loop. This Fox fellow

was good.

Jerry tried not to show his concern. "It's, it's my company,"

Jerry said. "We sell computer programs. You know, software."

"I see." Fox turned and focused upon Jerry.

"Made me a lot of money," Jerry said. He was still unsure where this was going, but he now knew that he had to end this inquisition soon, and reformulate his plan. "Look, Mister Fox," he said with a yawn, "I've given you your minute. I'm tired."

Fox nodded and looked around the room. "You said you live where?"

"I didn't say," Jerry said. He thought quickly. He knew the Corolla was registered to Anonymity, and the registration's address was Johnson City, Jade's old apartment. Jerry felt there could be no harm in telling Fox that.

"Johnson City," he said.

Fox nodded. He kept a poker face, but Jerry knew he wasn't buying what Jerry was selling. He kept squinting at Jerry in a funny way and Jerry was growing more than a little frightened that he had pushed his luck. But Fox just kept staring.

"She didn't tell you anything about the money, then?" Fox asked from out of nowhere. "Mrs. Shaw. The insurance money?"

"Sorry, Mister Fox," Jerry said. "She didn't say anything to me about insurance money. How much did you say was missing?"

"Well," Fox said, seeming almost embarrassed by it, "almost four million dollars."

Jerry whistled.

"Holy!" he said. "No, she didn't mention it. Didn't come up."

As he sat there, Fox decided that he, and Global, would have been better served had he waited them out. Had he done so, Holly Shaw and Flaherty and perhaps the third man might have led him to the money. Fox stood and a wave of relief coursed through Jerry.

"Well," Fox said and stuck out a hand, "good night, Mr.

Gordon. It's been a pleasure."

"Likewise," said Jerry, and shook Fox's hand.

Fox left the motel feeling that he had been a fool or made a fool of or a combination of both. Back at his hotel room, he Googled Alan Gordon and didn't find much, mostly irrelevant links. The name was just too damned common. He did a Lexis-Nexus, and visited several skip tracing sites the company had on retainer, and found out a lot about several Alan Gordon's, including a guy living in Queens who had attended the State University of New York at Binghamton during the time in question. He found a number and decided, despite it being almost two in the morning, he'd risk waking the guy up. An answering machine picked up and a metallic voice told him Alan Gordon was unavailable and to leave a message. Fox decided against that and simply hung up. He'd call back later.

Fox nodded off on his chair at the hotel desk peering

at his computer screen. He woke up at quarter to three in the morning with a start. An epiphany had hit him, the idea that this Gordon fellow may have been behind the incriminating emails, his way of removing Flaherty from Holly's life with him stepping conveniently into the void. Why not? A man in love would do almost anything for his beloved.

He yawned and decided he needed to get some sleep. He wanted to be up early to call back Alan Gordon. Fox turned out the light over his laptop, closed it and stumbled to bed. But he had a hard time falling asleep. That guy, Alan Gordon, kept bothering him. The story was bogus, he knew. The guy must be someone else. Fox just couldn't figure out who.

At some point, after tossing and turning a long while, sleep finally came.

Chapter Forty-One

The moment Fox left his motel, Jerry was on the phone with Holly.

"Major change of plans," he told her after she answered groggily. "We have to leave town tonight. Now. Pronto." After a pause, added, "So you aren't gonna have to testify against Jeff after all."

Holly asked what had happened, and he told her about Fox's visit.

Jerry knew that they didn't have much time. Fox's first order of business, no doubt, would be to check the Alan Gordon story. The proverbial house of cards would start to collapse after that. Hopefully, the search for Alan Gordon wouldn't start until the morning. By then, he and Holly needed to be long gone. The problem with it was that Holly would never get to testify against Jeff Flaherty once she became a fugitive, and that meant Jeff would likely go free. There would be no ultimate revenge against the one character who really deserved it. Well, so did Holly, but he was in love with her. But what other choice did he have now?

"So where we going?"

"Florida," he told her.

"But what about your girl?" Holly asked.

"Look, she's not my girl," Jerry said, knowing that wasn't true. She was his girl, but so was Holly. "I'll put you up in a hotel, down near my house. We'll figure something out later."

But he had no idea what he was going to tell Jade. And then the thought came to him— maybe he didn't have to tell her anything at all.

"What about that guy, Fox?" Holly asked. "What are you going to do about him?"

"Don't worry about him," Jerry said. "I don't think he has any idea who I am, or that we need to run."

"What do you think Jeff'll do?" she asked, "if he gets off without my testimony."

"We'll be long gone by then," Jerry said, Bastard might get off, Jerry thought. But Jeff wouldn't have a clue where to look for them. He'd be broke, tired. It was unlikely that they'd have anything to worry about from him. Still, it troubled Jerry that he'd always have to wonder where he was, whether he was looking. Or whether Holly would be tempted, and give in to the temptation, of contacting Jeff.

But Jerry couldn't think about all that now. He had to get them moving.

Allowing Holly back into his life had certainly added a stressful factor into the neat little equation for anonymous financial security and freedom he had calculated simply with Jade as the front solely for him.

Jerry looked at the time. It was late, way late, but he still needed to call Jade. She was likely already long past the panic stage.

The phone rang only once before she answered.

"Where the hell were you?" Jade asked. "Fucking that skank?"

"No way," he told her with a forced laugh. "I was here, sleeping. I fell asleep."

"When you coming home?" Jade asked after a time, more mellow now. "I saw on the internet that she pled."

"I'm leaving in the morning," he told her. "First thing."

"You still love her, don't you?"

The question came out of nowhere. Jerry stumbled around a few moments, pacing the room in his underwear and bare feet holding the cell phone to his ear, trying to get his bearings. "What? No. Course not. She's a fucking skank, like you said. She fucking wanted to kill me. She wanted me dead. I'm the one who is putting her in prison."

And he wondered for a moment what he was doing, rescuing that same woman. Still loving that same woman.

"What time you gonna be home?" Jade asked.

"Couple days. I'll make it to around Charlotte tomorrow. I'll call you along the way. Okay?"

Jerry wondered if she was buying anything he was saying. There was something about the tone of her voice…

"I have to get going. I need to get some sleep."

"I can't wait to see you," Jade said.

"Me too," Jerry said, and he didn't have to fake the sentiment. He did miss her.

After Jerry hung up with Jade, he called Holly. It was quarter to three.

"I'm on my way," Jerry said. "Be waiting for me out front.

Look out for any strange cars parked in front of your house."

"Strange cars?"

"Fox."

"Oh, Jesus."

"Okay," he said. "See you in a few."

"Hey, Jerry?"

"What, Ja— ah, Holly?"

"What? Jade? That whore–"

"No, please, Holly," he said, "stop it. I'm exhausted and hyperventilating at the same time." He sighed. "So what? What did you want to say?"

It was her turn to sigh.

"I was going to say," she said, "I love you." That surprised him. "Jerry?"

"Yeah," he said. "I heard you. I love you too. See you in twenty."

He hung up the phone, clutched his suitcase, and rushed out the door.

It took Jerry fifteen long minutes or so to make it to Northview Lane keeping exactly to the speed limit the entire time. He drove all the way down to the end of the street and turned around in a driveway. There were only a couple cars parked along the street, but none of them looked occupied. Fox was not there. Jerry pulled along the curb in from of

320 Northview and his heart raced when he saw Holly step out the front door carrying a small suitcase.

Jerry reached over and opened the door and Holly got in. She turned around and deposited her suitcase on the backseat. Before he was able to put the car in gear and get on with their journey, she leaned over kissed him.

"I meant what I said, Jerry," she whispered. "I love you." Jerry leaned in and kissed her. "Let's get out of this fucking town."

"Alright," she whispered. Someday, Jerry hoped to trust her again. Someday.

Jerry managed to drive twelve straight hours, stopping only twice to piss and once to grab burgers for both of them, before he had to stop just south of Columbia, South Carolina. Holly kept him awake with her constant chatter about movies and acting and the Anonymous Man and once, briefly, how sorry she was for doing what she did to him. For her affair with Jeff.

She fell silent for a time after telling Jerry that.

"Do you love him?" Jerry asked. The sun had just come up and everything was bathed in a gray hue.

"No."

"Did you?"

"I thought I did. Maybe."

"You plotted to kill me."

"That was all Jeff," she said.

"No," Jerry said. "You brought it up."

"No," she assured him. "You— you heard it wrong. I— I started out loving him but then I grew afraid of him. Jeff is, well, a little off, I think. He—he enjoyed killing that body guy. Enjoyed it.

"I tried to talk him out of it, you know. But he said we couldn't leave any witnesses behind." Holly sighed. "I'm so sorry, Jer. But all that is behind us. We've got each other now. We've gotten back what we lost."

But then, Jerry thought about Jade.

Chapter Forty-Two

Finally in Kissimmee, Jerry helped Holly settle into a room at a decent enough motel along Route 192 and then told her he had to go see Jade.

"Okay, Jerry," she said. "You gonna tell her about me or what?"

"Not just yet," he said.

"Aren't you gonna fuck me again?" she asked and gave him a mischievous grin.

Jerry laughed. "My dick is going to fall off, girl," he said.

He laid down next to her and brought her to him. She was thin and subtle and looked so much like Jade. A tug of something suggested that he start kissing her, but he resisted. He had to go home to Jade.

"This is short-term," he told Holly. "In a couple of weeks, you'll be in your own apartment. You'll get used to it. I'll take care of you. I'll see you."

"How are you gonna juggle her and me?"

"Let's just settle in," was his response. "Take it one

day at a time."

She got quiet and moved away from him and laid back.

Staring up at the ceiling, she said, "Okay, go then. Go to her, your precious Jade." She said the name, "Jade," like it was crap.

"C'mon, Holly," he tried to reason with her, but he knew that if the roles were reversed, he'd be feeling the same way. Vulnerable, left out.

"I can't believe this is happening," she said. "I left everything back there. Everything. My parents, my sister, my baby brother. I'll never see them again, will I? I wasn't the one who was supposed to become anonymous."

"Would it have been better to see them in jail?" he asked. "And maybe, somehow, we can get word to them, when the dust settles. You're a fugitive, not dead."

As Jerry held her, he considered blowing off Jade, calling her and telling her the car had broken down or something. But as he had told Holly, Jade was no dummy. She would see straight through that story, and both he and Holly might be on the street, with no one to interact with the world for them. While they might be able to last for some time without identities, Jerry believed that they ultimately needed some kind of cover.

Although he could likely find someone else, man or woman, to stand in as their front, he truly cared for Jade and trusted that she wouldn't squeal him out. They had a relationship beyond her being his front. She loved him, and he loved her, although his feelings for her had admittedly been muddled now that Holly was back in his life.

"I really have to go," Jerry told Holly as he slid away from her. "And at some point, I promise you, I am going to figure this Jade thing out."

She turned to her side and looked up at him. "Go then."

But as he went out the door, Holly did not say goodbye. And he was long gone by the time Holly opened the door to the motel room, peeked up and down the deserted parking lot, and walked out into a bright, clear afternoon. She walked toward the lobby, constantly alert for someone on her heels, looking back every few steps.

Holly left the lobby, walked across the street and entered the foyer of a diner. She sighed with relief when she saw the pay phone. She picked up the receiver and placed a call. At the other end, Jeff's cell phone chimed.

Chapter Forty-Three

The moment Jerry pulled the Corolla into the garage, Jade was out there, on him. She smothered him with kisses as he stepped out of the car but Jerry suspected she was sniffing for the scent of another woman on him rather than seeking romance.

"I missed you, hon," she said and hugged him close. "Let's fuck."

"Let me take a shower first," he laughed.

Jade let him go and Jerry took a long, hot shower. As he stepped out of it, Jade was waiting there in the bathroom holding his boxers.

"You've been with her," she said, not a question. Jerry bowed his head.

"I smell her stink all over these." She nodded to the laundry basket in the walk-in closet. "On all your fucking clothes."

Jerry wrapped the towel around himself and sulked as he leaned against the double sink cabinet.

"Yes," he admitted and looked up at her. "She came

back with me. I – I didn't know what else to do. I couldn't send her to jail."

"You fucking asshole!"

Jade ran at Jerry and slapped at his bare chest. He grabbed her wrists and started to twist them around.

"Jade! Jade!" he cried. "Let me explain. Please."

She yanked free of him and backed away into the bedroom in tears. She turned her back to him and took a few long breaths trying to regain her composure.

"You're a sick, weak fool," was all she said. "You keep fooling yourself that you've changed, become a superhero, but you're still a fat, scared little boy."

Jerry walked over and sat on the edge of the bed. He had chosen the wrong fork in the road and it was too late to turn back because he had run out of gas. But in the next moment, Jade surprised him by walking over, plopping down next to him, and placing his head on her bosom.

"No, you're not," she said. "You're not weak. You still love her, don't you?"

He let her console him for a time, rocking gently in her arms on the edge of the bed. But no, he couldn't leave it at that. He broke out of her arms and stood.

"No, I'm fucked up," he said and seemed to have reached a sudden, irrevocable conclusion. "I can't do this. I can't have both of you. What was I thinking? Look. I can never trust her again. Our love is over. The first night she screwed Jeff, it was over. And now, I love you. Only you.

"I don't know what the fuck I was thinking. It was as if she bewitched me back there. You were right, I should never have gone back. What was it for? All I need is you, the treasure you are."

Jerry leaned forward and kissed Jade. And she kissed him back. There was no doubt in his mind that she loved him. Not a shred of doubt.

"I need to do something about her." He looked away from Jade, cursing himself. "Why did I fucking have to bring her here? To spoil us?"

"It hasn't spoiled us, hon," Jade said. She looked deep into Jerry's eyes. "It's brought us closer together. Made us realize what we have. She made you realize who you are. Who you love."

Jerry nodded.

"I have to get rid of her," he said. "Tell her it's not going to work out between us."

Jade was shaking her head. "Just call the cops on her," she said. "There must be a warrant out for her arrest by now."

"Yeah, sure." Jerry's eyes went wide. "Yeah, I could do that. Blow her in. They'd come to the hotel and pick her up and I'd never have to see her again."

"And we live happily ever after."

"But that would be such a coward's way out," Jerry said.

Jade laughed and reached over and pulled him down to bed with her.

"Yes," she said, "but what sweet revenge." Jerry laughed.

"You are one evil bitch," Jerry said. He rolled on top of her and straddled her hips. "An evil whore is what you are."

She giggled and let him kiss her. "But I can't do it," he said softly.

"Well then go cut that bitch a break," Jade said. "But I think you will be sorry. Real sorry."

Chapter Forty-Four

With Holly having fled, all hell broke loose. McGraw had to go to Judge Pratt and get an order revoking her bail and obtain a bench warrant for her arrest. Stauber got wind of it and brought a motion to lower Flaherty's bail. Jeff was out of the county holding pen in less than an hour.

"You got any idea where she went?" Chief Reynolds wanted to know after Fox stopped by his office and broke the bad news.

"No," he said flatly. "Not a clue."

"Christ," Chief Reynolds said and scratched his chin for a time. "What about that Gordon fellow?"

"I checked it out. Gordon is some schlep living in Queens. Some accountant. He did go to school at SUNY Binghamton and he knew Holly Shaw and Jerry Shaw for that matter. But he hadn't seen them since college."

"And you haven't come up with how he, the guy you interviewed, came up with that name?"

"I have no clue on this one, Chief. I really don't. All my years, I never been this baffled."

"So where do we go from here?" the Chief asked.

"The speedy trial clock is ticking. If they don't bring Flaherty to trial in six months, the case gets dismissed. But going to trial without Holly Shaw is as good as a dismissal anyway. At least, that's what Miller thinks, and he was speaking for McGraw. It's my opinion as well."

"What a disaster," said the Chief. And it's all my fault, thought Fox. "Flaherty made bail," Fox added.

"So?" asked the Chief. "That good or bad?"

"Maybe good," Fox said. "He might just lead us to Holly."

"You think they're that stupid?"

"Why not?" Fox said.

"Alright," said Chief Reynolds. "Tail Flaherty. See what happens and we'll reassess in a week from now."

Jeff Flaherty looked both ways the moment he stepped out of his apartment. He hesitated momentarily, then walked gingerly down the hall to the steps leading to the parking lot of his building. In his right hand was a duffle bag. Of course, he had no idea that Jack Fox was in the lot, staking him out, settled in the past eight hours in an inconspicuous rented compact sedan.

Flaherty was still looking around as he got into his silver Lexus, the same one Fox had seen him driving to and from the Shaw residence within a few days of Jerry Shaw's funeral. He pulled out of the lot and drove toward the Thruway entrance. Fox stayed a safe distance behind him. He gave himself a symbolic pat on the back for having planted a GPS device on the inside of the Lexus' front wheel well not a half hour before Flaherty had come down from his apartment to go wherever he was going.

Fox stayed beyond the rearview mirror field of Flaherty's Lexus and used Global's GPS system to monitor his speed and direction. What it told him was that Flaherty was heading south a few miles per hour over the speed limit. To Holly.

Seven hours later, Fox was yawning and in serious need of sleep as Flaherty entered Virginia on Interstate 77.

"I think he's heading to Florida," Fox told Chief Reynolds.

He was holding a cell phone to his left ear. "Florida? How do you know that?"

"Just a feeling," Fox said. But it was a strong one.

"You think he's driving straight through?" Reynolds asked. "To Florida, or wherever he's going?"

"Wouldn't you?"

"I guess," said Reynolds.

"And he's younger than me," said Fox. "When I was his age I could drive straight through to California if need be."

"Well," said the Chief, "if you're feeling sleepy, stop. We got the GPS."

"At some point," said Fox, "he's gonna wonder about that, I think, if someone did that. Like us. I'm surprised he hasn't already. He's a smart guy."

As if on cue, in the next moment, Fox got a report from the GPS system that Flaherty's car had exited the interstate at a rest area. "And I think maybe he's finally done that," Fox told Chief Reynolds. "Figured it out. He's stopping."

"Or maybe he just has to take a leak."

The Chief was right this time. After the pit stop, Flaherty's Lexus entered the interstate, then sped up to seventy-five, and kept heading south. But not ten minutes later, Flaherty exited at an exchange and pulled into the first gas station. A couple minutes later, Fox exited at the same exchange and stopped in McDonald's across the state road onto which the exchange exited. He waited there for fifteen minutes, sipping a cup of coffee, wondering why Flaherty was taking so long. Finally, he decided to chance it and walk across the state road to the gas station, see if he could sneak around and spot the Lexus.

But the Lexus was nowhere in sight. Flaherty was gone.

Fox ran back across the street, almost getting hit in the process. He switched on the GPS and got nothing. It was dead, kaput. Shit! Fox said to himself as he sped out of the McDonald's lot, almost getting broadsided by a van. "Shit," he shouted. "Shit!"

Fox got back on the interstate, southbound, and sped up to eighty-five, then ninety. But there was no silver Lexus in sight.

Fox slowed down to around seventy and kept driving. After a time, he called Chief Reynolds.

"What is it?" the Chief asked.

"Chief, "Fox said, "we really got a cluster-fuck now. One major league cluster-fuck."

Chapter Forty-Five

When Jeff found the GPS tracking device, he cursed himself for being so stupid as to have not checked for it earlier, way back when he had taken off on this trip from the parking lot of his apartment.

Yesterday, not fifteen minutes after finally getting bailed from the rat hole that was the county holding center, he received a frantic call from Holly. She was calling from a pay phone in a diner down in of all places, that tourist trap, Kissimmee, Florida. Jeff had been there a couple times as a kid when his parents had driven him and his younger brother down to spend their hard earned money at Disney World.

"What the fuck you doing down in that shithole?" Jeff asked.

She told him how Jerry had watched the couple days of the trial, in the back of the courtroom and then he approached her. It was Jerry who convinced her to cop a plea, that it was her only ticket to freedom. She apologized profusely and Jeff let her sob for a time. While she cried, he thought back to the first day when he had glanced back to the guy who had walked in during the middle of the medical examiner's testimony. The guy had looked so goddamned familiar but back then he had not been able to place why. Now, he knew and he nodded briefly, impressed now all the more, thinking again that he and Holly had underestimated the size of Jerry's balls.

"Do you love him, Holly?"

"How could you ask me that?" she said. "I called you. I'm helping you."

"Help me? You wanna explain how you're doing that?"

"I found us a way out of this mess. That's what I'm telling you. Just listen to me. Trust me. I have a plan.

"Well, you better have," Jeff said. "Because otherwise we're screwed."

He listened as she went over it— she would become Jade, her look-a-like, and Jeff would become anonymous. After a minute, Jeff signed, then said, "So you want me to come down there, kill them both. Just like that."

"Yes," she said. "It's our only hope."

The trip down had been uneventful until Jeff found the tracking device. After Pittsburgh, there had been long stretches especially in the rolling hills of West Virginia, without any cars on the road, either in front of him or behind, making him feel confident that he wasn't being tailed. But there was something too easy about it that kept nagging at him. Then the idea struck him while leaving a rest area that someone could easily have attached one of those GPS tracking devices to his car. Jeff stopped at the very next exit, pulled into a gas station, and quickly found the device attached under the passenger side front wheel well.

"Bastards," Jeff said to himself as he pulled the tiny, inconspicuous thing off and tossed it far into a field behind the gas station. He quickly got in his car and took off.

During the whole ride down, Jeff had rehearsed killing Jerry and his girl by various methods. He decided that the best way to do so was for him to hide in the bathroom of Holly's cheap motel room and surprise Jerry upon his inevitable arrival to visit Holly. He'd brought a thick steel wire and read up on the Internet how to quickly use it to strangle someone, like those Mafia guys do. After killing Jerry, he'd drive over to Jade's place and strangle her the same way. Disposing of the bodies would be the next trick. He'd have to quickly find a decent swamp out in the boonies and dump the bodies.

No one would be looking for Jeff, and as for Jade, Holly had said they looked like twins and she could easily take her place, become Jade. She'd driven off with Jerry, an anonymous man, intent to serve his as a front. And Jerry had told Holly that Jade had no family. Except for him, she was essentially alone in the world. Thus, their situation played perfectly into their hands.

But thinking all that made him sour and sick. His murder toll would be up to three. And though each of his victims had major flaws, so did he. Killing the body guy had not really bothered him. He had lost no sleep, had no nightmares. Still, it worried him every now and then that someday he'd pay for what he had done. Hell or whatever.

Then again, maybe not.

Chapter Forty-Six

Before Jerry went to talk to Holly, he took a nap to clear his head. When he awoke, he yawned for a time on the edge of the bed, stretched his arms out before finally ambling out of the bedroom into the living room. He was surprised that it was daylight. He had slept all night, about ten hours or so. But no wonder. It had been a long last couple of days.

Jade was out on the pool deck having a cup of coffee and reading the *Orlando Sentinel* on her lounge chair. Jerry watched her for a time through the sliding glass doors leading from the living room to the pool deck as she squinted at whatever article she was reading, so interested and involved in it. Jade was certainly no dummy.

Jade looked up from the paper and saw Jerry standing in the living room staring at her. Jade quickly came inside and went to him.

"You're finally up, sleepy head," she said as she kissed his neck. "Want some breakfast?"

He took a deep breath and held her close. "Yeah," he

said. "I'm starved. What time is it?" "After eight," she said.

She fixed him scrambled eggs, bacon and toast and brewed a cup of coffee. He ate next to her at the kitchen table.

"Why so quiet?" she asked.

Jerry put down his fork and told Jade he still intended to see Holly.

Jade sat back and seemed drained of all resolve, hopeless.

"You won't come back," she said. "You'll see her and you'll change your mind."

He reached over and clutched her hand.

"No," he told her with certainty in his voice. "Well, go then," she said. "Get it over with."

"I'm coming back."

She nodded briefly then asked him where she was, what hotel.

"Why?"

"I just want to know," she said. "So in case you don't come back, I got a starting point where I can come look for you. Because if you betray me again, don't think I won't come after you, take my revenge."

He almost laughed at that but held it inside. It thrilled him that she said that, proving again that she truly loved him.

Jerry told her the place and she said, "That shithole."

"Well, what did you expect?" he asked. "Gaylord Palms?" Then, he said, "Give me an hour, If I'm not back by then, you can come after me, ring my neck."

"Don't think I won't."

Jade got up and took her plate and his over to the sink and started washing them.

"One hour," she repeated.

Jerry felt he had made a big mistake telling Jade the name of the hotel where Holly was at.

"You stay away from there," he warned. "I'll give her the money to rent a car and back she goes up to Buffalo. It's either that, or I blow her into the police. I tell her it just wasn't going to work out. I tell her, I love you. She can make up a story about needing to get away, tell them doesn't the fact that she came back show them good faith. Then she testifies against Jeff in a month, and they both go to jail. Out of our hair. Forever."

"I hope," Jade said. "I never met that bitch, but I don't trust her, and you shouldn't either."

"Look," he said, pulling Jade into his arms. "I can handle this. I can handle her."

Jade nodded sheepishly and broke free of him. "Go then," she said. "Get it over with."

He left the house and drove the twenty-minute ride to Holly's room. She opened the door with a wide smile.

"I didn't think you were ever coming back," she said with a hug and pulled him into the room. The door shut out the bright glare from the afternoon and for the moment, Jerry was blind. The next thing Jerry knew, Holly had him in her arms and was kissing him.

"Geez, Holly," he said, in between kisses. "Let me catch my breath."

Out of the corner of his eyes, Jerry saw something, a blur. There was someone else in the room, a presence. He strained to look that way, toward it, but Holly had turned him around and kept holding and kissing him. And then someone was on him, wrapping a string, a wire, around his neck. The sharp wire hurt as it sliced into his skin and a narrow line of blood oozed out.

Holly let go of Jerry and stumbled away. "Do it," she said to whoever was behind him.

Jerry stumbled forward, but as the wire tightened, he fell backward with it boring into him. Panicking, Jerry jumped backward and the force somehow pushed him and the figure using the wire onto the edge of the bed. They almost fell off together onto the floor, but Jerry pushed harder and was on top of the guy. Under him, the figure grunted and huffed, and now Jerry knew it was Jeff.

Jade had left the house not five minutes after Jerry and had driven over to Holly's motel. She had taken the pistol with her that Jerry had bought a few months back from her cousin as protection for them. "We need a gun," he had told her. "Just in case." Best thing was it was untraceable. "It's just like me," Jerry added. "Anonymous." And despite her initial skepticism and fear of the thing, Jade had taken some shooting lessons with Jerry. Now, she traveled everywhere with that pistol.

It was Jade's intention to find a spot in the lot near Holly's room and watch, see how long Jerry took to tell Holly what was what. If he lingered too long, she'd confront the situation head on. She'd go in and meet Holly if for no other reason than to slap the heartless bitch across her face.

Jade saw the Corolla parked in a space in the small lot in front of the motel and pulled into a spot next to it and waited. After a few minutes, she couldn't wait any longer. Something told her that she needed to get to that room and look Holly, and Jerry for that matter, straight in the eyes.

Stepping out of the car, she immediately heard some muffled sounds of distress, an altercation or something, voices and grunts, coming from somewhere on the ground floor of the motel. Holly was in Room 117, facing the parking lot about half-way along the side façade of the motel. Jade squinted momentarily then hurried her gait after finally realizing that the commotion, a struggle of some kind, might indeed be coming from Holly's room. Reaching the door, she listened for a moment. There was a gurgling noise and a woman's voice saying, "Finish him."

"Hold him down," said a man's voice. It wasn't Jerry.

Jade knew Jerry was in bad trouble. She took the pistol out of her handbag, stepped back, and pointed it toward the card-lock mechanism on the door. Jade had no idea what would happen when she shot, but there seemed nothing else she could do. So she shot. The bullet ripped into the lock and exploded, miraculously destroying it. She raised her foot and kicked open the door. It swung wide revealing a bizarre scene inside. Jerry was face up on the bed being strangled by a guy beneath him. A woman who looked incredibly like herself— Holly, no doubt—was standing at the corner of the bed, her face red, enraged. The guy under Jerry, squeezing piano wire around his neck, had to be the famous Jeff Flaherty.

Jade pointed the pistol at Flaherty as the gurgling emanating from somewhere deep in Jerry's throat had reached the ultimate panic stage.

"Take your fucking hands off him."

By now, a Puerto Rican housekeeper had stepped out of a laundry room next to the lobby and was squinting in the general direction of the commotion. No doubt in this place she had seen quite a lot of weird shit, but gunfire was gunfire.

"Do it, motherfucker," Jade shouted. "Take your motherfucking hands off him."

His eyes wide, bulging, Jeff eased off the piano wire a bit and looked over at Jade with a dumbfounded expression.

"Now, motherfucker!" Jade shrieked. "You got three more seconds."

Jeff released the wire and Jerry fell sideways onto the floor next to him, gasping for air.

"Get your ass away from him," Jade barked at Jeff. "Go over by that skank. And you make one move toward me, I'll blow your fucking head off."

Jerry was coughing on the bed, crumpled over. There was blood oozing out of the string marks on his neck.

"Go, mother fucker," Jade shouted.

Finally, Jeff rolled off the bed and stood next to Holly. "Get back against the wall," she said. "Now."

They stepped slowly back. "Jerry," Jade called.

She got worried when he just laid there, spitting blood, and she thought for a moment to just shoot Holly and Jeff and carry him out of there and make a run for it. A couple more housekeepers had stepped gingerly toward the open door where the commotion had been and were milling about ten yards from the lobby door peering down the way toward Room 117. A guest joined them and asked what all the noise was. Had a gun gone off?

"Jerry!"

Jerry finally stirred. He rolled off the bed and wobbling, came over to Jade. Now Jade saw that his neck was bleeding bad where the wire had cut in. Somehow, he found the strength to hobble over to where Jeff was standing and throw a wild haymaker that cut across the left side of his face. Jeff fell to the floor landing on his ass. Jerry then walked over to Holly.

"Mother-fucking bitch!" he said in a hoarse, barely audible voice. Then he reached back and slugged her straight in the nose. She fell backward with a groan and with her lying there before him, he kicked her in the stomach.

"Let's go, Jerry," Jade said with a measure of urgency. "We gotta go."

Jerry looked down at Holly's bloody face and smiled. Next to her, Jeff lay still. He could be faking it but Jerry's hand hurt bad.

"C'mon, Jerry," Jade pleaded.

Jerry looked at her in the doorway, nodded, then stumbled toward her. Arm in arm they trotted over to Jerry's car.

"Your keys," she ordered, looking back over a shoulder. "What about your car? We can't leave it."

"It's registered to that LLC, Anonymity. I'll come back to get it later."

He nodded and fell into her. She held him up and got him around to the passenger side, opened the door and slid him in. Making her way over to the other side, she saw blood on her shirt from Jerry's neck wound.

Now the housekeepers, a clerk from inside the motel and a couple guests edged forward toward the scene. Jade found that she was still holding the pistol. She lifted and pointed it at them as they approached.

"Look the other way, mother-fuckers," she yelled. The lead guy among them stopped in his tracks and looked down at the ground.

She got in and started the car.

"C'mon Jerry, stay with me," she pleaded.

"I'll be okay," Jerry said, his voice hoarse, a forced whisper.

Then, he looked up at her. "I'm so sorry."

"I love you, Jerry."

She drove out of the parking lot, hoping that no Joe Citizen had been sharp enough to have caught the license plate number.

By then sirens were screaming from somewhere, moving toward the motel. Jade prayed that fugitive warrants had been issued out of New York for Holly and Jeff.

She looked over at Jerry, who had finally passed out. She considered momentarily taking him to an emergency room but knew that would result in a host of problems. She had learned some things surviving alone on the road and cleaning out bad wounds was one of them. She'd clean it out and bandage it and make sure he settled down and didn't end up going into shock. Luckily, the ride back to their house should only take fifteen, twenty minutes. "Well, looks like you'll get your revenge after all," she said to Jerry as she drove as fast as she could back to their house.

Jerry stirred and moaned as if he heard that.

Chapter Forty-Seven

"I still don't get it," Chief Reynolds said. He put Fox's report down on his desk. "I just don't get it."

"They were caught down in Florida," Fox said. "In Kissimmee. Flaherty went down to meet up with her. Then, a drug deal or something went bad, and there was a fight or something in her room." Fox sighed. "I think it has something to do with that other guy, the one who lied to me that his name was Alan Gordon."

"Jesus Christ, Jack," said the Chief. "Nothing fits in this case."

"Yeah, I know," Fox said. "I don't get it either." He shook his head. "And do you know what Flaherty told the cops? That the insured, Jerry Shaw, isn't really dead. That they faked the murder to collect the insurance money."

"You don't think he's telling the truth, do you? That Jerry Shaw— that maybe that Alan Gordon imposter was really—"

"Jerry Shaw?" Fox sighed. "Yeah, I thought of that. But when I looked up some photos of Shaw, this guy looked nothing like him. Shaw was fat, jowly. This mysterious Gordon guy, or whatever his name is, was thin, built. A few years younger, I think, than Shaw.

"And Inspector Miller said the DA's not buying the story anyway. Holly Shaw isn't backing him up. Despite what she did, becoming a fugitive and all, she's still getting her plea. But for sure she's going away for at least seven years. And anyway, no way they're gonna change a murder charge to insurance fraud and grand larceny. Miller says they think Flaherty is reaching for straws because it's the only way to beat the rap. There's no way to independently prove what he says. The body they burned has turned to dust. No way to extract DNA from it."

After a moment, Chief Reynolds eyes lit up.

"What about all that blood that was in the room?" he asked. "The motel room? The cops said there was a lot of blood. And didn't Flaherty say he had cut Jerry Shaw in the fight he had with him in there before Shaw knocked him out and broke Holly's nose?"

Fox shook his head.

"No one suspected anything like that back then," he said. "So after they took Flaherty and Shaw in, housekeeping cleaned up the room. Washed everything they could, threw the rest out."

"Shit," said the Chief, shaking his head, thinking of another way to confirm Flaherty's claim.

"What about the Flaherty's story, though— about where they got the body. From the medical school."

"They never reported a missing cadaver," he told Chief Reynolds. "Miller checked that, first thing. Every last body the students cut up in the last ten years has been accounted for." Fox sighed. "But there was one thing."

"Yeah?"

"One of the school's anatomical preparators–"

"Their what?"

"Well," laughed Fox, "let's just call him a body guy. You know, the guy whose job it is to take care of the cadavers donated for dissection— one of those guys was murdered a few weeks after Jerry Shaw's death. Name was Willie Robinson. Stabbed not a couple blocks from his home, in well, a kind of dangerous neighborhood."

"What's that got to do–?"

"I know," said Fox. "Nothing. Just another odd quirk is all." Chief Reynolds nodded, looked away.

"Well, that's it then," he said. "They try Flaherty for murder, and with Holly Shaw's help, it looks like a lock. Flaherty will be spending the rest of his life in jail. And Global's money? That Shaw woman still claim she doesn't know where it is?"

"Yeah," said Fox, "unfortunately, she's sticking to that. And like I said, the DA doesn't seem to care much about pursuing that issue, or make it a condition of the plea."

They fell silent for a time, both trying to fathom what the facts showed. Because something bothered each of them about this case.

"So you don't believe him?" Chief Reynolds asked from out of nowhere.

"Who?"

"Flaherty. That Jerry Shaw is still alive."

"Only one way to prove that," said Fox.

"How's that?"

"Find him," Fox said. "Shaw."

Chief Reynolds shrugged.

"And I really don't think there much chance of that happening," Fox said.

"Why's that?"

"Well, if he is alive, he's anonymous."

Epilogue

It's my gravestone, thought Jerry Shaw.

Standing before it that morning were his father and his sister, Joan. His father was bent over, using a cane, looking even more frail and tired of life than he had been at Jerry's funeral nearly two years ago. They were oblivious, of course, to the fact that Jerry was watching them from a Toyota Corolla parked about fifty yards away along one of the narrow paved roads crisscrossing Holy Cross Cemetery. A small metal box containing the urn with Jerry's supposed ashes had been buried in Jerry's space of the plot. A week after Holly's sentencing, her lawyer had handed over the urn to a paralegal from the DA's office who, in turn, had delivered it to Joan.

Today was Jerry's thirty-third birthday, six months after Jeff's conviction and the dust had seemed to settle on the case. Jerry had driven up from Florida with Jade to visit his gravestone. Jade thought it was a morbid way to spend Jerry's birthday and the life his anonymity had left behind, but she had finally relented. She recognized that his anonymity weighed down on him at times, and he needed to reconnect, however tangentially, to the land of the living. Jade had stayed back at the hotel. She had told him she wanted no part in grieving over his former life.

Jerry noticed that Joan had lost a decent amount of weight since Jeff's trial and was looking good for someone who has just turned forty. Jerry missed their occasional calls to her and he would have liked to have told her about Jade, that he had found someone to replace Holly, and how Jade had saved his life.

Holly was remanded to the county jail after being extradited back up to Buffalo until she was called to testify against Jeff. Judge Pratt stayed true to his word and sentenced Holly to a minimum term of seven years imprisonment. With good behavior, she could be out in five years or so, but without a dime to her name, she'd have to figure a way to survive financially once she was paroled. At first, she'd probably go back to work, get a job as a secretary somewhere in some far away city. Jerry imagined she'd find some older guy, a sugar daddy of some kind, and use her acting skills to convince him that she really loved him. And so, in a way, she'd become an actress, and a whore just like Jade used to be.

For his part, Jeff kept quiet about his end of money, over two million dollars. Even though Judge Pratt had sentenced him to life in prison without the possibility of parole, Jeff had convinced himself that someday he would indeed get out and that when he did, he'd have a pile of Global's cash to make his remaining few years happy ones, at least. And if not, he'd have the satisfaction of keeping it from Holly.

All that seemed like ancient history to Jerry now, like a dream that faded with every waking hour.

Joan tugged at her father's arm and they turned and trudged out of the section back to Joan's car. Jerry watched them drive off, feeling sad, and walked to the gravestone. He stood before it, said a silent prayer in memory of his mother, and touched the top of the stone. Then he stepped back and regarded his name, and his date of birth, today, thirty-three years ago, and the date of his fake death. He laughed to himself because that date was now truly his birthday, his re-birthday, the start of his new life in anonymity.

"Happy birthday," a voice from behind Jerry said.

Jerry swung around. Standing no more ten yards away down the narrow path between gravestones was Jack Fox.

"Jerry Shaw, right?" said Fox in a calm, even voice. "I had a hunch you'd come here today."

Jerry thought for a moment of running for it, getting to his car. But Fox would likely call the police. The gig was up.

"Don't worry," Fox said. "I'm not going to turn you in." Jerry frowned. He wondered what this old, clever coot was up to.

"I quit Global right after Jeff's trial," Fox went on. "Enough was enough." He laughed. "Now I'm writing crime novels. I may use what you, Holly, and Jeff did as a premise."

He stepped forward and got within three feet of Jerry and stood eye to eye with him.

"And anyway, justice has been served. Flaherty's in jail— not for killing you, granted. Not for cheating Global. But he killed the medical school worker who got you the body. Right?"

Jerry nodded.

"You weren't in on that." It was a statement, not a question.

"No," Jerry said. "That was after I left town. He and Holly planned it. The guy was blackmailing them."

"And you were the one who gave the widow Robinson a hundred grand, weren't you," Fox said with a nod and a wink.

"So you found out about that," Jerry said with an admiring shrug. "Yes. I got it to her anonymously, of course. The least I could do. Actually, Willie Robinson wasn't a bad guy. Just looking out for his family."

"One thing I have to know," Fox said, "is how you operate. I mean, as an anonymous man. Even Batman had his Alfred." Jerry smiled.

"Well, let's just say, my Alfred's much better looking than that Alfred."

"I see," Fox said. "Jade Martin is your Albert's name." Again, Jerry shrugged.

"So you're really not going to report me?" he asked.

"I said I wasn't. Consider it your birthday present."

"Well," Jerry said after a time. "It was nice chatting with you."

Fox nodded. With a wave of the back of his right hand, he gestured for Jerry to get going. And Jerry did not hesitate.

A couple weeks later, Fox received a thick envelope in the mail. There was no return address. He tore open the top of the envelope and pulled out some kind of homemade comic book. And that was it. There was nothing else, no letter, no invoice.

Fox turned the comic book over in his hands and examined the cover for a time. There was a guy who vaguely resembled Jerry Shaw with his arms stretched out like a Christ figure looking upward into the title of the comic book and Fox smiled to himself when he saw what the title was:

The Anonymous Man.

More from Vincent L. Scarsella at Digital Fiction Publishing Corp.

Lawyers Gone Bad (A Lawyers Gone Bad Novel)

Infinity Cluster: Digital Science Fiction Anthology (Short Story Collection Book 6)

The Cards of Unknown Players: Digital Science Fiction Short Story (Ctrl Alt Delight)

Resurrecting Jack: Digital Science Fiction Short Story (Infinity Cluster Book 5)

About the Author

Vincent L. Scarsella is the author of speculative, fantasy, and crime fiction. His published books include the crime novels "The Anonymous Man" (2013) and "Lawyers Gone Bad" (2014), as well as the young adult fantasy, "Escape from the Psi Academy", Book 1 of the Psi Wars! Series released in May, 2015. Book 2 of the series, "Return to the Psi Academy", is slated for publication by IFWG Publishing in the summer of 2016.

Scarsella has also published numerous speculative fiction short stories in print magazines such as *The Leading Edge*, *Aethlon*, and *Fictitious Force*, various anthologies, and in several online zines. His short story, "The Cards of Unknown Players," was nominated for the Pushcart Prize and has been republished by *Digital Science Fiction*.

Scarsella's full-length play, "Hate Crime," about race relations in the context of a legal thriller, was performed in Buffalo on September 13, 2016 and is scheduled for a reprise in late May, 2016. "The Penitent," about the Catholic Church child molestation scandal, was a finalist in the June 2015 Watermelon One-Act Play Festival.

Scarsella has also published non-fiction works, most notably, "The Human Manifesto: A General Plan for Human Survival," which was favorably reviewed in September 2011 by the Ernest Becker Foundation.

The End

Visit **DigitalFictionPub.com**
for more great books. Thank you.

Copyright

Made in the USA
Middletown, DE
04 June 2018